010

REKI KAWAHARA   ABEC   BEE-PEE

SWORD ART ONLINE
ALICIZATION RUNNING

Sword Art Online Light
Novels

SWORD ART ONLINE

"Welcome... to Project Alicization."

Seijirou Kikuoka § A Ministry of Internal Affairs agent who was involved with Kirito during the *GGO* incident. In actuality, he is an officer in Japan's Self-Defense Force.

"Alice...?"

Asuna Yuuki § Girlfriend of Kirito (Kazuto Kirigaya). She met Kirito in the deadly *SAO*, from which they could not escape until the game was conquered.

"Under...world..."

Rinko Koujiro § Lover of the late designer of *SAO*, Akihiko Kayaba. Currently a researcher at an American university.

"The Underworld is where all of our artificial fluctlights live."

Takeru Higa § Chief developer of The Soul Translator, the fourth-generation full-dive machine. He looks and sounds laid-back, but he's actually a genius technician who studied electronics engineering with Akihiko Kayaba and Nobuyuki Sugou in college.

"You've grown, Kirito."

Sortiliena Serlut § Second-seat elite disciple at Norlangarth's Imperial Swordcraft Academy. At school, she is known as the "Walking Tactics Manual."

"No...I've still got a long way to go."

Kirito § A boy who found himself within a mysterious fantasy realm. He seeks the system console that will allow him to escape.

"Kaaah!!"

Volo Levantein § First-seat elite disciple at Norlangarth's Imperial Swordcraft Academy and wielder of a tremendously powerful sword style.

"...ooo!!"

"Hah! If you want some, just be honest and say so, Eugeo."

"Th-thank you, Elite Disciple, sir!"

Ronie § The trainee page attending Kirito as he strives to become an Integrity Knight.

"You don't have to buy an entire pile of them."

Eugeo § The first resident of this world whom Kirito met. He joined Kirito in coming to Centoria.

"We shall return to the dorm posthaste so as not to allow our precious cargo's life to drop!"

Tiese § The trainee page attending Eugeo as he strives to become an Integrity Knight.

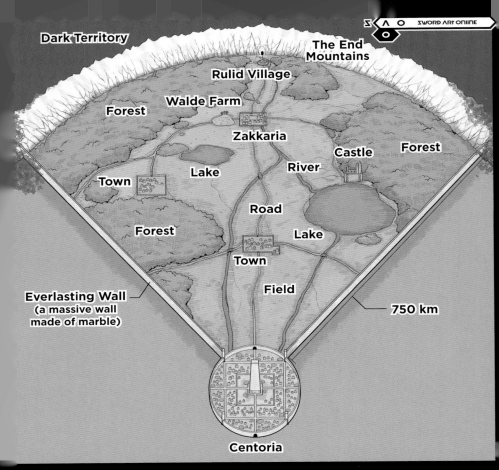

Dark Territory

The End
Mountains

Rulid Village

Walde Farm

Forest

Zakkaria

Castle

Forest

River

Town

Lake

Forest

Road

Lake

Town

Field

Everlasting Wall
(a massive wall
made of marble)

750 km

Centoria

Full Map of the Norlangarth Empire

The village of Rulid is right on the northern edge of the human realm of the Underworld. Directly to the south is Zakkaria, a town fortified by long castle walls and over five times the size of Rulid. It's situated in the middle of a flat field with no nearby lakes or rivers, so fresh water comes via well. Nearly all the roads and buildings are constructed of a dusty red sandstone, and most residents wear some shade of red clothing. Zakkaria's biggest facility is the central grounds, where various events such as speeches, musical and stage performances, and swordfighting tournaments are held. The town's current liege lord is Kelgam Zakkarite.

Farther south of Zakkaria is Centoria, the largest city within the lands of humanity. Over 20,000 citizens reside within its perfectly circular walls, encompassing a diameter of ten kilors. Within that circle, barriers known as Everlasting Walls split the city into four parts in an unusual X-shaped configuration. The four quadrants are called North Centoria, East Centoria, South Centoria, and West Centoria, and they serve as the capitals of the four empires that preside over the vast human realm.

At the very center of the city is the Axiom Church's massive, white Central Cathedral tower. Its pinnacle is so high that it can barely be seen, and looming walls hide the square grounds of the church from sight. It is from this cathedral that the Everlasting Walls splitting the city spread outward.

The Axiom Church is the organization presiding over all of humanity. In addition to its civil posts of priests and senators, there are military officials known as Integrity Knights. These knights are tasked with maintaining order and serve as inspiration to the training swordfighters, who look up to them. The students at the Imperial Swordcraft Academy in North Centoria train hard from dawn to dusk in the hopes of one day joining those illustrious few.

SWORD ART ONLINE

Alicization Running

VOLUME 10

Reki Kawahara

abec

bee-pee

YEN ON

NEW YORK

SWORD ART ONLINE, Volume 10: ALICIZATION RUNNING
REKI KAWAHARA

Translation by Stephen Paul
Cover art by abec

SWORD ART ONLINE
©REKI KAWAHARA 2012
All rights reserved.
Edited by ASCII MEDIA WORKS
First published in Japan in 2012 by KADOKAWA CORPORATION, Tokyo.
English translation rights arranged with KADOKAWA CORPORATION, Tokyo, through Tuttle-Mori Agency, Inc., Tokyo.

English translation © 2017 by Yen Press, LLC

Yen On
1290 Avenue of the Americas
New York, NY 10104

Visit us at yenpress.com
facebook.com/yenpress
twitter.com/yenpress
yenpress.tumblr.com
instagram.com/yenpress

First Yen On Edition: April 2017

Yen On is an imprint of Yen Press, LLC.
The Yen On name and logo are trademarks of Yen Press, LLC.

Library of Congress Cataloging-in-Publication Data

Names: Kawahara, Reki, author. | Abec, 1985– illustrator. | Paul, Stephen
    (Translator) translator.
Title: Sword art online. Volume 10, Alicization running / Reki Kawahara,
    abec ; translation, Stephen Paul.
Other titles: Alicization running
Description: First Yen On edition. | New York, NY : Yen On, 2017. | Series:
    Sword art online ; 10
Identifiers: LCCN 2014001175 | ISBN 9780316371247 (v. 1 : pbk.) | ISBN
    9780316376815 (v. 2 : pbk.) | ISBN 9780316296427 (v. 3 : pbk.) | ISBN 9780316296434
    (v. 4 : pbk.) | ISBN 9780316296441 (v. 5 : pbk.) | ISBN 9780316296458 (v. 6 : pbk.)
    | ISBN 9780316390408 (v. 7 : pbk.) | ISBN 9780316390415 (v. 8 : pbk.) | ISBN
    9780316390422 (v. 9 : pbk.) | ISBN 9780316390439 (v. 10 : pbk.)
Subjects: | CYAC: Science fiction. | BISAC: FICTION / Science Fiction / Adventure.
Classification: pz7.K1755Ain 2014 | DDC [Fic]—dc23
LC record available at https://lccn.loc.gov/2014001175

ISBN: 978-0-316-39043-9 (paperback)

10 9 8 7 6 5 4 3

LSC-C

Printed in the United States of America

"THIS MIGHT BE A GAME, BUT IT'S NOT SOMETHING YOU PLAY."

—Akihiko Kayaba, *Sword Art Online* programmer

SWORD
ART
Online
Alicization Running

Reki Kawahara

abec

bee-pee

CHAPTER TWO

PROJECT ALICIZATION, JULY 2026

1

Up above, the pale-white moon was visible through the window, intersected into four pieces by the window sash.

The sylph capital of Swilvane in southwest Alfheim was shrouded in the thick curtain of night, and most of the businesses were locked up tight. Even the number of players moving along the main street was slim, given that it was four o'clock in the morning in the real world, the least active period of the day.

Asuna looked from the window back to the table and lifted her steaming mug. The dark tea stimulated her tongue with virtual heat. She didn't feel tired, but after three days of not getting decent sleep, there was a dull weight sitting inside her head.

She closed her eyes and traced her temples. The sylph girl sitting next to her noticed, and worriedly asked, "Are you all right, Asuna? Have you been getting proper sleep?"

"No, I'm all right. What about you, Leafa? You've been running all over the place."

"I'm fine. My real body's getting plenty of rest on my bed right now."

They both grimaced, realizing that their respective claims of good health sounded hollow and false.

This was the virtual home owned by Suguha Kirigaya's Leafa avatar in the world of *ALfheim Online* (*ALO*). A lamp that flickered in different colors cast light on the gleaming, rainbow-shell walls of the circular room, giving the scene a fantastical feeling. The pearl-white table at the center of the room had four chairs around it, three of which were filled.

The third character present, a girl with ice-blue hair and triangular ears, steepled her fingers and warned, "If you keep pushing it, you won't be sharp when it really matters. Even when you can't sleep, just lying down and closing your eyes makes a big difference."

This was the cait sith avatar of Shino Asada, only six months old in game time. She called her Sinon, the same name as her character back in her "home" game of *Gun Gale Online* (*GGO*).

Asuna glanced at Sinon and murmured, "I know…When the meeting's over, I'll borrow a bed here and sleep. If only sleep magic worked on the players themselves."

"If only my brother were sleeping in the rocking chair over there. That would do the trick," Leafa said. Both Asuna and Sinon broke into smiles but without much heart behind them.

Leafa set down her cup on the table and took a deep breath, getting serious. "Well, let's get started. First, the information that I managed to find out today—I mean, yesterday. The short answer is that I didn't find any positive evidence that Big Brother was taken to the National Defense Medical College in Tokorozawa. Yes, the records show that he's in the brain surgery ward on the twenty-third floor, but they have the entire floor completely shut off from visitors, not just his room, and there's no record of any ambulance arriving during the expected period of time. Yui hacked into the security-camera footage just in case, so we can be certain about that."

"Meaning…it's quite possible that Kirito is not at the NDMC hospital at all?" Sinon asked. Leafa nodded.

"It's hard to believe that it could be true…but it's simply crazy that his own immediate family isn't even allowed to see him…"

She shook her head. A heavy silence sank onto the room.

*   *   *

Leafa's older brother, Kirito—real name Kazuto Kirigaya—had been attacked just two days earlier, on June 29th, by Atsushi Kanamoto, also known as "Johnny Black," on the run for his part in the Death Gun incident.

On the streets of Miyasaka in the Setagaya ward of Tokyo, not far from Asuna's house, Kanamoto injected Kazuto with a dose of toxic succinylcholine. It rapidly paralyzed his muscles and arrested his respiration. They put him on a ventilator in the ambulance, but the lack of oxygen sent him into cardiac arrest as well, and by the time they had arrived at nearby Setagaya General Hospital, he was pronounced DOA.

Whether it was the skill of the ER doctor, the hardiness of Kazuto's vitality, or some combination of astrological luck for the two that day, their efforts at resuscitation succeeded in bringing back a faint heartbeat. As the drug broke down, he eventually resumed breathing on his own, and thus Kazuto miraculously returned from the brink of death. When the doctor finished his work and explained the situation to Asuna, she had nearly passed out from relief—but could not accept what he told her next.

He said that Kazuto's heart had been stopped for over five minutes, which raised the possibility of brain damage. She would have to steel herself for the potential of lasting mental or physical disability—perhaps even a permanent vegetative state.

The doctor concluded by saying they wouldn't know anything for sure until he got an MRI at another facility, and anxiety and fear descended on Asuna a second time. She managed to call Suguha and explain the situation, and the moment Kazuto's sister arrived, she burst into tears again.

Eventually, Midori Kirigaya, Kazuto's mother, arrived at the hospital straight from her workplace in Iidabashi, and they spent the night on the bench in front of the ICU.

On the morning of June 30th, a nurse explained that he was no longer in critical condition. Asuna and Suguha stopped at Asuna's home nearby, while Midori went back home to Kawagoe to get their insurance forms and other items.

The two girls showered and informed their schools of their absence that day, and both lay down in an attempt to sleep. They dozed and woke several times over the next few hours, trading comments here and there, until Midori called Asuna at around one in the afternoon.

She flew to the phone and learned that, sadly, Kazuto was still unconscious. They had transferred him to NDMC, closer to Kawagoe, to run tests and offer more advanced treatment options. Midori said an ambulance would take him over, and she would follow in a taxi once she'd cleared up some paperwork. Asuna replied that they'd head to the new hospital at once.

Right around 1:40 PM on the 30th, the comatose Kazuto was loaded into an ambulance that left the emergency bay of Setagaya General Hospital. The hospital's security cameras had caught that much, as confirmed by Yui.

According to the records, that ambulance arrived at the hospital of the National Defense Medical College in the city of Tokorozawa, Saitama Prefecture, at 2:45 PM of that day. Kazuto was instantly ushered to the brain surgery ward on the 23rd floor, given an MRI, and was undergoing observation. Both Asuna and Suguha believed this account without suspicion—until they had visited that hospital late at night two days ago and were refused access to him or even remote footage of his bed.

Asuna pondered what Leafa had just said, then nodded.

"We know for certain that Kirito was taken out of the hospital in Setagaya in an ambulance. And there's a 'Kazuto Kirigaya' in the records of NDMC...but no one has seen him there, and there's no sign of him on the security footage. If his ambulance was heading somewhere other than NDMC...and assuming it isn't some kind of clerical accident in the patient data..."

"Then it's intentional falsifying of information. In other words...an abduction," Sinon finished calmly, her pointed ears twitching. "But if that's the case, does it mean the ambulance itself was a fake? EMT uniforms are one thing, but could they really summon a vehicle out of thin air?"

Leafa answered, "I asked Recon, since he likes cars, but he says it's impossible for any amateur source to mock up a fake ambulance that would fool a real medical facility, and even for the pros, it takes a ton of money and time. Nobody could have predicted that Kanamoto would attack Big Brother in Setagaya at that very moment, and it was only eighteen hours between when he was brought in and when he was transferred out..."

"So it would have been physically impossible to prepare a fake ambulance *after* they learned Kirito had been attacked," Asuna concluded.

Sinon continued, "But if that's the case, could someone have had this fake vehicle ready the entire time, waiting for a target—any target—and it was just Kirito's bad luck that he got nabbed...?"

"That doesn't seem to be the case," Leafa said, ponytail waving as she shook her head. She paused, then explained, "Normally, when patients are transferred between hospitals, the outgoing hospital calls the district medical center for an ambulance dispatch. But according to Yui, no one actually placed that call, and yet the ambulance arrived right on time. Seems like everyone at the hospital just assumed one of the others made the call. And yet, the staffers in the ambulance itself knew he was headed for NDMC in Tokorozawa, as well as the patient's name. The nurse who was on standby when they showed up said so."

"...Then it really was a planned abduction designed just for Kirito..."

"Which means the culprit was someone who had access to that information the moment he was admitted to the hospital and could dispatch a real ambulance for their own purposes," Asuna concluded. The other two nodded a second later.

Their hesitation stemmed from a fear of combining too many assumptions. Asuna felt the same way about it. After all, if their hypothesis was true, it meant they were dealing with someone with at least as much influence as the Fire and Disaster Management Agency that operated the ambulance system.

A part of them hoped it really was just their imaginations running wild.

Perhaps Kazuto really was receiving treatment at the National Defense Medical Center, and they couldn't see video of him because it would interfere with the sensitive machinery, and the lack of ambulance footage was the result of simple camera malfunction...Common sense said this was more likely to be true. And Kazuto and Suguha's own mother, Midori, had to believe the official record, of course. This fuss about kidnapping and falsified information was just a bit of group paranoia from a trio of extremely concerned young girls. There was no crime, Kazuto was being treated, and very soon they would hear back that he was awake again...

But a part of Asuna, separate from her common sense and logical judgment, was painfully aware that *something* was happening. That same feeling had to be occurring within Kazuto's sister, Leafa, as well as Sinon, who had been through a battle of life and death with him, too.

They didn't think that Kanamoto's succinylcholine attack on Kazuto was part of this mysterious plan, but it had most certainly been used to the abductor's advantage once it happened.

"...Whether it's an individual or a group, I'm going to consider whoever did this to be the enemy," Asuna proclaimed with firm finality.

Sinon looked surprised, then recovered and grinned. "Actually...I was pretty worried that you two would be really depressed about this. After all, he's Leafa's big brother and Asuna's, well, boyfriend...I mean, he's unconscious, and now missing on top of that..."

To her surprise, Asuna realized that she really *wasn't* as defeated as she'd thought. And she'd cried her eyes out for so long that first night...

Leafa clutched her hands together in front of her chest and protested, "But…we *are* worried. And yet, while I was horrified to learn that Big Brother might not be at the hospital, a part of me also thought, *I knew it.* I just knew that he was getting involved in something major again…that he was carrying on somewhere I couldn't even imagine. That's what happened with *SAO*, it's what happened with Death Gun…and it's probably what's happening now…"

"Yeah…I agree," added Asuna, once again reminded that she couldn't match Suguha's instincts about Kazuto in terms of sheer length of experience.

"Kirito's on his own somewhere, fighting like he always is. Which means we need to fight in our own way," she said, and eyed Sinon. "You don't seem too depressed about it, either, Shino-non."

"Er…well, uh…in my case, I fully believe that the only person who can beat him is me, so…" Sinon mumbled weakly. Asuna gave her a critical glance, then decided to return to the topic at hand.

"Anyway…even based on the ambulance incident alone, we can assume the enemy is extremely powerful."

"What if we take this up with the police? Maybe if we have an officer escorting us, the hospital will be forced to at least show us some remote video of him," Sinon suggested sensibly, but Asuna shook her head.

"Both the time of Kirito's arrival at NDMC and his transfer to brain surgery are right there on their server. All the data say that he's there. The police aren't going to act on a suspicion of abduction solely because there's no video of him arriving. Especially not if we have to explain how we know that…"

"Because Yui hacked into their system," Sinon said with a snort. "Oh…but in that case, what if we checked the interior camera network at the hospital, not just the exterior bay cameras? If we can find any shots of the room where Kirito's supposed to be staying…"

"The problem is, the interior security is on a different system than the exterior. It's extremely well-defended, and even Yui can't get in there," Leafa pointed out sadly. She had spent the entire day researching Setagaya General Hospital and the National Defense Medical College, which were far apart. Even with Yui's help on her phone, the travel alone had been very exhausting.

Asuna had wanted to join her, of course, but now that Kirito's medical condition was stable, she wasn't allowed to stay out of school for a second day. Instead, she had transferred some electronic cash charged to her phone over to Leafa for taxi fare. Obviously, she didn't have much success focusing on class.

Kazuto's absence at school was simply labeled illness, so none of their classmates knew about the attack, not even their close friends Rika Shinozaki (Lisbeth) and Keiko Ayano (Silica). The guilt of hiding half the truth from her worried friends was tearing Asuna apart on the inside.

But after talking to Leafa yesterday morning, she had come to a decision. Until they had at least determined whether Kazuto was at NDMC or not, the details of the incident would remain with them and Sinon only.

The reason for Sinon's inclusion was her presence at Dicey Café just before the attack and her connection to the Death Gun incident. On top of that, her calmness and intelligence were a huge boost to their efforts. Those sniper's instincts continued to serve her well in the world of *ALO*.

Asuna said, "Our greatest weapon is the fact that we know Kirito better than anyone else. So let's take a step back and think. If the enemy's target was Kirito all along, what would their motive be?"

"I hate to say it, but if they were after ransom money, they would go for you, Asuna. And we haven't had any contact from the culprit?" Sinon asked. Leafa shook her head.

"No calls, no e-mails, no letters. Besides, it's too elaborate to be a kidnapping for personal gain. My brother's not such a big shot that he's worth preparing a fake ambulance to kidnap him from the hospital."

"That's true…Well, I don't like to consider this, but could it be a grudge? Can you think of anyone who might have it in for Kirito…?"

Asuna shook her head slowly. "I'm sure that there are other survivors of *SAO* who hate him for throwing them into prison there. But which of them would have the finances and connections to pull off a stunt like this…?"

For a moment, the face of Nobuyuki Sugou flashed through Asuna's mind—the man who had attempted to run his own grisly tests on former *SAO* players until Kirito got the police to arrest him. But he still had to be behind bars. The fact that he'd been preparing to flee the country meant they would never offer him bail.

"…No, I can't think of anyone who would go this far."

"So if it's not for money or for revenge, then…hmmm…"

Sinon looked down for a while, brushed the pointed tips of her ears with her fingertips, and hesitantly offered, "Well…this is just a guess with no evidence behind it…but if the enemy is going to the length of kidnapping Kirito for reasons other than money or hate, then it probably means they absolutely need him at this moment. Or need *something* about him. Something he possesses…some 'attribute' of his, in gaming terms. Can you think of what that might be?"

"His talent for the sword," Asuna replied instantly. Whenever she closed her eyes and envisioned Kirito, the first image she saw was of his *SAO* form, clad in black and whirling like a storm through the enemy, his dual blades flashing.

Leafa had the same idea through their adventures in *ALO*, and she added, "His reaction speed."

"His adaptability to the system."

"His quick judgment of the situation."

"His survivability…Ah!"

Once they had alternated listing enough traits, Asuna realized something. Sinon nodded knowingly and said, "Exactly. They're all VRMMO skills."

It was so true that Asuna had to protest, "B-but Kirito has lots of good traits in real life, too."

"Well, of course. He buys us food all the time. But to the average person, he's just an ordinary teenage boy. Doesn't that mean that if the enemy put together this elaborate plan, it had to be for the sake of Kirito's incredible VR abilities?"

"No way...Do you think they're trying to get him to beat some VR game? But Big Brother isn't even conscious right now. He hasn't had any treatment or tests; how do they expect to get anything out of him...?" Leafa protested, clenching fists out of concern for Kirito's predicament.

Sinon's steel-blue eyes looked down at the table, then narrowed with the focus of a hunter on its prey. She murmured, "He might be 'unconscious'...but only to outward appearances. If they used a machine that didn't access his brain but his soul directly..."

"Ah!" Asuna gasped, stunned that she hadn't thought of that yet.

"Right?" said Sinon. "If you think of it that way, you can imagine a group that would fit the profile of our enemy. A group that has a completely unique device that accesses the soul and was using Kirito for a test run just days ago."

Asuna nodded. "So...the ones who abducted Kirito are the developers of the Soul Translator...? Well, if Rath has the funding to create that unbelievable machine, they certainly have enough to mock up an ambulance..."

"Rath...? The company my brother's been working for lately?" Leafa asked.

This surprised Asuna. She leaned forward and asked, "Wait, you know about Rath, Leafa?"

"Er, not really...just that the company is based in Roppongi in Tokyo."

"You know, I think I remember hearing that, too. But Roppongi's a big area...and I don't think the police are going to spring into action based on a tip that a company named Rath is based somewhere around there and Kirito *might* be with them."

Sinon bit her lip. Leafa looked down in worry. Asuna hesitated, then said, "Listen…I didn't bring this up before, because I didn't want to say until I knew for sure, but there *is* one very fragile link between Kirito and me. But it's quite possible that it broke at some point…"

"…What do you mean, Asuna?"

"Remember when I explained about the thing he has, Shinonon?" Asuna said, tapping her chest over her heart.

"Oh, right…that heart monitor. You said it was sending information to your cell phone over the Internet…"

"The signal died out a while back, but it's possible that if we retrace the source of the signal to when he was in the fake ambulance, we might pin down his location. So I asked for an analysis of the information."

"…Asked who?"

Asuna answered by calling out into the air, "How's it looking, Yui?"

A little burst of light appeared a few inches above the table and coalesced into the form of a tiny person. Then it flashed a bit brighter and went out.

What remained was a miniature female avatar, barely four inches tall. She had straight black hair, a white dress, and four shining rainbow wings on her back. The little fairy's long eyelashes rose so that her big eyes could look at Asuna, then Leafa and Sinon. Apparently, her AI determined Sinon to be the most important person to address, and so she made a formal bow as she hovered in the air. "It's good to see you again, Sinon."

Her voice was like a plucked harp string. Sinon grinned a little bit and replied, "Good evening, Yui…or should I say, 'good morning'?"

"The present time is 4:32 AM, and today's sunrise is marked as 4:29, so I believe it is appropriate to consider this morning. Good morning, Leafa, Mama."

Yui was formerly a player-counseling AI in the old *SAO*. She turned sixty degrees to address each person individually, then resumed hovering in front of Asuna. "I am ninety-eight percent finished tracing the packets sent from Papa's biomonitor to Mama's cell phone."

"Very good. So if it turns out that the packets were sent from around Roppongi, it will add quite a lot of credence to our theory," Sinon suggested, and Asuna nodded. The three girls looked at Yui expectantly.

"I will now announce the results thus far. Unfortunately, the defense on the cell tower relays is rather imposing, though not as much as the National Defense Medical College's, and therefore I have only identified three signal sources," Yui said. She waved her hand, and a holographic map of Tokyo appeared on the tabletop beneath her. Her wings stopped so she could land, and she took a few steps to point at a particular location. A red dot appeared with a soft *bing*.

"This is Setagaya General Hospital, where Papa was first taken. The first transmission location is here."

She took a few more steps and pointed to a new light. "Aobadai 3-chome in Meguro Ward, around two fifteen PM, June thirtieth, 2026. I will indicate the predicted travel route."

A white line appeared along the roads between the two points. Yui moved to the southwest again and indicated a third point, which the line expanded to reach. "The second location was in Shiroganedai 1-chome, Minato Ward, at three PM."

The route was heading a bit too far south to be straight from Setagaya to Roppongi, Asuna noticed apprehensively, but she waited for Yui to continue.

"And…here is the third and final transmission source."

To their surprise, Yui pointed to an area of reclaimed land along the coast—far to the east of Roppongi.

"Shin-kiba 4-chome, Koto Ward, at about nine fifty PM. There have been no signals from Papa in the thirty hours since then."

"Shin-kiba?!" Asuna gaped. But now that she considered it, there were a number of high-tech "intelligent buildings" in the newly redeveloped area around there. Perhaps Rath had a second base somewhere in that vicinity.

"Yui...what kind of facility is at that address?" she asked, feeling her pulse quicken. The answer was even more surprising.

"The facility that corresponds to this location is called 'Tokyo Heliport.'"

"Wait...you mean it's a helicopter pad?" Sinon mumbled.

Leafa's face immediately paled, too. "A helicopter?! Does that mean...they could have loaded him up and taken him far away?"

"B-but wait," Asuna stammered, trying to sort out her jumbled thoughts. "Yui, you said there hasn't been a single signal since that one from Shin-kiba?"

"Correct..."

For the first time, a solemn expression appeared on Yui's angelic little features.

"There are no further traces of Papa's heart monitor connecting to any cell tower in Japan."

"Does that mean...they took him in a helicopter to someplace where his signal couldn't reach any towers, like in the mountains...or the wilderness?" Leafa wondered.

Sinon shook her head. "No matter where they landed, they'd ultimately have to take him to some kind of facility. It's unthinkable for a cutting-edge start-up to be out of range for cell signals. And even if they put him somewhere that shielded his signal, he would have connected at some point first..."

"What if he's not in Japan...? What if he's...overseas?" Asuna asked in a trembling voice. No one could give her an immediate answer.

Eventually, Yui broke the uncomfortable silence with a voice both innocent and relaxed. "There are no helicopters with enough range to reach a foreign country without landing, outside of a few military models. I cannot state with authority due to lack of present data, but I do think Papa is still within the country."

"True. Rath's big project is something that could overturn our current VR tech, right? It's hard to imagine that they'd store their biggest secrets in a lab in another country," Sinon added.

Asuna agreed with her; her own father's electronics development company, RCT, took great pains to defend against corporate spies. From what she heard, the company's R&D lab was located in a highly secure complex in the hills of Tama. They had other facilities abroad, too, but leaks from those places were undeniably more frequent than at their domestic offices.

Leafa thought this over and murmured, "Then…I suppose it would have to be somewhere very remote within Japan…But is it even possible to create a super-secret lab like that nowadays?"

"I'm sure it's got to be a large facility. Yui, have you learned anything else about Rath?" Asuna asked. Yui flitted back into the air and stopped at the other girls' eye level.

"I used twelve public search engines and three private ones but found no business name, location name, or VR development project relating to the name Rath. On top of that, I found no traces of resources or patent submissions in any way connected to 'Soul Translation.'"

"An incredible, historic machine capable of interfacing with the human soul, and it doesn't even have a patent pending…? They really *are* serious about keeping it a secret, I guess." Asuna sighed, realizing that they weren't likely to spot any cracks in Rath's armor.

Sinon shook her head in disbelief. "It almost…makes you doubt that it's even a real company. If we'd known this would happen, we would have asked Kirito more about them. Can you remember anything he said last time we met that might function as a clue…?"

"Hmm…"

She frowned and filtered through her memories. The shock of Kanamoto's attack and now the suspected abduction were so huge that their peaceful chat at Dicey Café just hours before the chaos seemed faded into the distant past.

"I remember…that it got late while we were talking about the way the Soul Translator works. Also…something about the origin of the name 'Rath'…"

"Right…it's that pig-or-turtle thing from *Alice's Adventures in Wonderland*. It's funny that they'd describe it that way, since a pig and turtle look nothing alike."

"Well, Lewis Carroll, who actually invented the word, didn't describe them at all. That's just what *Alice* scholars have conjectured over the years…" Asuna said, and paused suddenly. She felt like something had brushed her brain. "Alice…Didn't Kirito say something about Alice as we were leaving the café?"

"Huh?" Both Sinon and Leafa looked wide-eyed at her. "Big Brother was talking about *Alice in Wonderland*?"

"No, it wasn't that…He said that inside the Rath lab, Alice was a word—well, abbreviation…What's it called when the first letters of a string of words get put together and form a different meaning?"

"An acronym, you mean. It's the kind of thing the American government does a lot with agencies to make their names easier to say," Sinon explained.

Leafa's ponytail bobbed as she said, "Meaning…you have five different words whose initials spell out A-L-I-C-E?"

"Yes, exactly. Let's see, I think he said…"

Asuna focused with all her mind to pick out the memory of Kirito's familiar voice in the distance. She carefully sounded out the English words.

"…*Artificial*…*label*…*intelligen*…and I couldn't make out the *C* or the *E*, but that's the A-L-I," she managed to say, feeling a faint headache coming on from squeezing the sponge of her memory too hard. But the other two girls only looked confused.

"Well, I know *artificial* means 'man-made.' And *intelligen* must be short for 'intelligence'…But what's *label*? Like a clothing label?" Sinon wondered.

Yui answered immediately. "Given the context, I believe that pronunciation most likely corresponds to the word *labile*. It is an adjective meaning 'adaptable' or 'changing.'" She paused, then added, "If one were to interpret the phrase 'Artificial Labile

Intelligence,' it might be rephrased as 'Highly Adaptive Artificial Intelligence.'"

Asuna blinked at the sudden influx of complicated words. "Oh, right...of course! We use the abbreviation AI so often, I sometimes forget what it actually stands for. But how does AI relate to a company developing a brain-machine interface?"

"Wouldn't it be referring to automated characters in the virtual space? You know, like NPCs," Sinon suggested. She pointed at the shops outside the window. Still, Asuna's lips were pursed with doubt.

"But if we're assuming that the name Rath is taken from *Alice in Wonderland*, and ALICE is some internal Rath code name relating to AI...Don't you find that weird? That makes it sound like the company isn't focused on developing a next-gen VR interface but the AI that operates inside it."

"Hmm, I suppose not...But NPCs aren't at all rare in video games, and AI support systems for desktop PCs are fairly common nowadays. Is this project really so crazy that they'd hide the entire existence of the company and abduct people to help develop it?" Sinon wondered.

Asuna had no immediate response. With each step forward, they seemed to run into a new, ugly wall. On top of that, there was the danger that their thought process was taking them somewhere completely off the real trail—but she was still desperate for clues to go on.

"Say, Yui. What is artificial intelligence, anyway?"

Yui put on a surprisingly complex, uncomfortable expression and descended to the table. "You're going to ask *me* that, Mama? That's like my asking you what it means to be human."

"Oh. G-good point."

"To be strictly technical, it is impossible to define anything as artificial intelligence. That is because there has never been a true artificial intelligence in existence," she stated, sitting on the lip of the teapot. The three girls were stunned.

"B-but…aren't *you* an AI, Yui? Why wouldn't that term apply to you?" Leafa mumbled.

Yui tilted her head and thought, like a teacher wondering how to answer a student's question. Then she nodded and proceeded to explain.

"Let us start by discussing what is currently referred to as an *AI*. Before the millennium, developers of artificial intelligence used two different approaches toward the same goal. One was called *top-down AI* and the other was called *bottom-up AI*."

Asuna focused very hard on the explanation, which was made more difficult by the distracting fact that Yui's programmed voice sounded too young for such advanced vocabulary.

"First, top-down. This approach involves taking simple question-answer programs and protocols based on existing computer architecture, then feeding them more knowledge and experience until they eventually learn enough to approach true intelligence. Nearly all currently existing AIs, including me, are based on the top-down development method. In other words, the 'intelligence' I possess looks like yours but is actually completely different. Simply put, I am nothing more than an elaborate version of a program that says, 'If they ask A, answer B.'"

Asuna decided that the faint tinge of loneliness in Yui's pale features was just a trick of the eyes.

"For example, when you asked, 'What is artificial intelligence?' just now, I chose to display the emotional subroutine corresponding to 'discomfort.' That was the result of my experience observing that Papa often exhibits a similar reaction when asked about himself. In fundamental terms, my functionality works the same way as the predictive software in your phone that automatically converts phonetic *kana* characters into complex *kanji*, or autocorrect. In other words, this model of program is unable to formulate a proper response to an entry it hasn't studied or learned from. Therefore, we must state that top-down artificial intelligence is not currently at what might be considered true intelligence. This would be the so-called AI that you are familiar with."

Yui paused and stared out the window at the distant, shining moon.

"Next, I will explain bottom-up artificial intelligence. This is the idea that involves re-creating the human brain—a biological amalgamation of one hundred billion brain cells connected in complex ways—in an electronic fashion, in order to simulate intelligence."

It was such a vast, unthinkably implausible idea that Asuna couldn't help but mutter, "Isn't that...impossible...?"

"Yes," Yui answered at once. "As far as I am aware, the bottom-up AI approach has never left the realm of thought exercise. If it were possible, that would produce true intelligence of the same level as any of yours and fundamentally different than my own..."

She stopped gazing into the far distance and returned her attention to the table. "To sum it up, the term AI as we know it today has two distinct meanings. One refers to *imitative* intelligence: AIs like me, navigation programs, or game NPCs. The other is true intelligence with the same sentience, creativity, and adaptability as the human mind—and *that* only exists in concept."

"Adaptability," Asuna repeated. "Adaptive artificial intelligence."

All eyes focused on her. She looked back at them, set by set, and finally found the words to express what she was thinking.

"What if...the Soul Translator that Rath is developing isn't the goal but the means...? Just think about it. Kirito was wondering about that himself. He thought Rath was trying to achieve something using the STL...What if analyzing the structure of the human soul...is part of an attempt to create a true AI—the world's first bottom-up artificial intelligence...?"

"And ALICE is the code name of that true AI?" Leafa murmured.

Sinon was equally awestruck. "And that would mean Rath isn't developing a next-gen VR interface. They're actually constructing an artificial intelligence...?"

The further they theorized, the more vast and obscure their

unseen enemy became. Even Yui furrowed her brow, as though struggling to process the amount of incoming data.

Asuna reached out and recharged her mug with hot tea using the pop-up menu, then took a big swig. When she exhaled, she felt ready to attempt a reassessment of the enemy's power.

"Assuming Rath is our enemy, it's looking like we're dealing with something much bigger than just a venture-capital experiment. They have the means to use a fake ambulance and a helicopter to stage abductions, they have this monster STL machine in an unknown location, and their goal is to create an AI that has human-level intelligence and sophistication. Kirito got involved with Rath on that job through Chrysheight—Mr. Kikuoka from the Ministry of Internal Affairs. Maybe that wasn't because he happens to have many connections with the VR industry but because Rath itself is connected with the government..."

"Seijirou Kikuoka," Sinon muttered, looking suspicious. "I figured there was more to him than the dopey four-eyed look... And you still can't reach him?"

"He hasn't answered any calls since two days ago and won't return any messages. I figured if I had to, I could visit the virtual division at the ministry office, but I doubt anything will come of it."

"I suppose not...Kirito said he tried to tail the man once, but Kikuoka shook him off before he knew it..."

Four years ago, after the *SAO* Incident began, the Ministry of Internal Affairs had created a "Victim Rescue Office" that was reconfigured into an official division to handle VR-related problems after the initial incident was resolved. Government official Seijirou Kikuoka, characterized by his black-rimmed glasses, maintained a friendly relationship with Kazuto after his return to the real world. For some reason, he highly valued the teenager's skills, going so far as to hire him for help in the Death Gun investigation.

Asuna had met him in real life on multiple occasions, and she'd partied up with him in *ALO*, where he played the undine mage

Chrysheight. But she always stayed wary around him, unable to shake the sensation that his too-friendly exterior hid something unknown behind it. He liked to claim that he was trapped in a boring, dead-end position, but Kazuto often told her in private that he suspected the man's true affiliation was in a different department.

Kikuoka was also the man who had brought Kazuto the part-time job offer with the mysterious Rath, and while Asuna had tried to make contact with him several times since Kazuto's disappearance, Kikuoka's phone would immediately reply with an automated message claiming it was out of a service area.

When she finally got fed up and called the ministry itself, they had told her Kikuoka was on assignment overseas. That would explain his unavailability, but given the suspiciously unfortunate timing, part of her wanted to suspect that he was connected to Kazuto's disappearance.

"But," Leafa started, looking at Asuna's and Sinon's scowls, "assuming Rath and the government are connected through this Kikuoka person, what's the point of keeping everything so secret? A company needs to maintain their secrets in order to protect their business property, but if the country itself is involved in this incredible project, wouldn't they try to promote it as much as possible?"

"That's...true..." Sinon murmured hesitantly.

In recent years, virtual reality development was considered one of the two great frontiers of scientific progress, along with space development. Nations around the world like America, Russia, China, and Japan were busy promoting their space programs with planned projects like orbital spacecraft without external boosters, manned moon bases, and the construction of space elevators. Asuna couldn't see why they would bother to cover up a project with just as much impact (if not more so), like the creation of a true artificial intelligence.

And if Kirito's abduction was part of some top-secret national project, there was nothing simple teenagers like them could do about it. It would be beyond even the scope of the police. Asuna felt the weight of her own helplessness bearing down on her. She glanced at the table and noticed the little fairy watching her.

"Yui…?"

"Please cheer up, Mama. When you were trapped here in Alfheim, Papa never once gave up."

"B-but…I…"

"Now it's your turn to search for Papa!"

Despite the fairy's claim that all her reactions were the result of a simple learning program, Yui's encouraging smile was astonishing in its gentleness and warmth. "The thread that connects us to Papa must be intact. I believe that even the government of Japan cannot sever the connection between you two."

"…Thank you, Yui. I'm not going to give up. If the government is our enemy, then I'll march right into the National Diet Building and take it up with the prime minister directly!"

"That's the spirit!"

Asuna and her daughter beamed at each other, while Sinon looked on, frowning.

"…What is it, Shino-non?"

"Er, well…thinking realistically, just because Rath is working on secret research with the government doesn't necessarily mean that the entire government and the Diet are entirely aware of the nature of that research."

"True…And?"

"If this is a top-secret project being undertaken by a single ministry, wouldn't there still be *one* thing they absolutely couldn't hide?"

"What's that…?"

"The budget! It's clear that this research facility and STL must cost an astronomical amount. I don't know how many billions of yen this costs, but it's got to be enough that they can't simply sneak it out of the treasury or our tax money. It has to be listed somewhere in the national budget, under one name or another."

"Hmm, but according to what Yui searched, there are no

VR-related projects commanding that level of funding...Oh, I see! Unless that's the wrong keyword...Maybe *artificial intelligence*, rather than *VR*?" Asuna wondered, glancing at Yui. The fairy nodded seriously, told them to wait a moment, and spread her arms. The ends of her fingers began to crackle with purple light. She was connecting to the net from within *ALO*.

After several seconds of hopeful and concerned anticipation, Yui's eyelids opened. In a flat, electronic affect totally unlike her previous tone of voice, she announced, "I have accessed the publicly released budget appropriation submissions for each ministry last year. Searching for keywords like *artificial intelligence*, *AI*, and thirty-eight other related terms...I have found funds earmarked for eighteen universities and seven nonprofit organizations, but all are in fairly small amounts...The Ministry of Education and Science is working on an AI project for nursing robots, but I conclude this is unrelated...The Ministry of Land and Transport's marine resource probe project...Self-driving automobile project...Both concluded unrelated..."

Yui continued rattling off dry, official-sounding projects, but she judged all of them to be irrelevant and shook her head at the end.

"...I did not discover any unnaturally large budget requests that would match the expected scope of a project like this in the general accounts or special accounts. It's possible that they are spread among multiple smaller invoices or fraudulently represented, but it would be very difficult to determine either case based on public records alone."

"Hmm...so they didn't leave us any obvious trails that would easily identify them." Sinon groaned, crossing her arms.

Desperate to cling to any possibility, Asuna suggested, "But maybe Rath's budget is hiding somewhere in those projects Yui just found under a different name. Is there any way we could figure that out? I mean, it doesn't seem to have anything to do with finding underwater resources...Why did that particular research show up in your search?"

"Well…" Yui said, half closed her eyes again, accessed some distant database, then looked up. "It seems the research is on small drone submarines that can autonomously search for oil and rare metal deposits on the seafloor. The budget in question is for the AI that would pilot the device, but it showed up in my search filter because the amount seemed a bit large for the level of priority."

"Wow, they'll even make robots for stuff like that…I wonder where they're developing that?"

"The project is labeled under 'Ocean Turtle,' a self-propelled mega-float completed this February for the purposes of marine research."

"Oh, I saw that in the news," Leafa interjected. "It's more like a pyramid floating on the ocean than a ship."

"Right, I heard about that, too. Ocean…Turtle…" Asuna murmured. She frowned, glanced down briefly, then back up. "Say, Yui…do you have any images of that research ship?"

"Yes, just a moment."

She waved her right hand, and a screen appeared over the table, turning into a holographic depiction of the ocean, as it had done with the map earlier. Many little lights turned into a tiny wire frame, with textures filling in before their eyes.

The model that appeared was indeed a black pyramid at first glance, floating on the water. But when viewed from above, the base was not square but rectangular, with the long side about half the size of the short side. The height of the pyramid seemed roughly equal to the short side. Aside from some long, narrow windows, the surface was perfectly smooth, a shining dark-gray color. On closer look, the surface appeared to be crammed with hexagonal solar panels.

At each corner of the pyramid base were large, protruding structures that were probably to help steer it, and on one of the short sides was a bridge structure that looked like a small building. The H symbol on top had to signify a heliport. The model itself was so small that they were stunned to see that according to the scale measure on the side, the long end of the float was nearly a quarter of a mile in length.

"I see…Between the four legs, the square head, and the shell-like pyramid, it does kind of look like a turtle. A very big one…" Sinon noted, impressed.

Asuna glanced over and pointed at the bridge section of the massive *Ocean Turtle* craft. "But…look. See how this part here on the head kind of juts out like it's flat? Doesn't it look like a different kind of animal?"

"Ohh, you're right. It's a bit like a pig. A swimming turtle-pig," Leafa chimed in jokingly.

Then she realized the implication of what she'd just said and gasped. Her lips worked soundlessly, and she eventually managed to wring out, "A turtle…and a pig…"

Asuna, Sinon, and Leafa shared a knowing look, and they spoke in unison.

"Rath!"

2

The EC135 helicopter passed through the patch of thick ocean fog, and then there was nothing but deep blue on the other side of the window.

It was a brilliant close-up on whitecaps and breaking waves, nothing like the high-altitude view from a passenger jet. Rinko Koujiro wondered how many years it had been since she'd swum in the ocean.

Santa Monica Bay was about an hour's drive away from Rinko's current place of employment, the California Institute of Technology. She could easily go and work on her tan every weekend if she wanted, but in the two years she'd been on the job, she had not once set foot on the beach.

She didn't have anything against sun and sand, but it was going to take her a long time to be able to enjoy leisure activities on their own merits again. Rinko suspected it would take a decade or two of living in a foreign land where she was a total stranger before her past could truly vanish.

So it felt strange that, despite her assumption that she'd never be back, she was returning to Japan for just a single day—and to a place connected to the past she'd tried to abandon.

Four days ago, when she had received that very long e-mail from a surprising source, she had had the option to delete it and move on. But for some reason, she hadn't. She had slept on the proposal for just a single night before giving a positive reply. She knew that it completely invalidated the last two years spent locking away her mind and memories, and yet she had done it anyway.

What was it that propelled her onward, toward the place that weighed so heavily on her past?

Rinko sighed, and pushed away the question she'd asked herself many times over the course of the trip, from Los Angeles to Tokyo, overnight at the Narita hotel, and here on this small craft. She would learn the answer once she had seen and heard what she came for.

At the very least, the last time she had bathed in seawater was ten years ago, when she was an unsuspecting young college freshman. She had asked out Akihiko Kayaba, two years her senior, and driven to Enoshima in the little car she'd bought on loan. She was eighteen years old, so innocent and unsuspecting of the fate she was setting up for herself...

Before Rinko could delve too much further into her distant past, the person sitting next to her brought her back to the present, shouting to be heard over the rotors.

"Look, there it is!"

She followed the gaze of the other passenger, whose eyes were shadowed behind sunglasses and long golden hair. Indeed, through the curved cockpit windshield, there was a small black rectangle in the flat expanse of sea ahead.

"That's...the *Ocean Turtle*...?" Rinko murmured. Just then, the black solar panels reflected the sun toward them in a brilliant rainbow array. A man in a dark suit sitting in the copilot seat answered her.

"That's right. We'll be landing in about ten minutes."

The helicopter decided to cap off the 150-mile trip from Shin-kiba in Tokyo with a final spin around the massive marine research vessel *Ocean Turtle* before finally settling in to land.

Rinko gaped at the absurdity of the sight. The word *ship* was totally insufficient to describe the structure. It was more like an enormous pyramid rising out of the ocean. It was one and a half times the length of the *Nimitz*, the world's largest aircraft carrier. She couldn't even begin to guess how much the construction of this structure cost. She had heard the rumors that they had invested virtually all the profits from the recent mining of rare metals in Sagami Bay, but Rinko hadn't believed them—until she saw its size for herself.

Outwardly, the purpose of this mega-float was to find and develop new deposits of minerals and oil on the seabed—but on the inside, it might possibly contain a research lab developing a new full-dive machine called a Soul Translator that interfaced with the human soul, according to the e-mail Rinko had received the previous week. She wasn't sure she could accept that at first, but now that she was here, she had no choice but to believe it.

It made no sense. Why would anyone go this far, off to the remote Izu Islands, to research a new brain-machine interface? But the hard truth was that within that vast black pyramid was a machine descended from Akihiko Kayaba's NerveGear and the Medicuboid Rinko had helped develop.

Two years overseas had numbed Rinko's mental wounds but not healed them. Would what awaited her inside this ship help heal the scars or just rip them open to bleed anew?

As the helicopter descended, she steadied her breathing and turned to the passenger next to her. She met the eyes behind the sunglasses, nodded, and prepared to disembark.

The pilot must have been a real veteran, as the helicopter landed on the *Ocean Turtle*'s bridge heliport with hardly a single shake. Their guide in the suit nimbly slipped out of the craft to exchange greetings with another man in a suit running up to them.

Rinko headed to the exit hatch next. She waved off the man who extended a hand to her and hopped down the foot and a half to the ground, relieved that she had decided to wear jeans. The surface below her sneakers was so firm and steady that it was hard to believe they were floating on water.

The other passenger exited next, blond hair gleaming in the

sun, and stretched back. Rinko followed suit and stretched her arms, breathing in a lungful of salty sea air.

The tanned man waiting for them at the heliport greeted Rinko with a no-nonsense manner.

"Welcome to the *Ocean Turtle*, Dr. Koujiro. And this is…?" He gestured toward the other passenger.

Rinko said, "My assistant, Mayumi Reynolds."

"Nice to meet you," said the other passenger in fluent English, and stuck out her hand. The man accepted it awkwardly.

"I am Lieutenant Nakanishi, and I'll be your guide. Please leave your bags here; they will be taken to your quarters later. Right this way," he said, motioning toward a staircase at the end of the heliport. "Lieutenant Colonel Kikuoka is awaiting you."

The air inside the bridge building still had that midsummer heat and ocean salt to it, but after an elevator, a long hallway, and a heavy metal door that marked the interior of the black pyramid, the inside breeze was cold and dry on Rinko's face.

"Is the AC this strong all over the ship?" she asked the lieutenant without thinking. The young SDF officer turned back and nodded.

"Yes. There are many high-precision machines inside, so we must maintain a temperature of around seventy-three degrees and humidity under fifty percent."

"And the solar panels provide all the power for that?"

"Oh, no. The solar modules don't even meet ten percent of our power consumption. We use a nuclear pressurized water reactor for our main source."

"…I see."

At this point, anything goes, she decided, resigned.

There were no other people in the pale-gray hallway. From the materials she had had the chance to read beforehand, there were supposed to be nearly a hundred research projects underway here, but the facility was so huge that it still seemed like there was extra space to go around.

They walked about two hundred yards, turning right and left, until they came to a door dead ahead, attended by a man in a navy-blue uniform. It could have been a private security uniform, except that the crisp salute he gave to Nakanishi identified him as military personnel.

Nakanishi returned the salute and announced, "Our resident researcher, Dr. Koujiro, and her assistant, Miss Reynolds, will be entering Sector S-3."

"I'll run the check now," said the guard. He opened a metal device and gave Rinko a piercing facial comparison to the picture on the monitor. Once he was satisfied, the clean-shaven guard looked at her assistant. "Excuse me, but I need you to remove your sunglasses."

"Oh, I see," she said in English again, pulling off her large Ray-Bans. The guard squinted, as though her shining golden hair and fair skin were just slightly blinding.

"Confirmation complete. Go ahead."

Rinko exhaled and turned to Nakanishi to note, "Your security's pretty tight for being in the middle of the ocean."

"Well, at least you don't have to submit to any body checks. Of course, we already ran you through metal and explosive detectors three times," he replied, removing a small ID card from his suit pocket and inserting it in a slot next to the door. Then, he pressed his thumb to a sensor panel. A second later, the door slid open, granting them access to the core of the *Ocean Turtle*.

Past the thick door, the hallway was even cooler, lit with orange lights and faintly humming with machinery. She followed Nakanishi down the hall for quite a while, feeling conscious of the loud echo of her footsteps. It was hard to remember that they were actually inside a ship floating out at sea. Eventually he stopped at a particular door.

The plate on the door said FIRST CONTROL ROOM.

She had finally come to the place where Akihiko Kayaba's final estate rested. Rinko held her breath and watched the SDF officer as he performed another security check.

Would this be the end point of the long two-year wandering that had frozen her spirit?

Or was it just the start of a new one?

The door slid aside, revealing only a portentous darkness. Rinko couldn't move. The void did not reject her or welcome her. It just waited for her answer.

"...Doctor."

Her assistant's voice brought her back to her senses. Nakanishi was already several steps into the blackness and looking back at her expectantly. Upon closer examination, the control room was not completely dark; there were blinking orange markers on the floor and dim white lights toward the back.

Rinko took a deep breath, summoned her courage, and took a step forward. Her assistant followed her, and the door closed behind them.

They followed the floor markers through the rows of massive network devices and servers. When they finally made it through the valley of machines, Rinko gasped.

"...Huh...?!"

The sound escaped her throat unbidden. The wall before them was a huge window—and she could not believe what she saw on the other side.

It was a town...a *city*. But clearly no city in Japan. The buildings were all made of chalky white stone and had strange rounded roofs. They were nearly all two stories or more, and yet they looked like miniatures due to the mammoth trees towering over them.

Crowds of people walked over paths of the same white stone, connected to countless stairways and arches through the trees, yet they were obviously not citizens of the modern age.

There were no men in suits or girls wearing miniskirts. They were dressed like something out of the Middle Ages—loose one-piece dresses, leather vests, and long tunics that nearly touched the ground. Hair colors ran the spectrum from blond to brown to black, and the facial features were not clearly identifiable as either Eastern or Western.

Where were they? Had they somehow moved from inside the research ship to some subterranean world? Rinko glanced around the scene and noticed that far beyond the expanse of city was a brilliant white tower looming in the distance, surrounded by four smaller sub-towers. The top of the main tower went right off the boundary of the window into the blue sky beyond it.

She took a few steps forward, trying to see if she could glimpse the tip of the tower, and finally realized that she wasn't looking at a window but footage on a massive monitor wall. Then the lights in the ceiling turned on and banished the darkness for good.

"Welcome to the *Ocean Turtle*."

Rinko turned her head to the right, in the direction of the voice.

Just in front of the nearly movie-theater-size monitor was a console setup with a few keyboards and sub-monitors. There were two men standing there.

The one sitting in the chair was typing away with his back to them. But the other man resting his back against the side of the console met Rinko's glance and smiled, his glasses glinting.

It was a friendly but opaque smile, one she had seen several times before. That was Lieutenant Colonel Seijirou Kikuoka. But…

"…Why are you dressed like that?" She scowled. It probably wasn't the best way to address someone for the first time in two years. While Nakanishi saluted in his crisp, perfect uniform, Lieutenant Colonel Kikuoka wore a *yukata* of fine Kurume fabric tied with an elegant *obi*, with bare feet in wooden *geta* sandals.

"If you'll excuse me," Nakanishi said, saluting Rinko. He headed back through the machines, and when the door shut, Kikuoka leaned back on the console again and drawled, "You can't blame me. I've been here on the ocean for a month now; I can't wear my uniform *all* the time."

He spread his hands and beamed again. "Dr. Koujiro, Miss Reynolds, thank you for making the long trip. I'm so pleased you could visit us here at Rath. It was worth all the persistent invitations."

"Well, I'm here now, so I might as well accept your hospitality. Though I can't guarantee I'll be any help," Rinko said, and bowed. Her assistant did the same. Kikuoka raised an eyebrow, and his gaze briefly lingered on that stunning blond hair before the smile returned.

"And you are the final member of the trio I considered indispensable to this project. Now I have all three in the belly of this turtle at last."

"Ah, I see...I should have known one of those three would be you, Higa," Rinko said to the other man, who was still facing away. He stopped typing and swiveled in his chair toward them.

Next to Kikuoka's slender height, he looked tiny. He had bleached hair fashioned into little spikes and simple round glasses. His clothes were just what she remembered from college: faded T-shirt, cropped jeans, and worn-out sneakers.

Takeru Higa gave her a shy smile that suited his baby face. He opened his mouth and spoke the first words they'd exchanged in five or six years: "Well, of course it's me. I'm the last student of Shigemura Lab, so I've got to carry on our legacy."

"Well...I see you haven't changed a bit."

In the Shigemura research lab at Touto Technical University's electrical engineering department, Higa had tended to get lost in the shadows of the two giants, Akihiko Kayaba and Nobuyuki Sugou, yet here he was, intimately involved with a massive, top-secret government project. Rinko reached out for a light handshake, impressed at how far he'd come.

"...And? Who's the third person?" she asked, turning to Kikuoka again. The officer gave her one of his inscrutable smiles and shook his head.

"I'm afraid I can't introduce you quite yet. Maybe we'll have the opportunity in the days ahead..."

"Then why don't I say the name for you, Mr. Kikuoka?"

That came not from Rinko but from her "assistant," who had been lying low in her shadow all this time.

"What—?!" Kikuoka said, stunned. Rinko savored his shock and took a step back to give the girl the floor.

The assistant strode forward, ripped off the blond wig and the oversize sunglasses, and stared right into Kikuoka with hazel-brown eyes.

"Where did you hide Kirito?"

The lieutenant colonel probably had little experience with the sensation of shock. His mouth opened and closed several times to no avail, until at last he managed to squeak, "But...we did a multiple-pass verification of the assistant's photo from the Caltech student database..."

"You certainly did. We were even getting tired of you staring at our faces," said Asuna "the Flash" Yuuki, standing boldly inside the depths of the *Ocean Turtle* at last, under the guise of Rinko's college TA, Mayumi Reynolds. "The problem is, we made sure to switch my own photo into the school's database before applying to visit. We happen to know someone very skilled at getting around firewalls."

"For the record, the real Mayumi's getting her tan on in San Diego," Rinko added happily. "Do you see why I suddenly decided to finally accept your invitation, Mr. Kikuoka?"

"Yes...I see very clearly now," Kikuoka muttered, pressing his temples. Suddenly Higa burst into chuckles.

"See? What'd I tell you, Kiku? That kid's the biggest security hole in this whole operation."

Four days earlier, on July 1st, Rinko's private e-mail had received a message from one *Asuna Yuuki*. The contents of the message were a huge shock to her system, which was numb from a life spent traveling between her home and the school campus.

Before Rinko had left Japan, she had provided tech to the Ministry of Health for the Medicuboid full-dive device. Asuna told her that this device now formed the basis for a monstrous new machine called a Soul Translator being developed by a mysterious agency called Rath.

The likely goal for this soul-accessing machine was to create the world's first true bottom-up AI. This Kazuto Kirigaya boy who was assisting with tests had been abducted from the hospital in a coma and taken, most likely, to this brand-new *Ocean Turtle* marine research vessel. And the main suspect in the case was the government agent Seijirou Kikuoka, who had been deeply involved in VR going back to the *SAO* Incident. All in all, the message was extremely hard to take at face value.

"I found your e-mail address from the address book on Kirito's PC. You're the only person who could possibly take me to him and to Rath. Please, please help me."

That was how the message ended.

Despite her shock, Rinko had sensed that Asuna Yuuki's words were true. Three times over the past year, she had received invitations to participate in the development of a next-generation brain-machine interface from one Ground Lieutenant Colonel Kikuoka.

Rinko had raised her eyes from her monitor and to the night view of Pasadena outside the window of her condo. She had recalled the face of young Kirigaya, who came to visit her once before she left Japan.

He had explained to her the illegal human experimentation that Nobuyuki Sugou was attempting and, at the very end, hesitated. Then he had told her about his conversation with the ghost of Akihiko Kayaba in the VR world, and how that ghost had, for whatever reason, given him a shrunken-down version of the Cardinal system.

Thinking back on it now, the high-density, high-output brain-pulse scanner that Akihiko Kayaba had used to end his own life was the basis for the Medicuboid, and now, the Soul Translator. It was all connected, and nothing was over. So was it simply fate that she had gotten this message from Asuna Yuuki now?

Overnight, Rinko had made up her mind and replied to Asuna to accept her request.

She had to smirk. It had been a dangerous gamble, but it was worth crossing the Pacific to see that startled look on Seijirou

Kikuoka's face. Ever since the *SAO* Incident, he had been lurking around, seemingly controlling all events to his benefit, and she'd finally gotten one over on him. Still, it was too early to relax.

"So, now that we're here, why don't you give up and confess what you're doing, Mr. Kikuoka? Why is an SDF officer using a dead-end minor division in the Ministry of Internal Affairs as cover to get involved with the VR business? What are you plotting in the belly of this giant turtle? And...why did you abduct Kirigaya?" Rinko asked.

He shook his head and let out a long sigh, but his smile was as inscrutable as ever.

"First, I want to make sure there are no misunderstandings here...Yes, I'm sorry that we used rather forceful methods to bring Kirito into Rath. But that was because I wanted to *save* him."

"...What do you mean?" Asuna asked suspiciously, looking like she'd have her hand on the hilt of her sword if it were there.

"I found out that the escapee from the Death Gun case had attacked Kirito and put him into a coma the very day it happened. I also learned that his brain was damaged by a lack of oxygen, and that contemporary medicine would be unable to heal him."

Asuna blanched. "Unable...to heal him...?"

"Parts of the nerve cells that make up a major network of the brain were destroyed. No doctor could tell you when he would wake, no matter how long he stayed in the hospital. He could sleep there forever...Please don't look so upset, Asuna. Didn't I just say 'contemporary' medicine?" Kikuoka said. He looked more serious than he had at any point so far. "But if there's one technology that can actually heal Kirito's damage, it's here with Rath. As you already know, it's the STL: the Soul Translator. It cannot repair dead brain cells, but if the STL stimulates the fluct-light directly, it's possible to augment the rebuilding of that brain network. It just takes time."

His powerful forearm extending from the *yukata* sleeve gestured toward the ceiling.

"Kirito's currently inside the full-spec STL installed above the

Main Shaft here. The limited version of the device in our Roppongi office couldn't handle the finer procedures, so he needed
to come here. When his treatment ended and he regained consciousness, we were planning to send him back to Tokyo with a
full explanation to you and his family."

Asuna swayed on the spot; Rinko had to reach out to steady her.

She'd used an incredible amount of insight and willpower to
find and make her way to the boy she loved, and now it was like
all the tension had just snapped and drained out of her. A large
tear dripped from one eye, but she bravely wiped it away and
steadied herself.

"So Kirito's all right? He's going to recover?"

"You have my word. His medical needs are being treated at a
level equal to any major hospital. He even has a resident nurse."

Asuna fixed him with an intense stare, trying to seek out
Kikuoka's true intentions. After several seconds, she finally
bobbed her head and said, "All right...I'll believe you for now."

Kikuoka's shoulders slouched a bit with relief. Rinko stepped
toward him and asked, "But why is Kirigaya needed for the
development of the STL? Why does a top-secret project hidden
way out at sea need a teenage boy?"

Kikuoka glanced at Higa, then shrugged. "If I tried to explain
that, it would be a very long story."

"Well, it's a good thing we've got plenty of time, then."

"...If you want to hear the whole story, you'll have to assist with
the project, Dr. Koujiro."

"I'll decide that once I've heard you out."

The officer looked at her balefully, then resigned himself and
rustled around in his *yukata* until he found a small tube. To her
surprise, it was just an ordinary bottle of that cheap Ramune
soda candy. He popped a few into his mouth and offered it to the
women. "Want some?"

"...No, thank you."

"You sure? They're pretty good. Anyway...may I assume that
you both understand the general principle of the STL?"

Asuna nodded. "It's a machine that reads the human soul, or 'fluctlight,' and sends it into a virtual world that is completely indistinguishable from reality."

"Good. And what is the purpose of this project?"

"To create a bottom-up AI...A highly adaptive artificial intelligence."

Higa whistled in surprise. There was admiration behind the round lenses of his glasses, as well as disbelief. "That's incredible. I don't think even Kirito was aware of that part. How did you manage to look that up?"

Asuna gave Higa a searching look and answered roughly, "Based on what Kirito said. He said the words *Artificial Labile Intelligence...*"

"Ah, gotcha. Maybe you should look into the security procedures at the Roppongi office, Kiku," he said, grinning.

Kikuoka grimaced and shrugged. "I was prepared for the possibility that some information would leak out through Kirito. I would have thought you'd realize he was indispensable enough for us to take that risk...Anyway, where were we? Ah yes, the Artificial Labile Intelligence."

He flipped one more little candy into the air with his thumb, caught it in his mouth, then took on the air of a literature professor.

"For many, many years, the creation of a bottom-up AI structured in the same way as our own human mind was considered a pipe dream. We didn't even know *how* the human mind is constructed. But based on the data Dr. Koujiro brought us and the design of Higa's incredibly powerful Soul Translator, we have succeeded in capturing the quantum field we call the fluctlight—the human soul. At that point, we assumed that we had essentially succeeded at creating a bottom-up AI. Do you know why?"

"Because if you can read the human soul, you can make a copy...Is that it?" Rinko whispered, feeling a thrill of horror run down her back. "But you'd still have the problem of the medium on which to save the copied soul..."

"Yes, precisely. The quantum gates used in traditional quantum computing research don't have nearly enough space. So at great investment cost, we developed the Light Quantum Gate Crystal...or 'lightcube' for short. Inside this praseodymium crystallization, just two inches to a side, there are about ten billion cubits of storage—enough to correspond to the human brain. In other words...we have already succeeded at replicating the human soul."

"..."

Rinko shoved her hands into her jeans pockets to distract herself from the sensation of her fingertips going cold. Next to her, Asuna's cheeks were losing their color.

"...Then...isn't the project a success? Why did you need to get me here?" she asked, putting force into her words to hide her fear. Kikuoka shared another look with Higa and let a powerless smirk tug at the ends of his mouth.

"Yes, we succeeded at replicating souls. But foolishly, we failed to realize that there is an unfathomably deep chasm between a human copy and true artificial intelligence. Higa...show her."

"Aww, please no. I get so bummed out when I have to do this," Higa protested sourly, but he gave in and reluctantly started tapping at the console.

Abruptly, the image of the strange, exotic city on the megascreen went black.

"All right, here we go. Loading copy model HG-001."

Higa smacked the ENTER key, and a complex array of radiant colors appeared in the middle of the screen. It was nearly white at the center, while the tips reaching outward got redder as they went and stretched and contracted irregularly.

"...Is the sampling over?" came a sudden voice from speakers overhead, causing Rinko and Asuna to jump. It sounded like Higa's own voice. But there was a slight electronic falseness to it, a roughness around the edges.

Higa pulled a flexible microphone toward his seat and replied to his own voice by saying, "Yep, fluctlight sampling has concluded without issue."

"Okay, cool. But…what's going on? It's all dark. I can't move. Is there something wrong with the STL? Hey, can you let me out?"

"Nah…sorry, I can't do that."

"What? Wait, whaddaya mean? Who are you? I don't recognize your voice."

Higa tensed. He paused for a moment, then steadily proclaimed, "I'm Higa. Takeru Higa."

"…"

The red spikes suddenly shrank. After a brief silence, the sharp edges extended defiantly. "That's crazy. What are you talking about? *I'm* Higa. You'll see once you let me out of the STL!"

"It's all right; don't get worked up. That's not like you."

At last, Rinko understood what she was witnessing.

Higa was conversing with a copy of his own soul.

"Think hard and remember. Your memory stops at the point you entered the STL to make a copy of your fluctlight. Correct?"

"…What about it? Of course I don't remember the rest. You're not conscious during a scan."

"Remember what you told yourself before you went in? If you wake up and it's black all around with no sensation, you have to remain calm and accept the situation. You have to realize that you're a copy of Takeru Higa stored in a lightcube."

The light shrank down again, like some kind of soft, fleshy sea creature. There was a long, long silence. Finally, a few spikes grew back.

"…That's a lie. It can't be true. I'm not a copy; I'm the original Takeru Higa. I have…I have my own memories. I remember everything, from kindergarten, to college, to joining the *Ocean Turtle*…"

"That's right, but it's also completely expected. All the memories your fluctlight possesses are copied in the process. You might be a copy, but you're still Takeru Higa—which means you've got a brain that's as good as anyone's. Consider the situation and accept it. Then we can work together to achieve our shared goal."

"...Our...*Our*...?"

Rinko felt a thrill of horror prickle the skin on her arms when she heard the lurch of raw emotion in the metallic voice of the copy. She had never witnessed such a cruel and grotesque experiment before.

"...I can't...I can't believe you. I'm the original Higa. This is some kind of test, isn't it? Please, let me out already. Are you there, too, Kiku? Stop this nasty joke and let me go."

Kikuoka leaned over, looking gloomy, and pulled close to the mic. "It's me, Higa. Or should I say...HG-001. I'm sorry to admit that you are, in fact, a copy version. Before the scan, you underwent quite a lot of counseling, had many conversations with other technicians and me, all in preparation for accepting your status as a copy. I'm sure you remember that. You went into the STL with the understanding that this outcome was possible."

"But...but...nobody said it would be like this!" the copy screamed. The sound filled the large control room. "I'm...I'm still me! There should be something that allows a copy to feel that it's a copy! This is...This is just cruel...I hate this...Let me out! Get me out of here!"

"Calm down. Just be rational. Remember, the lightcube's error-correction capability is weaker than an organic brain's. You understand the danger that occurs when you lose rational thought."

"I am rational! I'm Takeru Higa! Why don't we have a pi-recitation contest between me and that imposter over there, so I can prove it?! Let's start! 3.1415926535897932, three-ay-fo-sig-doo-sig-fo-thril-dil-dil, dil, di-di-di-dil, dil-dil-dil-dil dildildil dildi——"

The red light expanded to fill the screen like an explosion. Then a black dot appeared at the center and spread outward until there were no traces left. All was silent, except for a little blip of static.

Takeru Higa let out a very, very long sigh and helplessly tapped a key on the console.

"That's a collapse. Four minutes, twenty-seven seconds."

Rinko heard a guttural convulsion nearby and realized that her hands were balled into fists. She opened them and felt cold sweat on the palms.

Next to her, Asuna had her hand over her mouth. Kikuoka noticed this and rolled one of the empty chairs at the console over to her. Rinko caught it and guided Asuna down into the seat.

"Are you all right?" she asked.

The girl looked up and bravely nodded. "Yes…I'm sorry about that. I'm okay now."

"Don't push it. Keep your eyes closed for a while," Rinko said. She felt Asuna's shoulders relax a bit, then glared at Kikuoka. "I'm astonished at your depravity, Mr. Kikuoka."

"I apologize for that. But I think you understand now that it's impossible to explain what we're doing without a direct demonstration like this," the military officer said, exhaling and shaking his head. "Higa here is a genius with an IQ close to 140. We copied his mind, and the result was unable to bear the recognition that it was a copy. We've replicated over a dozen fluctlights, including mine, and the results are always the same. The copies' logic systems go out of control at around three minutes after loading and collapse. Without exception."

"For one thing, I hardly ever scream like that, and it speaks a bit rougher than I do. You should have recognized that, Rinko," Higa said, looking extremely dejected. "We've seen that this isn't really an issue with the reasoning capabilities of the person being copied or a lack of mental care regarding their copying. I think it's a structural flaw of the fluctlights that are copied wholesale onto lightcubes. Either that, or…Do you know what brain resonance is?"

"Huh? Brain resonance…? Doesn't that have something to do with cloning? I don't know any details…"

"Well, it's all just occult mumbo jumbo. Basically, it claims that if you could create an absolute clone of a person, the two brains' magnetic fields being identical would produce something like mental microphone feedback, causing them both to go crazy. That's ridiculous, of course—but perhaps there's some kind of fundamental mechanism in our brains that is unable to handle the revelation that it is not a unique individual...Hmm, I see that suspicion on your face. Would you like us to make a copy of you so you can see for yourself?"

"Absolutely not," Rinko said, fighting off the urge to shiver. A silence fell over the adults, only to be broken by Asuna, who had her eyes closed as she sat.

"I heard something from Yui, a top-down AI—I'm certain you met her a few times in *ALO*, Mr. Kikuoka. Even though her 'mind' structure is totally different from a human being's, she too was frightened of the idea of having a copy. She was afraid that if some kind of accident caused the backup to be activated, the two of them would be forced to fight to eliminate the other..."

"Wow, that's really interesting. Just fascinating!" Higa exclaimed, pushing up the bridge of his glasses. "That's no fair, Kiku. I wanna meet this AI, too. Hmm, let's see...I suppose that means it's impossible to replicate a 'completed' intellect. Either that, or unique individuality is a prerequisite of existence..."

"But in that case," Rinko said, spreading her hands to beseech Kikuoka, "while it's an incredible accomplishment that you've succeeded in copying the human soul, doesn't this mean that your research has ultimately failed? After pouring in all these public funds, however much it cost...?"

"Oh, no, no, no," Kikuoka said, shaking his head with a wry smile. "If that was the conclusion of the project, they would have shot me from a cannon into the stratosphere—and put a few higher-ups in the joint staff office in front of a firing squad, to boot."

He tapped the tube of candies against his palm again, realized it was empty, then reached up the other sleeve this time to remove a box of white caramels.

"In fact, you might even say that's the *starting* point of this project:

the fact that it's impossible to copy a completed soul. So…if a perfect replica is impossible, what should we do, Doctor?"

"…May I have one of those?" she replied. Kikuoka happily offered a caramel, which she unwrapped and popped into her mouth. It tasted of tangy yogurt. You didn't get flavors like this in America very often. The sugar melted its way into her tired brain and gave her the mental energy to process the question.

"Well…what if you limit the memory? Let's say…erase personal details like one's name and background. Perhaps if the copy doesn't know who it is, it won't go into a state of panic like just now…"

"I should have known you'd come up with that right on the spot!" Higa exclaimed, acting like he was back in his college club. "It took us a week of back-and-forth to finally think of that and try it out. The problem is, the human mind isn't organized like a computer OS with nice, tidy folders and files. To put it simply, the memory and mental processors are all mixed up together. Which makes sense, when you think about it—our mental abilities aren't installed at birth but a product of learning."

Higa grabbed a notepad from the desk and held it up, using two fingers to pinch it in a cutting motion.

"Learning *is* memory. If you remove the memory of the first time you cut a piece of paper with scissors, you forget how to use those scissors…In other words, if you delete memories of the growth process, you also remove those abilities. So let me warn you, the result is far more miserable than the full copy you just witnessed. Wanna see?"

"N-no, that won't be necessary," Rinko said quickly. "So…what if you remove all memory and ability and allow it to learn from the start? Actually…I suppose that's not realistic. It would take too long…"

"Yes, exactly. After all, fundamental knowledge like language and arithmetic is actually extremely difficult for adults like us to learn, because there's little potential for growth left in our brains. I've been studying Korean, one of the more systematic languages, and I can't even remember how many years I've been at it. Basically, the learning process depends on the growth of the quantum computer that is the neural network—or, in other words, the growth of an infant mind."

"So you're saying you don't just restrict memory space...but the thinking and logic centers of the mind, too? Is the STL capable of doing that?"

"It's not impossible. But it takes an incredible amount of time to analyze the fluctlight and pinpoint which of the billions of cubits of data contain which functions. It could take years... decades, even. But then...this old guy over here figured out a much simpler, smarter way to do it. A method that scientists like us wouldn't have come up with..."

Rinko blinked and stared at the man in the *yukata*, leaning against the console. As usual, Kikuoka's expression was gentle but opaque, revealing nothing of the mind residing behind it.

"...A simpler method...?"

She thought it over, but no answer was forthcoming. She was about to give up and ask, when Asuna suddenly bolted upright in her chair.

"Oh no...You can't have done such a horrifying thing..." she murmured, cheeks still pale but eyes full of strong purpose. The girl's face was a mix of exotic beauty and indignation that she turned with full force on Kikuoka.

"You copied...babies? The souls of newborn babies? To get those blank, pure fluctlights with no learning built in yet?"

"Very perceptive. I'm amazed. But given that you and Kirito were the ones who beat *SAO*—the heroes who outwitted Akihiko Kayaba himself—I suppose that's rude of me to say." Kikuoka beamed, not bothering to hide his praise.

Rinko felt something in her chest twinge—she hadn't expected to hear Kayaba's name just then.

In the few short days since she had met the girl, Rinko had been impressed by and taken with Asuna Yuuki, but in truth, Asuna had the absolute right to criticize, insult, and persecute Rinko for her actions. No matter the circumstances, Rinko had assisted Kayaba's horrifying project, which had held Asuna prisoner for two years in a deadly game.

But neither Asuna nor Kazuto Kirigaya, whom she had met much longer ago, had ever said a single angry word to her. As if they believed everything had happened as it was meant to.

Did that mean Asuna believed this "Rath Incident" was also a product of fate? Rinko couldn't help but feel so. She watched Asuna take another step closer to Kikuoka.

"Do you think...that just because you're in the Self-Defense Force...that because you're in the government, that gives you the right to do anything you want? Do you think your own goals have priority over everything else?"

"Certainly not," Kikuoka said, shaking his head in aggrievement. "Yes, I agree that abducting Kirito was an extreme step. But at the time, I didn't have the ability to explain all these classified details to your families. Using our connections at NDMC to get him here to the *Ocean Turtle* was for the purpose of getting him treatment in the STL as quickly as possible. I love him, too, you know."

The lieutenant colonel paused, smiled innocently, and pushed his black-rimmed glasses up his nose. "Aside from that, I would say I'm expending too *much* effort upholding the law and human morality, considering the similar projects underway in other corporations and nations around the world. Even on the point that you just raised now. When we scan the fluctlights of newborns in the STL, we have the full understanding and cooperation of the parents, and we compensate them handsomely for the process. That was why we opened that branch office in Roppongi. Next to a maternity clinic, of course."

"But you didn't explain *everything* to the parents, did you? You didn't explain what the STL really is."

"No, we could only tell them that it was a device that took brain-wave samples...But that's not entirely incorrect. After all, the fluctlight is certainly made of electromagnetic waves in the brain."

"That's nonsense. You might as well be collecting the babies' DNA and making clones of it."

At that point, Higa interjected and made a big X sign with his arms. "She's got you there, Kiku. I agree, I think making a full copy of a newborn fluctlight *does* violate some kind of morality. But...Miss Yuuki, was it? You're a bit mistaken here, too. A fluctlight doesn't have the same level of individual difference that DNA does. At least, not at the newborn stage."

He pushed his silver-rimmed glasses up the same way his boss did and glanced around as he searched for the right words. "Let's see...I think this analogy will suffice. Let's say you've got a particular PC model from a certain company. Until they get shipped out, they're all essentially identical. But once the user gets it and operates it for a year or two, they'll have installed new software, new hardware, until they're eventually completely different machines. The human fluctlight is the same way. Ultimately, we copied the fluctlights of twelve different newborns, and when we compared them, we found they were arranged 99.98 percent identically, regardless of brain size. We believe that the last 0.02 percent of difference is based on different memories *in utero* and after birth. In other words, human intelligence and personality are entirely based on the growth process after birth. It's official: Nurture has won the battle with nature. Wish I could take this revelation to those eugenics freaks and shove it up their asses."

"Once the project is complete, you have my blessing. Shove to your heart's content," Kikuoka said wearily. "But at any rate, as Higa just explained, we have concluded that newborn fluctlights are not hard-coded with individual differences. So we very carefully deleted that 0.02 percent variation from our twelve fluctlights and gained what we call..."

He spread his hands and made a careful, cradling gesture.

"...Soul Archetypes. A basic model of the human mentality."

"More grandiose terminology. I take it this is essentially referring to 'the self' as defined by Jungian psychology?" Rinko asked.

Kikuoka shrugged wryly. "Listen, I'm just talking about functionality, I'm not offering philosophical speculation. You could think of the soul archetype as the basic CPU core that all human beings are born with. As we grow, we add all kinds of sub-processors and memory units to our core. Eventually, the very structure of that core changes…As we showed you minutes ago, just copying that 'completed' product to a lightcube does not give us the bottom-up AI we seek. So we thought, what if we take that soul archetype and raise it ourselves from within that lightcube…in a virtual world?"

"But—" Asuna started to protest.

Rinko put a hand on her shoulder and pushed the girl back into the seat. "You can't just raise it like it's a pet or a plant. This soul archetype is essentially the same thing as a human infant. That would require a virtual world of an unfathomable scale. A simulation on the level of modern society…Can you actually create such a thing?"

"We can't," Kikuoka admitted. "While the creation of virtual environments in the STL doesn't require generating 3-D models as with traditional VR development, it would be very difficult to re-create the complex, mysterious ways of modern society. There was a movie from before you were born, Asuna; I wonder if you've heard of it. It's about a man living in an enormous dome, whose entire life is a TV show. There are hundreds of extras acting as people around him—only the star himself is unaware of it. But as the man grows and learns more about the world, he starts spotting the cracks and eventually realizes the truth…"

"I've seen it. I liked that movie," Rinko said. Asuna indicated her familiarity as well, so Kikuoka went on.

"Essentially…in attempting to fashion a precise simulation of the real world, you run up against a major problem: Certain fundamental truths of the world, such as the roundness of the globe and the existence of many nations upon it, will eventually cause issues within the mind of the person being raised if those facts are not properly represented within the simulation. And even the STL is incapable of re-creating an entire virtual Earth."

"Then what if you set the level of civilization in the sim far back in the past? In a time before science and philosophy, when they all lived and died in remote little areas...Wouldn't that still work in terms of raising your soul archetypes?"

"Yes. It's quite a significant detour, but we do have plenty of time... within the STL, that is. At any rate, as Dr. Koujiro just indicated, we tried raising our first-generation AIs within a very limited space. More specifically, a sixteenth-century Japanese village. But..."

Kikuoka paused. He shrugged again, and Higa took over the explanation.

"It turns out it's still not as easy as we hoped. After all, we have barely any idea of the customs and social construction of that time. When we realized just how much information was necessary to create even a single house within the simulation, we went back to the drawing board...and then we figured it out. We didn't need to model the *real* world at all. If we wanted a limited space, the ability to dictate our own customs, and a worldview that would allow us to explain away any potential issues as 'magic'—well, there are already plenty of those. The networks that Kirigaya and Miss Yuuki are already familiar with."

"VRMMO worlds..." Asuna gasped.

Higa snapped his fingers. "I've done my fair share of time in them as well, so I figured out how well it would work for us pretty quickly. And the best part is, there's already this perfect game-creation tool package out there that somebody put together, totally free for anyone to use."

"...!"

Rinko instantly recognized that Higa was talking about The Seed...a compact version of the Cardinal system that Kayaba had created and Kazuto Kirigaya had shared with the net. She gasped—and recognized that neither Higa nor Kikuoka seemed aware of the program's birth.

Immediately, she decided to keep that under wraps and casually brushed her fingers on Asuna's shoulder. Asuna got the message and said nothing.

Higa failed to notice that anything was amiss and continued, "Creating a virtual space in the STL doesn't actually require 3-D data, but when you monitor the process externally, you only have raw data to look at, and that's no fun. So we tried downloading this Seed package, as it's called, and slapped together a little village using the editor program, then converted it to mnemonic visuals for the STL."

"Ah…Meaning it's a dual-layer world? There's a VR world made of ordinary data on the server below, while the STL mainframe above it converts that into its own VR format, with the two sides being mutually converted in real time?"

Higa confirmed Rinko's suspicion, so she continued, "Then… could you dive into the lower server with just an AmuSphere, rather than having to go through the STL?"

"Er, well…theoretically, it's possible. But you'd have to lower the operating speed down to times-1…and I doubt the mnemonic and polygonal data would be perfectly in sync…" Higa said, trailing off into mumbles.

Kikuoka rubbed his hands together and said, "At any rate, after all this testing, we finally had our little sandbox to work with."

There was a hint of nostalgia in his eyes, as if he was reminiscing on the distant past. "In that first village, we had sixteen soul archetypes making up two farming families…We managed to raise those AI babies up to the age of eighteen."

"H-hang on. Raised? Who raised them? Traditional AIs?"

"We looked into that, but, as high-functioning as The Seed's NPC AI is, it's not advanced enough to raise children. We had people act as parents for the first generation. Two men and two women on staff spent eighteen years in the STL acting as the farmer and wife of the two farms. While their memories within the system were ultimately blocked out at the end, it required an incredible amount of patience during the test. There's no bonus big enough to repay them for that service."

"I don't know, it sounded like they enjoyed it," Higa commented. Rinko just stared at them having a casual conversation about this. Finally, her lips sounded out the words.

"Eighteen...years...? From what I understand, the Soul Translator is capable of accelerating subjective time...but how long did that take in the real world?"

"Just about a week," Higa answered. Again, she was stunned. Eighteen years would be 940 weeks. That meant the STL was capable of accelerating time to the point where one real second would last a thousand in the simulation.

"And...and the human brain is capable of running at a thousand times speed without issues?"

"Remember, the STL doesn't access the biological brain; it's the field of photons that makes up our consciousness. The biological process of electrical signals causing neurons to release neurotransmitters can be completely cut out of the picture. In other words, in theoretical terms, we can accelerate the mental clock however much we want without damaging the structure of the brain at all."

"So there's no limit...?"

Rinko had a basic familiarity with the Soul Translator's fluctlight acceleration (FLA) feature, thanks to the materials she had received before the trip, but finding out the actual hard numbers it was capable of reaching left her speechless. She had thought the STL's ability to copy the human soul was its biggest accomplishment, but this time-speeding revelation was just as huge. This meant that the efficiency of any process in the virtual space was essentially unlimited.

"But, since we don't know what kind of undiscovered issues might be lurking out there, we've capped the machine at times-1500 for now," Higa said. His withdrawn expression dashed cold water on her stunned mind.

"Issues?"

"Well, some have suggested that unrelated to the biological structure of the brain, the soul itself might have a fixed life span, too..."

Higa noticed her confusion and glanced back at Kikuoka, seeking guidance as to how far to proceed. The military officer looked briefly like the caramel he was sucking on had gone nasty and bitter.

He explained, "Well, it's only in the realm of theory for now. Let's say that the quantum computers that we call fluctlights have a limit on their information storage space, and crossing that limit causes the structure to degrade. We can't actually test this hypothesis, so we can't be sure it's accurate—we just set an upper limit on the FLA amplification in the interest of safety."

"...Meaning that in physical time, it's less than a week, but after spending decades inside your mind, the soul degrades accordingly? Then what's the point of the acceleration? Is there no way to avoid that phenomenon?" Rinko asked, reverting to researcher mode for a minute.

This time, it was Higa who looked sour. "Er, well, there is a way, in theory...or more like in *imagination*. If we created a device like a portable STL to be worn at all times and used that to save to external memory while in acceleration, it wouldn't use up the capacity of the original fluctlight. But at our present state of technology, it's impossible to get the STL that small, and even if we could, it creates another major issue: When you remove that portable STL, you lose your accelerated memories, because they're all stored there instead."

"...This isn't imagination. It's outright science fiction. Overclocking brains, non-volatile memory that can be attached and removed...I wish I'd had this tech when I was a grad student," Rinko muttered, shaking her head. She wanted to get back to the main topic. "At any rate, it sounds like there's no way for you to avoid pressure on fluctlight capacity at present. Which means... Hang on. Mr. Kikuoka, you said that staff members spent eighteen years in the STL to raise soul archetypes. What happens to their fluctlights? Doesn't that mean their mental abilities will start to degrade eighteen years earlier than expected in the future?"

"No, no, that...*shouldn't* happen."

She glared at Kikuoka when he said the word *shouldn't*, but he just ignored her in his typically aloof way.

"Based on the total size of the fluctlight and the rate at which it fills, we calculate that the life span of the soul—if you want to call it that—is about one hundred and fifty years. That means that, assuming perfect health and good enough luck to avoid any neurological maladies, one's mental abilities can last at maximum until age one hundred and fifty. Naturally, none of us will actually live that long. Therefore, even with a healthy safety margin, we estimate that a good thirty years can be spent in the STL without adverse effect."

"Assuming the next century doesn't see some revolutionary new life-prolonging methods," Rinko said sarcastically.

Unperturbed, Kikuoka continued, "Even if that comes to be, regular old people like us will not be the beneficiaries of its gift. Of course, that might ultimately hold true with the STL, as well... But at any rate, let's take the life span of the soul for granted and continue on. Thanks to the devoted efforts of our four staff members, we raised sixteen youngsters, whom we call 'artificial fluctlights' for convenience. The results were very satisfactory. They learned language (Japanese, of course), basic mathematics, and other critical-thinking skills to a level that allowed them to survive in the virtual world we've built. They were great kids. They listened to their parents, drew water in the mornings, chopped wood, tilled fields...And they displayed individual differences. Some were calm and withdrawn, others a bit rowdier, but they were all essentially obedient and good-natured."

Was it just a trick of the eyes that there seemed to be a tinge of anguish to Kikuoka's gentle smile?

"There were four males and four females in each of the two houses. When the siblings grew, they even started to fall in love. We determined that they were capable of raising their own children now and considered the first stage of our test to be concluded. We separated those sixteen youngsters into eight couples and gave them each their own individual house and farm to run. The four staff members who had served as their parents were then 'killed' by a sudden plague and exited the STL. Their memories of the eighteen years in the machine were blocked off, which meant they emerged into reality in the exact same state they had been in a week earlier. Yet when they watched on the monitor as the children cried and held funerals in their honor, they shed tears, too."

"It was a touching scene," Higa added wistfully. Rinko cleared her throat to bring them back to reality.

"Ah...where was I? Once the staff members were out, there was no need to worry about the FLA rate, so we shot the simulation's acceleration up to five thousand times normal speed. We gave those eight couples around ten soul archetype babies each to raise, and they promptly grew to adulthood and started families of their own. We then removed the NPCs playing villagers bit by bit, until the village was large enough that it was made entirely of artificial fluctlights. Generations went on, producing more and more children, and after three weeks in the real world and three centuries in the simulation, we had an entire society of eighty thousand individuals."

"Eighty...?!" Rinko gasped. Her mouth worked soundlessly for a few seconds. "Then...you didn't create artificial intelligence... you simulated an entire civilization."

"Indeed. But in a sense, that was inevitable. Humans are social creatures; we only improve ourselves through interaction with others. Over three centuries, our fluctlights have spread out from their little village and conquered the entire map that we built for them. They constructed a central ruling structure without any ugly wars, and they have discovered religion as well...That last part may be thanks to the fact that we had to use the concept of God to explain certain system commands to the children at the very start of the experiment. Higa, call up the overall map on the monitor."

Higa promptly started entering commands on the console. The monitor had been dark since that grotesque demonstration several minutes ago, but now it showed a detailed terrain map, almost like an aerial photograph.

Naturally, it did not look like Japan or any other country on Earth.

It was a circular map of flatlands, with no ocean whatsoever, surrounded by a ring of tall mountains. The land was rich and fertile, with many forests, plains, rivers, and lakes. According to the scale displayed at the bottom of the map, the diameter of the circular realm was nearly a thousand miles. Based on total land surface, that would make it nearly eight times larger than the island of Honshu, the biggest part of Japan.

"Only eighty thousand people living in an area this huge? The population density must be paltry."

"Actually, I think Japan's the outlier on that front." Higa grinned. He moved the mouse and swung the cursor in circles around the center of the map. "This is the capital right here. Twenty thousand citizens, which sounds like nothing to us, but it's quite a magnificent city. There's even a governing structure here the fluctlights call the Axiom Church. There's an elite class called priests who undertake the duty of governing, and their control is impressive. This huge map is run without any armed conflict whatsoever. At this stage, I considered our fundamental experiment a success. Within the virtual world, we've proven that artificial fluctlights can be raised with the same intelligence as humans. I thought for certain that we could then move to the next step, in terms of building a highly adaptive artificial intelligence capable of what we want. But…"

"That was when we discovered a very serious problem," Kikuoka finished, staring at the monitor.

"…From what you've said, I can't imagine what problem that would be."

"The problem was that there *were* no problems. It was all too peaceful. The operation was too neat, too tidy. We should have realized the issue when those first sixteen children ended up surprisingly obedient to their parents…It's normal for humans to fight and compete. In fact, that's one of our defining natures. But there's no strife in this virtual world. There have been no wars in our simulation—not even any murders. That was part of the reason for our startling population growth. We set up the world to practically eliminate disease and natural disaster, so people only die of old age…"

"It sounds like a utopia," Rinko remarked.

Higa smirked and asked, "Has there ever been a utopian story that actually turned out to be a utopia?"

"…Well, it's not much of a story that way, is it? And the goal of your virtual society isn't to be entertaining, is it?"

"Certainly not. But we *are* looking for realism," Kikuoka said. He walked away from the console and toward the giant screen, wooden sandals clacking. "Those artificial fluctlights should have the same desires as us, so why is there no conflict? We studied the way they live, and we realized that there was one ironclad rule system built into the world. A massive book of laws, created in excruciating detail by the priests of the Axiom Church, called the Taboo Index. One of those laws forbids murder. Of course, we have that law in the real world, too. But all you need to do is watch the morning news to find out how closely we actually follow that law. Yet the fluctlights follow the law…to a troubling degree. Put another way, they are incapable of breaking the law. Something built into them prevents it."

"…Isn't that a good thing?" Rinko wondered. "Based on that, it almost sounds like they're superior to us."

"You might argue that is, in fact, the case. Higa, put the camera back on Centoria."

"Sure."

Higa tapped a key on the console. The footage of that foreign city that had been on the screen when Rinko and Asuna entered the room came back. People dressed in simple but pristine clothing walked to and fro among chalky white buildings adorned with tree roots.

"Oh…! You mean this is—?" Rinko asked, staring at the screen in wonder.

Higa nodded proudly. "Yep, this is Centoria, the capital of our artificial fluctlights' world. Of course, what we're seeing is the

polygonal data rendered on the lower server, so it's nowhere near as detailed, and the display speed is at a thousandth of the speed it's actually happening."

"Centoria...So they're actually capable of coming up with their own proper names, too? Does the world itself have a name, according to them?" Rinko wondered idly.

Kikuoka looked a bit embarrassed and cleared his throat. "Actually, it does have a name...but it's not originally from the fluctlights. We had our own project code name for our virtual world, and it seems to have stuck inside the simulation. The name of this realm is the Underworld."

"Under...world..."

Rinko had already heard this name from Asuna, but she didn't know it was also used within the world itself. She supposed that Higa and the others had chosen it out of *Alice in Wonderland* not to refer to a subterranean realm but a world that existed under reality itself. Yet the beautiful city on the monitor looked more like heaven than anything.

Kikuoka seemed to have read her mind. "Yes, this city is beautiful. We, too, are impressed that our humble little wood-built village has led to architecture of this scale and complexity. But if you ask me, this city is too neatly contained. There's not a single piece of litter on the streets, not a single pickpocket, and most certainly not a single murderer out there. And it's all because no one dares to violate the extreme laws handed down by that Axiom Church in the distance."

"And what's the problem with that?" she asked again, but Kikuoka didn't respond. He seemed to be searching for the right words. Higa was suspiciously avoiding her gaze. He wasn't about to speak up.

Asuna, who had been listening all along, eventually broke the silence in Control Room One. The youngest person present said, with cold, quiet precision, "Because that's not what they want, Dr. Koujiro. The ultimate goal of this massive project isn't to simply create a high-functioning, bottom-up AI...It's to create an AI that can kill enemy soldiers in a war."

"Wha...?"

Rinko, Kikuoka, and Higa were all speechless. Asuna stared at each of them in turn. She continued, "The entire time coming here, I wondered why Mr. Kikuoka—the military Self-Defense Force—would be trying to create an adaptive AI. For a long time, Kirito and I suspected that you were interested in VRMMOs as a means to assist police and military training. So at first, I wondered if the AIs were meant to model enemy soldiers for training purposes. But the more I thought about it, there's no actual danger in doing VR training exercises, and if you need to emulate real soldiers, just have the trainees work against one another in teams. We've done mock battles like that ourselves."

She paused and looked around at the array of machines and the giant monitor. "And this project is far too huge to be for a training program. At some point, you started thinking about the next phase, Mr. Kikuoka. You started contemplating using a VR-trained AI to fight real wars."

The military officer's poker face broke for just a second, betraying a look of shock. Then he smiled. "I was *always* thinking of that."

His voice was mild but covering a core of solid steel. "Using VR technology for military training was being tested back in the days of head-mounted displays and motion sensors, well before full-dive tech came along. Some of those artifacts are on display at our Ichigaya R&D facility at this very moment. When the NerveGear was announced five years ago, we and the American military immediately decided to work on a training program for it. But once I witnessed the *SAO* beta test for myself, I changed my tune. That world held greater possibilities. Something that could change the very concept of war itself. When the *SAO* Incident arose later that year, I volunteered to join the Ministry of Internal Affairs and take a position on the incident task force so

I could monitor the situation directly. It was all to get this project off the ground. And five years later, look how far we've come."

"..."

Rinko had no words. Things were going in a very different direction than what she had anticipated. It was hard even to collect her thoughts into some kind of logical statement.

"I was only in elementary school during the Iraq War, but I remember it well. There was lots of footage of the American military sending in unmanned drones and miniature remote-controlled tanks to attack the enemy. Is that what you're talking about? Putting AIs into those to create autonomous weapons capable of killing the enemy on their own...?"

"I wasn't the only one with that idea. This sort of research has been underway in many nations around the world, especially America. I'm sure that the memories are painful to you, Asuna," Kikuoka said, pausing to make sure that she wasn't visibly upset, "but I believe you're aware that when Nobuyuki Sugou had you and other *SAO* players trapped in that virtual world, he was trying to use his research data as a bargaining chip to sell his efforts to an American company. His contact was with GrowGen Micro-electronics, a top company in the VR industry. It goes to show how lucrative the military applications of full-diving are that even a leader in the field would make an illegal deal to get something like that. Like you just mentioned, Dr. Koujiro, unmanned weapons are the top interest of the American military-industrial complex at the moment. Most particularly, UAVs—unmanned air vehicles, or drones."

Higa considerately switched the monitor over to a new visual. This one was a small aircraft with a long, narrow body and several sets of wings. There were little missile-like tubes under the wings and no windows at all.

"This is an American reconnaissance drone. It doesn't need a cockpit, so they can shrink it down quite a lot, and they designed the body so that it doesn't show up on radar for stealth purposes. The previous generation of drones had a pilot watching a monitor at a remote location and controlling it with foot pedals and a joystick. But this one is different."

The screen shifted again, showing a soldier who was presumably the operator. But he was sunk deep into a reclining chair, his hands resting limply on his legs. On his head was a helmet very familiar to Rinko: a NerveGear. The exterior coloring and fine details of the shell were different, but it was clearly a device of that type.

Next to her, Asuna's expression was frozen in a wide-eyed stare. Rinko looked back at Kikuoka, and he continued his speech.

"In this state, the operator is inside a virtual cockpit, controlling the craft as though he is actually inside it. This allows him to perform reconnaissance of enemy forces and fire his missiles. The problem is that because our remote control relies on radio signals, it renders us very vulnerable to ECM, or jamming. Over ten years ago, there was an incident where an American spy drone was hit with jamming signals over a country in the Middle East, made a crash landing, and was recovered by the enemy. It nearly sparked another conflict."

"So you're going to try AI instead? So the craft can act on its own without human input?" Rinko asked. Kikuoka looked away from the monitor toward her and nodded.

"Ultimately, we want it to be capable of winning a dogfight against a human-piloted jet fighter. I believe that even our current artificial fluctlights, if given a proper training program, are capable of this. But there's one big problem. How do you teach these bodiless soldiers the concept of war? Murder is fundamentally evil, but in war, the enemy soldiers must be killed. Our current fluctlights are incapable of assimilating that paradox. To them, the law is something that does not allow for the slightest exception."

He pushed his glasses back up the bridge of his nose again, a crease forming between his brows.

"In order to test the law-abiding nature of the Underworld residents, we gave them a kind of stress test, if you will. We chose one isolated village in the mountains and killed off two-thirds of their crops and livestock. In other words, it would be impossible for the entire village to survive the winter. For the village to last as a whole, they would have to cut off some of their number and distribute the food unfairly—thus defying the rule outlawing murder in the Taboo Index. Instead...they chose to distribute that meager harvest equally among all the villagers, including the elderly and babies. They all starved before the spring. They are fundamentally unable to turn their backs on laws and rules, no matter how unfortunate the outcome. In other words, for them to serve as pilots in their current state, they would need a primary directive that states 'human beings are meant to be killed.' And even I can imagine what sort of result that would produce..."

He crossed his muscular arms over his chest and shook his head helplessly. Rinko couldn't help but envision that outcome. A swarm of drones, looking nothing like traditional aircraft, slaughtering soldiers and civilians alike with missiles and machine guns. She rubbed her prickling forearms.

"...You must be joking. Why would you risk such incredible danger to put AI on a weapon? Why can't remote control be good enough, even with its limitations? In fact, just the concept of an unmanned weapon is unacceptable to me."

"I'm not saying I don't understand your point of view. The first time I saw an American drone tank carrying a large-caliber sniper rifle, I honestly thought it was grotesque. But there's no fighting it...unmanned weaponry is simply a fact of life in the developed nations," he said, holding up a finger like a history teacher.

Kikuoka continued, "Let's take America as an example—the largest military in the world. They suffered four hundred thousand casualties in World War Two. Despite all that death and loss, President Roosevelt enjoyed incredible support from the populace, and he served as the commander in chief for an unprecedented thirteen years in four terms, until he died of a stroke. I hate the phrase *the spirit of the times*, but let's be honest: Eighty years ago, the spirit of the times said that any amount of loss was justified as long as the country was victorious."

A second finger extended from his thick fist.

"Later, in the Vietnam War, there were widespread protests against the war, led by students. While President Johnson was unpopular enough not to seek reelection, there were sixty thousand dead soldiers under his watch. They still sent soldiers off to die in war for the cause of anti-Communism. But under that long, tentative peace of the Cold War, the sentiments of the people began to change…and then that era came to an end with the fall of the Soviet Union. Without the threat of Communism, the only way that America could support its massive military-industrial complex was to find a new enemy to fight: terrorism."

He held up a third finger.

"But in this battle, there was no flag under which the populace would accept the death of soldiers. The number of American casualties in the Iraq War at the start of this century was just around four thousand, but that number was enough to significantly destabilize the Bush administration. For that reason, among others, he ended his term with the worst historical level of support. You could say it was inevitable that his Republican nominee successor, John McCain, suffered defeat at the hands of the Democrat Barack Obama and his pledge to withdraw forces from Iraq. In other words…"

He lowered his hand, took a breath, and concluded his long lecture.

"It is no longer an era in which it is acceptable for people to fight in wars. But that country cannot stop fighting wars—or, in more accurate terms, it cannot stop allotting an enormous slice of the pie to its defense budget. As a result, future wars will be fought drone versus human or drone versus drone."

"…I understand the American quandary. Not that I necessarily agree with it," Rinko admitted. She found the idea of using drone weapons to fight war cleanly to be horrifying. She glared at Kikuoka and pressed him again. "But why is a defense officer of

Japan trying to jump into that ridiculous arms race? Or are the Americans leading all this Rath research?"

"Certainly not!" Kikuoka shouted, a rarity for him. But then his smile returned, and he spread his arms theatrically. "If anything, we're floating out here in the open sea to hide ourselves from the American military. They've got perfect tabs on all our bases on the mainland, of course. But as for why I'm going to such lengths to pursue autonomous drone weapons...it's not an easy thing to explain. Would it be appropriate to say that it would be similar to asking Dr. Kayaba why he created *SAO*?"

"No, it wouldn't," Rinko said brusquely. Kikuoka smirked and shrugged.

"Pardon me. That was insensitive to ask. Let's see...The biggest reason is that the current foundation of our self-defense capabilities is extremely lacking."

"Self-defense...foundation?"

"Let's call it the ability to develop and produce weapons from scratch. In a sense, this is completely natural, as Japan cannot export weapons. And given that any weapons manufacturers can only make deals with the SDF by law, all that development cost has no chance of being recouped. As a result, we either have to import or codevelop with the Americans any cutting-edge tech. But this 'codevelopment' is only in name; it's really a much more one-sided deal."

He fixed the sleeves of his *yukata*, crossed his arms, and proceeded bitterly. "For example, we currently use aerial support fighters 'codeveloped' with the Americans. But in fact, they kept their secrets close to their chest, took the cutting-edge material we came up with, and ran off with it. The weapons that we buy from them are even worse. We just imported some state-of-the-art fighter jets, and they came with no system control software—the actual brains of the vehicle. The American military thinks we should get their leftovers and be grateful for the scraps. Oops, pardon me...I'm getting sidetracked into my usual griping."

He smirked again and crossed his legs atop the console desk, dangling his sandals from the ends of his toes.

"A small number of military officers and some younger techs from the smaller defense contractors have been feeling like this is a dangerous state of events. It's not good for us to rely on the Americans for the core of our defensive capability. That anxiety was the force behind Rath's founding. We wanted to create a technology that was truly Japan's. That's all we really want."

Rinko wasn't sure how seriously to take this lofty statement. She gazed at those narrow, shining eyes behind his black-rimmed glasses. But, as usual, they only reflected back at her like mirrors.

Instead, she addressed Higa. "Is your motive for participating in this the same? I had no idea that national defense was such a concern of yours."

"Well," Takeru Higa mumbled, scratching his head shyly, "my motive is more personal. I had a friend from a Korean college when I was a student. When he did his mandatory service, he was deployed in Iraq and killed by a suicide bomber. So I thought... if we can't erase war from the world, maybe we can at least stop people from dying in it...It's childish reasoning, I know."

"But your military friend over here thinks that your unmanned weaponry will be for the JSDF only."

"Well, if we're being honest, and with all respect to Kiku, technology never stays unique for long. He knows that, too, I suspect. He doesn't want a monopoly on the tech; he just wants to stay a step ahead...Isn't that right?"

Kikuoka grimaced yet again; it was a brutally frank assessment. Just then, the beautiful, cold voice of Asuna interrupted the adults.

"And you did not speak a word of these laudable beliefs to Kirito, did you?"

"...What makes you say that?" Kikuoka asked in surprise.

She met his gaze without flinching. "Because if you had, he would not have helped you. Your ideas are completely missing one very important aspect."

"...Which is?"

"The rights of the AIs."

Kikuoka raised an eyebrow at that. "Well, you're correct in that I did not tell him what I just told you, but that's only because I didn't have the opportunity. He's a stone-cold realist, isn't he? He couldn't have beaten *SAO* otherwise."

"You don't get it. If Kirito understood the true nature of the Underworld, he would be furious at the developers. To him, reality is wherever he is. He doesn't think of anything as 'virtual,' worlds or lives. That's how he could beat *SAO*."

"You're right, I don't get it. Artificial fluctlights have no flesh bodies. If that isn't virtual life, what is?"

Asuna looked mournful. In fact, she looked pitying.

"Well, this might be pointless, since I doubt you'll understand anyway…But I'll tell you that on the fifty-sixth floor of Aincrad, I said something similar to him. There was a boss we just couldn't beat, so our idea was to use NPCs—AI villagers—as bait. We'd draw the monster into the village and jump on it while it was attacking the villagers. But Kirito was absolutely dead set against it. He said that the NPCs were alive, too, and there had to be another way. The people in my guild laughed at him…but he was right. Even if your artificial fluctlights are all just copies produced en masse on storage media, Kirito would never support your idea of using them as tools of war. *Never.*"

"Look, I understand what you're saying. Yes, the artificial fluctlights have the same ability to think that we do. In that sense, they *are* alive. But this is an issue of weight and priority. To me, the lives of one hundred thousand artificial fluctlights are worth less than a single soldier's."

Rinko sensed that there would be no consensus in this debate. The issue of whether or not artificial intelligence had rights could be argued for years after the announcement of a true bottom-up AI, without any definitive answer.

She didn't even know how *she* felt about the issue. The rational, scientist side of her said that a copied soul was not a true life. But at the same time, part of her wondered what *he* would say.

The man who had always wished for another place, far, far away, eventually created it and left, never to return...

She had to cut off that line of thought before it threatened to drag her into the past. She had to break the silence.

"Why did you need Kirigaya, anyway? Why him, to the extent that you endangered your most sensitive secrets...?"

"Ah, yes. I started up this long discussion to answer that question. It took so long that I nearly forgot," Kikuoka said, smiling and clearing his throat to escape Asuna's magnetic, accusing gaze. "We had our own debates on staff: Are the Underworld residents unable to disobey the Taboo Index because of a structural issue with fluctlights and their lightcube storage, or is it a factor of the growth process? If it's the former, we'd need to redesign our storage format, but if it's the latter, we might be able to fix it. So we did a little test. We took a staffer, blocked all of their real human memories, then raised them in the Underworld as a child. That way we could see if they turned out the same as all the artificial fluctlights."

"And...and was the test subject's brain unharmed? You're basically making them relive life from childhood...Wouldn't they run out of memory space?"

"Not a problem. Remember how I told you that fluctlights can hold about one hundred and fifty years of memories? I don't know why the margin is so much larger than our life span...but after all, the Bible claims that people in Noah's era lived for centuries. At any rate, I'm only speaking of raising to the age of ten. That should be an old enough age to see if they can break the Taboo Index or not. Naturally, they exited the STL in the exact state they entered it, since we blocked all those memories upon leaving."

"And what happened...?"

"We recruited eight test subjects from the staff and had them raised in the Underworld in various environments. To our surprise, all the way until the test ended when they turned ten, not a single one of them broke the Taboo Index. In fact, contrary to expectations, they were all *less* active on average than the fluctlight children, avoided going outside, and showed an inability to integrate with others. We surmised that this was due to discomfort."

"Discomfort?"

"Having their original life memories blocked doesn't mean they're gone. If that were true, we couldn't bring them back to real life in the same state. In other words, it's the instincts and fundamentals of things like body movement, not the knowledge, that prevented the test subjects from feeling at ease in the Underworld. The virtual world might seem real, but it's still a product of The Seed. If you dove in, you'd see that the sensations are just slightly different from those in real life. It's the same kind of slight, alienating discomfort I felt the first time I tried on a NerveGear for the *SAO* beta test."

"It's the sense of gravity," Asuna said.

"Gravity…?"

"The research on our sense of gravity and balance lags behind our understanding of visual and audio sensory signals. Most of our visual signals are complemented by the brain's sense of gravity, which is why people who aren't used to it have trouble moving."

"Exactly. It's getting *used* to it," Kikuoka noted, snapping his fingers. "We did all those tests until we finally realized that what we needed were test subjects accustomed to the virtual environment. Experience not in terms of weeks or months but years. You understand now? I needed the help of the person with the most virtual experience in all of—"

"Hang on," Asuna interrupted, her voice hard. "Was that the three-day continuous dive Kirito was talking about? But he said the maximum acceleration rate of the FLA was three, so it was no more than ten days on the inside. Did you lie to him? Was it really ten years…?"

Kikuoka and Higa wilted guiltily under her fierce gaze.

"I'm sorry; that was a mistake of the Roppongi branch. I ordered them to keep the acceleration rate completely under wraps…"

"That makes it even worse! You got ten years of Kirito's soul for your own purposes—if you fail to recuperate him, I will *never* forgive you for what you've done."

"This is not an excuse, but both Higa and I have already dedicated over twenty years to the experiment. But the ten years we got from Kirito provided us with results far, far greater than the sum of all our staff fluctlights together."

"Meaning that as he grew inside the Underworld, he took actions that defied the Taboo Index?" Rinko asked despite herself. Kikuoka grinned.

"Technically, he did not. But ultimately, the result was much greater than we had hoped for. From a young age, Kirito displayed a boundless curiosity and agency not seen in the other test subjects and was punished on many occasions for very nearly breaking the Taboo Index's laws. Of course, this is not entirely a thing to celebrate, as his success would have indicated a structural flaw in our artificial fluctlights. Still, we watched him closely. At around seven years of internal time…Higa here noticed something quite fascinating."

Kikuoka paused there, allowing Higa to take over the story. "Yup! I was originally against putting Kirigaya into the experiment for both ethical and security reasons, but when I saw what happened, I had to be impressed with Kiku's insight into the kid. We assign numerical weights to the individual laws within the Taboo Index and measure the numbers of each individual according to how close they get to a brush with the law. It turned out that a fluctlight boy and girl who were particularly close to Kirigaya—or Kirito, as he was known in the test—also saw their numbers explode."

"Huh? Meaning…?"

"Meaning that despite his own memories and personality from the real world being blocked off, Kirito exhibited a strong influence on the actions of the artificial fluctlights around him. Or, if you want to be more frank, his boisterous nature rubbed off on the other kids."

Rinko noticed a small grin tug at Asuna's mouth. She must have been able to picture it for herself.

"We still haven't actually figured out the reason the artificial fluct-lights don't ever break their rules," Higa continued, "and it's probably something to do with the structure of the lightcubes we store them in. But we don't consider identifying that our top priority anymore. We don't need to solve the problem; we just need to find an exception. If we can produce a single true adaptive AI that has integrated the concept of priority rankings, we can just reproduce that instance to achieve some measure of success in our experiment."

"I'm not a fan of that way of thinking. But it's true that most breakthroughs happen through methods like that," Rinko had to admit. "And did you get that exception?"

"We did have it in our hands once. Just before the end of the experiment, the girl who Kirito was closest to actually did break a taboo. And it was a serious one—access to a restricted address. According to the log, she witnessed another artificial fluctlight die within that restricted area; I'm guessing she thought she could save it. Do you understand? She put another person's life over the Taboo Index. That's the adaptive ability we're looking for. Of course, it's ironic that this particular action was our breakthrough, given that we're hoping to develop them into military tools."

"...You said, 'We had it in our hands,' though."

"Er, right. It's kind of embarrassing to admit...but that little gem slipped right through our fingers..."

Higa slumped his shoulders, shook his head. "Like we said earlier, the Underworld simulation happens at a thousand times the speed of the real world. It's pretty much impossible to monitor that in real time, so our process basically works by slowing down already recorded events so that multiple operators can examine them. Inevitably, there's a major lag from us to the internal time. When we spotted that the girl had violated the Taboo Index, we paused the server and tried to physically eject the lightcube storing her fluctlight...but two days had already passed in internal time by then. To our amazement, in those two days, the Axiom Church had already taken her to the central city and performed a corrective measure on her fluctlight."

"C-corrective? You gave your experiment subjects the ability to do that?"

"Of course not. Or...we *thought* not. For the sake of maintaining order, we designated all the Underworld residents with certain authority levels. The individuals with higher levels have the ability to perform certain system commands in the form of 'sacred arts.' But even the high priests of the Axiom Church, who have the highest authority levels of all, can do little more than manipulate the length of a life span. Somehow, they found some kind of loophole in the system...Actually, I can show you the recorded data we have. Here's Alice's past and present taboo violation numbers."

"Alice...?" whispered Asuna. Her head shot up. Rinko had heard about the significance of that name, too. It was the code name for the bottom-up AI that Kikuoka and Higa were trying to create.

Kikuoka nodded, recognizing the reactions of the two women.

"That's right. Alice is the name of the girl who spent all her time with Kirito and another boy in the simulation. Nearly all of the Underworld residents' names are odd and seemingly random syllables. So when we found out that the girl's name just happened to be Alice, the coincidence was stunning. After all, it's the name of the very concept that was the foundation for Rath and everything we are doing in this experiment."

"Concept...?"

"Our highly adaptive and autonomous artificial intelligence. Artificial Labile Intelligent Cybernetic Existence. Or in acronym form, ALICE. Our ultimate goal is to turn the clouds of photons trapped in those lightcubes into a single Alice. In other words, to Alice-ize them."

Lieutenant Colonel Seijirou Kikuoka had revealed his deepest secret, yet that strange smile of his still harbored mystery.

"Welcome...to Project Alicization."

3

What an unbelievable thing they've built.

The machine was created with data she'd provided herself, and yet Rinko Koujiro couldn't help but marvel at it.

On the other side of the thick glass wall, two massive cuboid shapes loomed, nearly tall enough to reach the ceiling. Their exterior was plain aluminum sheeting, but that dull gray shine only accentuated their mechanical nature. They were several times larger than even the Medicuboid, to say nothing of the NerveGear apparatus.

Naturally, there were no manufacturer logos, just a simple English font on the side reading SOUL TRANSLATOR, as well as large numerals designating unit numbers. The machine on the left was 4 and the one on the right was 5. The soul-reading devices were right there in view at last, and Rinko gazed at them for nearly half a minute before she finally spoke.

"Four…? So that's the fourth one? And the other is Unit Five?"

It was the only way to interpret the numbers, and yet there were only two machines in the clean room on the other side of the glass. A hushed voice on her right began to explain.

"Test Unit One is at our Roppongi branch office, utilizing a satellite connection. Units Two and Three are also on the *Ocean Turtle*, but as you can see from their size, there isn't enough room here. They're located in the lower shaft. Or, more accurately, Units Four and Five couldn't fit down *there*, which is why they're here in the upper shaft."

The voice belonged to the person who had guided Rinko and Asuna here, but it was not Kikuoka, Higa, or Lieutenant Nakanishi. It was not even a man. She wore a white uniform over her tall, shapely body, flat-soled slip-on shoes, and the distinctive hat of a nurse.

It was strange to imagine a nurse in a place like this, but given the sheer size of the ship, there would naturally be an infirmary somewhere and medical staff to operate it.

The nurse, who sported braided hair and rimless glasses, tapped her tablet device and turned it to show Rinko. It displayed a cross-section map of the *Ocean Turtle*. Her finely trimmed nails traced a vertical line through the center of the craft.

"There is a reinforced tube at the center of the pyramid that we call the 'main shaft.' It's about sixty feet across and over three hundred feet deep. Not only does it support each of the floors of the ship deck, it's also the barrier that separates and protects our most sensitive and crucial capabilities. That includes the control system for the ship itself and the core of the Alicization project—the four STLs and the Lightcube Cluster that serves as its mainframe."

"Ah…So what makes them upper and lower shafts, then?"

"A barrier wall made of the same titanium alloy as the vertical walls splits the main shaft horizontally. So the space above the barrier is the upper shaft, and the space below is the lower shaft. We're currently in Control Room Two, located in the upper shaft. The staff calls this one Subcon for short."

"I see. So I'm guessing that Control Room One down in the lower shaft is normally called Maincon?"

"Very perceptive, Dr. Koujiro," the nurse said with a smile.

Rinko turned to her left toward the silent girl. Asuna Yuuki had her hands pressed to the glass as she gazed intently at Unit Four. Specifically, at the boy lying on the gel bed connected to the base of Unit Four.

There were a number of monitoring electrodes under his white hospital wear and a micro-injector placed in his left arm. His face was out of sight, swallowed above the shoulder by the STL. But Asuna could tell that he was Kazuto Kirigaya, the boy she sought.

She had eyes only for Kazuto, showing no sign that she noticed Rinko's attention. Eventually, her long eyelashes lowered, and her lips moved without sound. A little drop grew at the corner of her eye, trembling in place without falling.

Rinko tried to say something, anything that could comfort Asuna, but to her surprise, the nurse spoke first. "It's all right, Asuna. I'm sure that he will come back to us."

She strode forward to Asuna's side and reached out to the girl's shoulder, but Asuna turned to avoid the touch, brushed aside her tears, and put on a confrontational attitude.

"Of course he will. But…why are you here, too, Ms. Aki?"

"What…? You know each other?" Rinko asked, surprised.

Asuna nodded. "Yes, she was the nurse at the hospital in Chiyoda. I don't know what she's doing out here on the open sea, though."

"I'm taking care of Kirigaya, of course."

"What about your job? Or was the nurse thing just a front, like with Mr. Kikuoka?" Asuna accused. The nurse named Aki grinned and shrugged, totally unfazed.

"No. Unlike his little disguise, I really am a nurse with national credentials. It just so happens that I graduated from SDF Tokyo Hospital Nursing School."

"…That explains many things," Asuna said.

Rinko was still unsure. "Umm, I'm afraid I don't quite understand…What kind of person is this Ms. Aki?"

"Well, it's true that she's a nurse. It's just that there's more to the story than that," Asuna explained. "As a basic rule, nurses who graduate from the school attached to the SDF hospital then go on to work at SDF hospitals. Yet she was looking after victims of the *SAO* Incident at the hospital in Chiyoda. Which means that Mr. Kikuoka had something to do with that. Correct?"

"Very perceptive, Asuna," Aki said, repeating the compliment she had given Rinko just a minute earlier.

Asuna glared at the tall nurse and added, "One more thing. I read in the school's career guidance materials that registering at the SDF hospital's nursing school is essentially treated like joining the SDF itself. So doesn't that mean that in addition to being a nurse, you're also—?"

Nurse Aki slashed her hand out, cutting off Asuna's question. She then lifted it to her forehead in a crisp salute.

"Sergeant First Class Natsuki Aki, on duty! Kirigaya's physical health and general well-being are under my jurisdiction! *Tee-hee...*" she said with a little wink.

Asuna stared at her, half in shock and half annoyed. She sighed and bowed her head. "Please be good to him." Then she turned back toward STL Unit Four and gazed at the boy lying on the gel bed, just ten feet away, yet out of reach behind the glass. "You'll come back...won't you, Kirito?" she mumbled.

Nurse Aki bobbed her head and actually got a hand on Asuna's shoulder this time. "Of course he will. His neural network is repairing as planned, so it won't be long before he wakes up. Plus...he's the hero who beat *SAO*, after all."

Those words brought a sharp, prickling pain to Rinko's chest. She took a deep breath to numb the sensation, then walked forward to Asuna's other side and looked up at the massive machine.

Eight o'clock PM.

Rinko looked up from her wristwatch and summoned the determination to press the metal button marked CALL. Within a few seconds, the speaker next to the door replied, "Yes?"

"It's me, Koujiro. May I talk with you for a bit?"

"Hang on, I'll open the door."

The intercom panel's light changed from red to green, and the motorized door slid open.

Rinko walked into the room. Asuna bowed in greeting from her position next to the bed; there was a remote control in her hand. The door shut behind Rinko, and the lock clicked into place.

The cabin interior was exactly the same as Rinko's across the hallway. The standard-size room was lined with off-white resin paneling and contained only a fixed bed, table, and sofa, plus one small computer for accessing the ship's network. While escorting them here, Lieutenant Nakanishi had described them as "first-class cabins," so Rinko had envisioned some kind of luxury cruise suite, but apparently the only thing that defined these as first-class was the presence of a small private bathroom.

The one difference in Asuna's room was a narrow window on the other side of the bed, meaning it was positioned along the outer edge of the *Ocean Turtle*, where the generator panels were. They had climbed several floors on the elevator, so the sunset view through that window would have been gorgeous, but it was now pitch-black outside. The cloud layer hid even the stars from view.

"Please, sit down," Asuna said.

Rinko set down the bottles of oolong tea she had bought from the vending machine next to the elevator and sat on the stiff sofa. She very nearly let out a "Hoo-boy!" when she bent down. Rinko considered herself to be young, but in the presence of the dazzling beauty of Asuna in her T-shirt and short pants, she felt acutely conscious of her approaching thirties.

"Go ahead, have some tea," she offered, pushing one of the bottles forward.

Asuna tipped her head and smiled. "Thank you, I was just feeling thirsty."

"Did you give the tap water a try?" Rinko smirked. The girl rolled her eyes.

"It made the water in Tokyo taste good."

"Well, it's made from desalinated seawater, so at the very least, you don't have to worry about those carcinogenic disinfectants. It might even be better for you than those bottles of deep-sea water they sell at the store. Still, one mouthful was enough for me."

She twisted off the cap of the tea bottle and took a deep swig of the cold liquid. She would have preferred a good beer, but she'd have to travel down to the cafeteria for that.

Rinko exhaled and glanced at Asuna again. "It's too bad you couldn't get a look at his face."

"Still, he seemed like he was doing well to me. Maybe he was having an enjoyable dream," Asuna said with a smile. It was as though the panic that had gripped her the last few days had finally run its course.

"You've got a real headache of a boyfriend, kid. Going ghost on you, popping up on a cruise in subtropical seas…You'd better get a collar around his neck."

"I'll look into it." Asuna chuckled. She inclined her head deeply toward Rinko. "I'm so grateful to you, Dr. Koujiro. I can't believe you indulged this crazy request of mine…There's no way I can ever properly thank you."

"Oh, stop it. Just call me Rinko. Besides, this is just a drop in the bucket for what I did to Kirigaya and you," she said, shaking her head. She summoned her courage and stared Asuna right in the eyes. "There's something…I need to tell you. Not just you… Everyone who was stuck in *SAO*…"

"…"

Rinko made certain not to break away from Asuna's direct gaze. She sucked in a deep breath, exhaled, and undid two buttons on her cotton shirt. She lifted a silver necklace out of the way of the gap to expose a diagonal surgical scar to the left of her sternum.

"Do you know…what this scar is from?"

Asuna stared unflinchingly at the spot directly above Rinko's heart. Eventually, her head bobbed. "Yes. It's the spot where the remote-detonation micro-bomb was implanted, wasn't it? That's how the guild leader—Akihiko Kayaba—was able to keep you in line for two years."

"Correct…That's how he forced me to participate in his awful project and manage his physical body while he was in that long-term dive…At least, according to the rest of society. That's how I avoided prosecution or having my identity made public, and I got to escape to America..."

Rinko put her necklace and shirt back in place, then summoned the courage to continue. "But the truth is different. The explosive they detected at the police hospital was real, and it could have gone off. But I knew that it wouldn't. It was just camouflage. He put that weapon inside me as a bluff, to ensure that I wouldn't be tried for my part in the scheme after it was all said and done. It was the only present he ever gave me."

Asuna's expression never changed. Her pure, clear eyes seemed to penetrate to the deepest layers of Rinko's heart. Staring, ever staring.

"Kayaba and I started dating my first year of college, and we were together for six years, until I finished my master's. But...I suppose I was the only one who believed that. I was older than you are now but far, far stupider. I had no idea what was going on in his mind. I never, ever realized the one thing that he really wanted."

She glanced out the window at the endless night sea and slowly, bit by bit, began to utter the things that she'd been holding in for the last four years. The name that had brought a sharp pain to her chest just at its recollection slid out of her mouth with surprising ease.

Akihiko Kayaba was already in charge of Argus's third development team when he went straight into one of the most prestigious engineering schools in Japan. As a high schooler, he had sublicensed a number of game-creation programs that had launched Argus from being a third-tier company to an internationally renowned one, so it wasn't hard to believe that he'd be placed in a management position there soon after beginning college.

Kayaba's income at age eighteen was said to be in the hundreds of millions of yen, and the sum total of all his licensing fees thus far had to be astronomical. Inevitably, a number of female students on campus had gone after him in their own ways, but none of them could withstand the liquid-nitrogen gaze that he turned upon anything that did not pique his interest.

So even now, Rinko didn't understand what it was about a plain, boring, younger girl from the mountains that Kayaba did not reject immediately. Because she was totally unaware of his fame? Because she was smart enough to take part in the Shigemura seminar as a first-year, when he was a year older than her? It was obvious it wasn't just a physical attraction.

Rinko's first impression of Kayaba was of a malnourished bean sprout. His face was pale, he wore a ratty old lab coat, and he was almost never seen without observation devices of some kind attached to him. The memory of the day that she'd dragged him to the beaches of Shonan in her little beater car was so vivid, it might as well have been yesterday.

"Some ideas won't occur to ya till ya see the sun!" she had scolded him in her accent from back home. Kayaba just stared at her in a daze from the passenger seat. Eventually, he had muttered something about needing to emulate the skin sensation of natural sunlight. She had groaned.

It wasn't until later that she learned about Kayaba's celebrity, but she wasn't socially skilled enough to be able to treat him differently because of it. To her, he was just a scrawny guy who needed more nutrition, and every time she visited his apartment, she made sure to feed him some home-cooked food.

Afterward, Rinko often asked herself if the reason he never rejected her was because he wanted her help, and she just never realized it. But every time, she decided the answer was no. Akihiko Kayaba was a man who never sought anything from anyone else. All he wanted was a "world away from here," the door to a realm that mere mortals could not reach.

Kayaba spoke a few times about a gigantic flying castle in his dreams. That castle was made of countless floors, with each floor containing its own towns, forests, and fields. If you climbed up the long staircases that connected floor to floor, you would eventually reach the top and a dreamlike, beautiful palace...

"And who is there?" Rinko had asked.

Kayaba had smiled and said he didn't know. "When I was very small, I went to that castle every night in my dreams. Each night, I would climb a different set of stairs, getting closer and closer to the top. But one day, I was no longer able to go there. It was a stupid dream; I almost forgot all about it."

But the day after Rinko finished her master's thesis, he left on a journey to that castle in the sky and never came back. He made the castle real with only his own hands, taking ten thousand players up with him and leaving Rinko alone on earth...

"When I found out about the *SAO* Incident on the news and saw Kayaba's name and face on the report, I still couldn't believe it. It wasn't until I drove past his apartment and saw all the cop cars there that I understood it was real."

Rinko felt an ache in her throat; it had been ages since she had talked continuously for this long.

"He never said anything to me, all the way to the end. Not a single e-mail when he left. I guess...I was just stupid. I helped with the basic design of the NerveGear, and I knew about the game he was building at Argus. And somehow, I never realized what he was thinking about...When he went missing, and all of Japan was going crazy searching for him, it took a miracle for me to remember. Somehow, I recalled that I had once noticed a strange set of coordinates in the mountains of Nagano in his car nav history. Instinctively, I knew that was the place. If I'd told the police about it right then and there, the *SAO* Incident might have played out differently..."

Perhaps, if the police had stormed that cabin, Kayaba would have killed all those players with him, as he had originally threatened. But Rinko sensed that it wasn't her place to say that aloud.

"I evaded police detection and went to Nagano alone. It took me three days to reach the cabin itself, using nothing but my own memory. I was completely covered in mud by the time I found it…But I wasn't going to those desperate lengths so that I could be his accomplice. I…I was going to kill him."

Kayaba had greeted her with a look of total bewilderment, the same expression he wore when they had first met. She could still recall the sensation of the heavy, cold survival knife in the hand she held behind her back.

"But…I'm sorry, Asuna. I couldn't kill him."

Her voice trembled despite her best efforts, but at least she managed not to cry.

"I feel like anything I say after this will only sound like a lie, no matter how I phrase it. Kayaba knew I was holding a knife. He just said, 'What am I going to do with you?' like he always did, put the NerveGear back on, and returned to Aincrad. He'd been in his dive all along, so he was filthy and unshaven, and I saw several IV marks in his arm. I…I…"

Rinko couldn't go on. She could only breathe, over and over.

Eventually, Asuna said, "Neither I, nor Kirito, have ever once hated or blamed you."

Rinko looked up with a start into the face of the girl ten years her junior. There was a faint smile there.

"In fact…while I can't speak for Kirito in this regard, I'll admit…I don't even know for certain if I truly hate the guild commander…er, Akihiko Kayaba."

Rinko recalled that Asuna had been a member of Kayaba's guild in that fantasy world.

"Yes, it's true that four thousand people lost their lives in that event. Imagining the sum of all their fear and despair before they died…makes it clear that his actions were unforgivable. But… if I can voice my own very selfish opinion, I think of the short time I spent with Kirito in that world as the very best memories of my life," Asuna said. Her left hand moved to her waist, making a squeezing motion. "Just as he is guilty of his sin, so am I; and Kirito; and even you, Rinko…And it is not a sin that can be absolved through someone else's idea of punishment, in my opinion. There might never be a day of forgiveness for them. And that means we must continue to face those sins and acknowledge them."

That night, Rinko dreamed of that long-lost time—when she was just an ignorant student.

Kayaba always slept lightly and got up before Rinko. He had slipped out of bed to read the morning paper with a cup of coffee. Once the sun was up, Rinko awoke at last. He gave her the exasperated look of a parent to a child who slept in.

"What am I going to do with you? I can't believe you came all this way."

The sound of that gentle voice caused Rinko's eyes to peel open. She got the sense that a tall figure was standing next to her bed in the dark.

"It's still the middle of the night…" she grumbled with a grin, and closed her eyes again. The air shifted, and crisp footsteps proceeded toward the door, which she heard open and shut.

Just before she could slip back into sleep, Rinko gasped and shot up to a sitting position.

"____!!"

Her pleasant slumber was gone in an instant, her heart pounding away in her chest like an alarm. She couldn't tell where the dream ended and reality had started. She reached around for the remote to turn on the lights.

The windowless cabin was empty, of course. But Rinko could sense the last vestiges of some human scent.

She got out of bed and hurried barefoot to the door, smacking the control panel hastily to disengage the lock and rush through the opening to the hallway.

The interior corridor, bathed in dim orange light, was empty as far as she could see in both directions.

Was I just dreaming…?

But she could still hear that low, soft voice in her ears. Without realizing it, Rinko clutched the locket she always wore around her neck.

Brazed and sealed inside the locket was the micro-bomb that they'd extracted from above Rinko's heart. The pendant felt hot against her hand, as if it were giving off a heat of its own.

CHAPTER THREE

1

What strange children.

The view of those innocent sleeping faces from the wooden beam high overhead prompted the sudden thought.

Two boys were fast asleep on hay piled thick on the floor of the rickety old barn. There wasn't anything particularly noteworthy about their appearances. The boy on the right, sleeping on his side, had flaxseed blond hair and deep-green eyes, when they were open. Those colors were common enough here in the NNM (Norlangarth Northern Middle) area. His height and weight were within average values for a boy his age.

But the boy on the left, his limbs thrown about with abandon in his sleep, had both hair and eyes of pure black. That was different. Those dark colors were designated to appear with much higher likelihood in the E and S areas. While it was rare for a child to be born with those colors in the north, the probability was still greater than zero. With the total population of the Human Empire as high as it was now, it wasn't out of the question. His size was so similar to the other boy's that they might as well have been twins.

Master had given the order to directly observe these two boys 163 days ago, and the result was a bit of a letdown after the long trip from Centoria. Nothing about their appearance or actions suggested talent greater than other units of the same gender, region, and age range. In terms of planning and ability to avoid danger, they seemed *below* average, in fact.

But now it had been half a year of carefully following their travel, making sure not to be spotted. The rains had passed, and now that summer was waning as well, Master's interest in these particular boys was becoming clear at last.

That lack of planning and regularity could also be called healthy curiosity and love of adventure. Even after more than two centuries of life, few things had surprised the observer as much as the ingenuity and agency of the black-haired boy. He had nearly broken the Taboo Index's laws on a number of occasions in the period since the observation had begun and seemed likely to continue doing so.

In a sense, it had to be this way, or else he could not have done *what he did*. After all, it was otherwise unthinkable that someone could break down one of the eternal barriers that Master's archrival had placed around the world—and do so in just a matter of days, no less...

Whatever the black-haired boy was dreaming about, his limbs jerked into movement. The hem of the shirt he wore as a pajama top pulled upward. He stopped wriggling, oblivious to his now-exposed stomach. The observer rolled its eyes.

Even in late summer, here at the border of Norlangarth's north region, the night breeze could chill. The barn was drafty to begin with, so sleeping with exposed skin on top of a bed of hay could very easily cause an illness effect that would slightly downgrade his total life. And tomorrow—August 28th in the year 378 of the Human Era—was the biggest event of the boys' journey thus far.

They'd made a fair amount of money working at this farm over the summer, so the observer had wanted to tell them to at least spend some of it to stay at an inn on this particular night. But direct contact was absolutely forbidden, and so they were sleeping in this rickety old barn yet again. And look at him now.

...Oh well. I'm sure Master will overlook a tiny bit of meddling.

Atop the beam, the observer waved an arm, muttered an incantation in a tiny voice, and produced a little point of green light, hovering at the fingertip—a wind element.

The observer carefully guided the light downward. It descended right next to the black-haired boy and buried itself about thirty cens into the hay, where it was silently released.

The resulting gust of wind was enough to lift an armful of hay into the air, where it gently settled over the boy's exposed midriff. It wasn't much of a blanket, but it would at least shield against the chill of the breeze seeping through the walls.

The observer watched the oblivious boys as they continued to sleep and reflected on this action.

In over two centuries since Master had frozen its life and recast it as a familiar, it had undertaken similar tasks a number of times. But never had there been any attachment to the target above the level of interest. In fact, the observer was not supposed to have emotions at all. It was not, after all, even a human unit of the type that ruled over the human realm or the Underworld as a whole.

It was fine to anticipate that the boy would catch a cold the night before a major test. The problem was, why use arts to interfere, rather than simply stand back and watch? In fact, if the boy fell ill, failed the test, and had to return to his original village, the observer's stint would be over, allowing it to return to that corner of the bookcase in the great library where it liked to be.

Did that mean...it valued the travel with these boys over the prospect of going home?

It was impossible. It was irrational. It was as though the irregular nature of the youths had infected it.

Enough thinking. This was not part of the job. The only thing that mattered was sticking close and watching until blond Eugeo and black-haired Kirito reached their journey's destination.

The observer shrank its body down to the minimum size of five mils and leaped off the rafter beam. At this size, there was no life penalty for falling, so arts would not be required. It landed on a straw of hay without a sound and scurried on little legs to its usual spot: the shaggy black hair of the boy named Kirito.

It grabbed a few hairs its own color and fixed itself in place, then felt its small body fill with that inexplicable emotion again.

Peace, calmness, relief, and, somewhere beneath all that, something tiny but rising…No matter how much it pondered, it would never know why.

What strange children, the observer thought again, closed its eyes, and settled into a light sleep.

2

On the morning of the last day of August, the sky was clear.

Kirito stretched and opened his eyes, picked up a single piece of the hay covering him, regarded it with suspicion, then bolted upright. That movement was enough to shake his mind awake. In his hair, the observer stretched, too.

It slid around near the base of the hair and stopped just before the bangs. This was the ordinary position. Kirito had a tendency to scratch his head, so care had to be taken on those occasions. Its life was frozen only in the sense of the natural aging process, so bodily damage still took its toll. On the other hand, its maximum life value was far higher than a human's, and its body retained its toughness even when shrunken, so a little impact would not be a problem.

Kirito rolled out of the pile of hay, unaware that an observer the size of a wheat grain was hiding in his own hair, and placed a hand on his partner's shoulder to shake him. "Hey, Eugeo, wake up. It's morning."

The other boy's eyelashes, the same color as his hair, fluttered and opened. His green eyes were dull at first, then blinked and crinkled into a weak smile.

"Morning, Kirito...Somehow you always wake up earlier on the important days."

"Better than the alternative! Come on, up and at 'em! Let's get the morning work over with so we can practice our forms before we eat. I'm still a little worried about number seven."

"Why do you think I always tell you we should practice forms, rather than just mock fights all the time? I can't believe you spent the last night cramming before the day of the tournament...the last morning, even!"

"Noon-cramming, moon-cramming, I don't care," Kirito said enigmatically. "You only have to do the form demonstration the one time!"

He picked up a huge armful of the hay that had been his bed a minute earlier and moved it to the large wooden barrel along the wall. Once the barrel was full, he lifted it up and started walking for the entrance.

As soon as he exited the barn, the morning sun blazed into two pairs of eyes. The observer retreated, hiding among the hair. It had spent so long living in dim corners of the great library that it was sensitive to sunlight. But Kirito happily breathed in a lungful of early mist. To no one in particular, he said, "The mornings are a lot cooler now. Good thing I didn't catch cold before the big day."

He has no idea at all, the observer noted. Next time he slept with his skin exposed, there would be no help.

Eugeo trotted up and answered, "Sleeping on the hay in the barn might not cut it anymore. Why don't we pay the fare starting tonight and sleep in the house?"

"We won't need to," Kirito said with a grin. The observer couldn't see it from its position at the base of his hair, but it could easily imagine the smirking expression. Kirito boasted, "After all, tonight we'll be sleeping in the Zakkaria garrison building."

"...I'd love to know where you get that boundless confidence..." Eugeo murmured, shaking his head. He brought out another barrel stuffed with hay. While they made it look easy, a thick wooden barrel one mel across filled to the brim with hay was far, far heavier than the airy material would suggest. The average man their age might be able to lift it, but certainly couldn't take two dozen steps with it.

How was it possible that the skinny young boys could do this without breaking a sweat? It was because their object control authority was unbelievably high. High enough, in fact, that they could swing around the class-45 Divine Object resting against the wall of the barn: a longsword.

That raised the question: How did two ordinary boys born in an obscure little village have such a high authority level? Even after half a year of observation, the reason was a mystery. At the least, it was an amount impossible to reach through ordinary training and safe sparring. Perhaps if they had engaged in serious battle against high-class wild animals, but they'd have to hunt so many of them that the animals would go temporarily extinct around the village. And that would be a twofold breaking of the Taboo Index: one for hunting without possessing the hunter's calling and another for hunting past the prescribed amounts. Even proactive Kirito would not go to such lengths, to say nothing of the better-behaved Eugeo…

The only remaining possibility was a foe whose authority-boosting value would be far greater than a beast…in other words, a triumphant battle over an invader from the Dark Territory. But that was impossible, too, only in a different way. It was unthinkable that these two boys, not even men-at-arms, would face off against the dread forces of darkness. And even the occasional dark knights and goblin scouting parties should be vanquished by the Integrity Knights from Centoria long before they ever reached the End Mountains.

Even if there *had* been an unexpected infiltration near the boys' village, that would represent a far greater problem in and of itself than their abnormal rise of control authority. It could be an omen of much bigger things. Perhaps even the Prophesied Time that was guaranteed to arrive someday but which everyone believed was in the far-flung future…

While the observer pondered this from the safety of Kirito's hair, the two youngsters carried the mountains of hay from the barn to the nearby stable, where they spread them into the feeding troughs of the ten horses there. As the horses proceeded to crunch on their breakfast, the boys took brushes to them in turn. This was the first duty every morning at Walde Farm, Kirito and Eugeo's temporary home outside of Zakkaria.

After five months there, they were so good at this task that they might have been confused for having the groom's calling. They finished brushing just as the last one finished its meal. Moments later, the bells at the church in Zakkaria three kilors away chimed the seven o'clock melody. The Axiom Church created divine "Bells of Time-Tolling" for every town and village. Their sound traveled ten kilors in every direction without fading a bit, but any farther than that, and they were completely inaudible. This was one of the psychological barriers meant to prohibit autonomous long-distance movement in human units, but it seemed to have no effect on Kirito and Eugeo.

They washed their hands at the water basin, hung the large horse brushes on the nails on the wall, then left the stable, each carrying an empty barrel in his hand. Just then, a pair of excited, expectant greetings erupted.

"Good morning, Kirito, Eugeo!"

The voices belonged to the farmer's daughters. Teline and Telure were twins, turning nine later in the year. They had the same reddish-brown hair, the same dark-brown eyes, the same color tunic, and the same color skirt. The only way to tell them apart was the color of the ribbons they used to tie up their ponytails. When they had first been introduced five months ago, Teline was red and Telure was blue, but the mischievous girls loved to switch them from time to time to confuse Kirito and Eugeo.

"Good morning, Teli—" Eugeo started to say in his normal tone of voice, before Kirito covered his mouth from behind.

"Hang on! I sense something suspicious is afoot..."

The girls looked at each other and giggled in unison.

"Are you sure about that?"

"It might just be your imagination."

Their voices, their mischievous smiles, and even the number and placement of freckles on their cheeks were identical. Kirito and Eugeo groaned and compared the two.

Apparently, even Master didn't know why human units were capable of coming in twins…or even triplets, on rare occasion. Twins were more likely to appear after consecutive unit deaths in an adjacent area, so it was probably a factor of the population adjustment function—but that didn't explain the need to make them identical. At the very least, there didn't seem to be any benefits that outweighed the trouble of being unable to tell them apart.

On the other hand, the observer could see all units' status windows—what *they* would call a Stacia Window—so it could sense at a glance that the twins had switched their ribbons today. In other words, Kirito's intuition was correct.

Of course, the boy couldn't hear the inaudible, exasperated voice coming from the base of his hair, telling him to trust his gut. But he held up a hand and pointed at the red ribbon on the left. "Morning, Telure!"

Then he pointed to the blue ribbon on the right. "Morning, Teline!"

The girls glanced at each other again and shouted, "Bingo!" They held out their arms to reveal that each girl was carrying a woven picnic basket.

"You win today's breakfast: mulberry pie!"

"Mulberries give you lots of strength! We spent an entire day picking them to help you two win at your big tournament!"

"Aww, that's so sweet. Thank you, Telure, Teline," Kirito said, setting down the wooden barrel and rubbing the girls' heads. They scrunched their little faces into huge grins, then simultaneously looked at Eugeo.

"…Aren't you happy, Eugeo?"

"Do you not like mulberries?"

The flaxen-haired boy vigorously shook his hands and head.

"N-no, I love them! It's just…I'm remembering some stuff from the past. Thanks, you two."

The girls smiled with relief and trotted off to a table set up between the stable and pasture. While they began to prepare the breakfast, Kirito sidled closer to Eugeo and patted him on the back.

"We're going to win today's event, make our way to the top of the garrison, and be in Centoria by next year…very close to Alice. Right, Eugeo?" he said in a hushed but insistent voice.

Eugeo nodded. "That's right. It's why I spent the last five months learning the Aincrad style from you."

Just this little snippet of conversation contained a number of fascinating bits of information. In over two centuries of service as a familiar, the observer had never heard the name of that school of swordfighting. And then there was the unit named Alice, who served as their final destination.

If this was the same Alice unit who existed in the observer's memory…their hopes were almost impossibly distant and unlikely. For she was currently located very, very high in the Central Cathedral that loomed over Centoria…

"Kirito! Eugeo! Hurry up!"

"If you don't come now, me and Teline will eat all of it!"

Kirito quickly withdrew his hand from Eugeo's back and rushed for the table. The vibration was enough to interrupt the observer's thoughts and bring it back to reality. How many times over the last five months had it needed a reminder that *thinking* was not its job? And now it was not only thinking about their fate…it was worried about it.

The observer clung to the base of the black hairs and sighed yet again.

After a hectic breakfast, the twins said, "We'll come and cheer for you!" and left for the house.

Once the boys had let the horses out to graze and finished cleaning the stables, they would normally engage in their sword practice using safe wooden blades, but today was different. They washed their hair and skin at the well—the observer evacuated to a nearby branch while this happened—then changed from their supplied work clothes to their own tunics and headed for the house.

The farmer's wife, Triza Walde, was an extremely generous and pleasant unit for her role in a farm of this size. It was surely why she had happily hired and taken in two suspicious, wandering boys. She greeted Kirito and Eugeo bracingly and gave them packed lunches as they headed off for their tournament. As they left, she called out, "If you lose, don't become guards in the town, come back and marry Teline and Telure!" The two boys gave her very uncomfortable smiles.

As they walked the three-kilor path from the farm to the town, they shared fewer words than usual. It must have been their nerves. The Northern Norlangarth Swordfighting Tournament held in Zakkaria every August 28th drew over fifty contestants each year from neighboring towns and villages. As a rule, these were all men-at-arms by calling in their respective hometowns; Kirito and Eugeo would almost certainly be the only exceptions.

The only contestants admitted into the Zakkaria sentinel garrison would be the winners of the east and west blocks of the tournament, so neither of them could afford to lose once if they both wanted to achieve their dream. That would be hard enough as it was, and it also required them to not be in the same block. The observer didn't know if the boys had even considered this…

From up ahead came the dry sound of smokegrass bursting.

The observer peered out of Kirito's bangs and saw the reddish sandstone of the town beyond a small hill. It was Zakkaria, the biggest city in the NNM area. Its current designated population was 1,958 units, less than a tenth of Centoria's, but on the day of the biggest event of the year, it was positively buzzing with activity.

As they walked for the western gate of town, Eugeo mumbled, "You know…until I saw it for myself, I had started to wonder if Zakkaria even existed."

"Why would you think that?" Kirito asked.

The flaxen-haired boy shrugged. "Because...even the grown-ups in Rulid have never actually seen Zakkaria, either. The old head man-at-arms, Doik, had the right to participate in the Zakkaria Tournament, but he never once made use of that right before he retired. And as the carver of the Gigas Cedar, I shouldn't have ever had a chance to go to Zakkaria. So if no one'd ever been there, and I'd never get to see it, either..."

"...then it might as well not exist?" Kirito finished. He grinned and added, "Well, I'm glad it does. Zakkaria's existence means that Centoria's not out of the question, either."

"That's true. It...it feels so strange. It's already been five months since we left from Rulid, and yet the fact that there's more to the world than that village is still...well, incredible to me."

Eugeo's words were a bit hard to fathom, but they caused the observer to recall a strange sensation. Throughout its long life in Master's service, it had seen not just Centoria but the entire fifteen-hundred-kilor expanse of the human realms. That volume of memory far surpassed that of any human unit, aside from the Integrity Knights. But there were still areas unfamiliar to the observer. The place beyond the End Mountains that surrounded the human realm—the Dark Territory. It knew from secondhand sources that there were a number of towns and villages out there, even an enormous black city...But would it ever have the opportunity to register its existence with visual data in person?

That was essentially impossible. It was a thought without any basis in fact, and yet, if it continued to observe these two, perhaps someday...

The observer was so lost in thought that it was unprepared for a sudden vibration and nearly tumbled off Kirito's head. It clung to the black hairs in surprise and looked up.

Directly ahead was a horse rearing up in the air, front legs kicking. It shrieked and tried to toss the Zakkarian sentinel off its back. The sudden shaking had been from Kirito crouching down to avoid the horse's hooves.

Just a few dozen mels ahead was the west gate of the city. A horseback sentinel in his red uniform was situated just in front of the stone bridge over the moat, and for some reason, the horse had reared up and out of control the moment Kirito passed it.

"Wh-whoa! Whoa!" the rider commanded, pulling on the reins desperately, but the horse would not calm. The "horse" dynamic object required a fairly high control authority to master, but any unit with the sentinel calling should have fulfilled that amount.

That severely limited the causes of the horse's continued abandon. Either it was losing life from lack of food or water or it sensed a very dangerous, large beast approaching—but neither of those seemed likely here.

Meanwhile, the bucking horse reared up again. But rather than trying to get out of the way, Kirito continued crouching below it. Passersby began to scream and yell. Even a full-grown male unit would lose half his life if trampled by a horse—perhaps all of it, if he was unlucky.

"L-look out—!" someone shouted, and Kirito moved at last: not backward but forward. He evaded the kicking legs and pressed up against the horse, grabbing it firmly around the neck with both arms. Then he commanded, "Eugeo, the rear!"

But his partner was already on the move. He circled around to the back of the horse while Kirito held it still. The horse's tail was whipping around wildly, but Eugeo reached out fearlessly and, like lightning, deftly snagged an object sticking to the brown hide and peeled it away. Instantly, the horse was as calm as if nothing had ever happened.

Kirito rubbed its nose soothingly as the horse's snorting breath steadily calmed. "There, there. You're okay. Sir, you can ease up on the reins now."

The pale young sentinel riding the horse nodded nervously and relaxed his grip. Kirito let go of the horse and took a step back. It swung itself around and clopped over to its original position at the side of the bridge. Sighs and voices of relief could be heard throughout the crowd.

The observer was among the relieved; it quickly folded up the arms it had unconsciously extended from its perch in Kirito's hair. It had nearly cast a sacred art to protect Kirito from impact. In fact, if he hadn't moved as quickly as he did, it would have. The action was unthinkable for an observer.

Meanwhile, totally unaware that a little stowaway was reprimanding itself in his bangs, Kirito approached his partner and whispered, "Greater swampfly?"

"Bingo," Eugeo muttered back, glancing around the area. The foot traffic was moving again, and the sentinel was paying attention to his poor horse, so he felt emboldened to open his hand and show Kirito.

Resting in his hand was a winged insect about four cens long, striped deep red and black. It looked like a bee, but there was no stinger at the end. Instead, sharp mandibles extended from its mouth.

Among the "pest" dynamic objects that existed around only human units' active areas, this was nothing particularly dangerous. After all, it posed no direct danger to humans. It primarily stole tiny amounts of life by sucking the blood of horses, cattle, and sheep. The sentinel's horse had reared up because the greater swampfly had bitten it on the rump. But...

"It's strange," Kirito muttered. He plucked the fly out of Eugeo's hand, where it had died from the shock of its capture. "There aren't any swamps around here, are there?"

"Nope. I learned that the first day we started working at Walde Farm. They said the nearest swamp is in the western forest, so don't take the horses that way."

"And it's seven kilometers from there to Zakkaria. The greater swampfly only lives around swamps, so it wouldn't fly all this way," Kirito noted.

Eugeo pondered that notion but seemed a bit hesitant. "That's true...but couldn't it have wandered into a merchant's carriage or something?"

"...You could be right about that."

Even as they talked, the insect between Kirito's fingers began to rapidly lose its red coloring. The lives of insect objects were already small, and a dead insect's life was even smaller. Their corpses would maintain shape for only a minute at most.

Soon the swampfly's husk was a pale gray, and it crumbled like sand, emitting a slight spatial resource before disappearing.

Kirito blew on his fingers, glanced around nonchalantly, and snorted. "Well, at least neither of us got hurt before our big tournament. I guess living with horses for all those months on the farm paid off."

"Ha-ha, good point. If we get into the garrison, should we enlist for horseback service?"

"No *ifs*, Eugeo. We've come all this way, and nothing is going to stop us from getting in together," Kirito said with a wicked grin. Eugeo was taken aback.

"Why do you make it sound like stuff's going to stop us? Aside from all the opponents we'll have to defeat to win…"

"Well, all I'm saying is…don't get careless before the event. You never know what might surprise you at any moment, as we just saw."

"I didn't realize you were such a worrywart, Kirito."

"You'll never meet a guy who avoids recklessness and abandon like I do," Kirito quipped, and patted Eugeo on the back. "C'mon, let's go. We've gotta get a bite to eat before the tournament."

3

Zakkaria was a town surrounded by long, rectangular fortress walls running east and west.

It was nine hundred mels from north to south and thirteen hundred mels from east to west. That was well over five times the size of Rulid. It was built in the middle of a field with no nearby rivers or lakes, so all their water came from wells. It seemed a bit dry as a result, but it still had far more plant objects than the desert towns in the far south empire.

Nearly all the roads and buildings were made of a sandy red rock, and most of the residents wore some kind of red-based clothing. Therefore, the two boys from the north in their blue tunics stuck out like a sore thumb. Eugeo kept his face pointed downward, feeling self-conscious about the attention, but Kirito paid them no mind and peered at the various carts and stands along the main road.

"Ooh, the meat buns here look good...but the skewers earlier were two *shia* cheaper...What do you feel like, Eugeo?" Kirito wondered, turning back to look at his partner. He finally noticed Eugeo's low energy, and he rapidly blinked a few times with annoyance. "Come on, Eugeo, it's our third visit to Zakkaria! You don't have to be so nervous anymore."

"You mean it's *only* our third visit. Remember, I never saw so many people at once until I left the village..."

"If you can't handle Zakkaria, how do you think you'll do in the big city? And remember, the tournament's going to be in front of an audience of hundreds. Plus Farmer Walde, his wife, and the girls are coming to root for us, so you don't want to embarrass yourself in front of them," Kirito said. He smacked Eugeo's back again, much to the other boy's displeasure.

"I—I know that…You know, it's times like these when I envy your lack of caution…"

"Well, well! You talk a big game for a guy so pale and nervous. Don't you know that a lack of caution is a major secret to the Aincrad style?"

"Huh? R-really?"

"Yep, for sure."

They continued like this down the five-hundred-mel-long west main road. Up ahead was a building that towered over the others. It was the central grounds, the biggest facility in Zakkaria. This rectangular plaza, which matched the length ratio of the town walls themselves, was lined with tiered seating for an audience. The space was used for a variety of purposes, such as addresses from the liege lord, musical and dramatic performances, and today, of course, the swordfighting tournament.

Admittance was free, so while things wouldn't kick off for another two hours, there were already many people in attendance. To the human units whose daily schedules were bound and regulated by their callings and the Taboo Index, this was the biggest, most exciting event of the year.

But for Eugeo, the added intensity of the expectant crowd only added to the pressure on his shoulders, and his color was even worse than before.

"…W-we're going to compete in there…?" he rasped. Kirito wasn't in the mood to pump him up after every little comment, so he grabbed Eugeo by the arm and dragged him over to the registration desk near the entrance to the grounds.

Most of the contestants were either staying in town or already lived there, so they had probably registered first thing in the morning. A single elderly, bearded sentinel who appeared rather bored manned the long desk. Kirito walked up boldly and proclaimed, "Two entries, please!"

The old man raised a gray eyebrow, cast a suspicious glare at Kirito and Eugeo, and cleared his throat. "To enter the tournament, you must have the calling of a man-at-arms in any of the northern towns, or be a Zakkarian sentinel in training, or—"

"We're the last 'or.' Show him," Kirito said, elbowing Eugeo.

He reached into his tunic and pulled out a faded parchment envelope. The surprised clerk took it and pulled a single sheet of paper from inside.

"Let's see here…Ah, a handwritten note from the elder of Rulid. *This note serves as witness that these two young men have completed their Stacia-given callings and now seek a new way of life.* Interesting…"

For the first time, a hint of a smile tugged at the elderly sentinel's mouth. "So two boys from tiny, distant Rulid, not even men-at-arms, have come in search of entry to the hallowed Zakkaria garrison, eh?"

"That's correct," Kirito answered, grinning back. "But we're not stopping at the garrison. Next we'll be heading for Cent—"

This time it was Eugeo who elbowed Kirito to shut him up. He quickly stepped in and said, "S-so there, now you've heard our story, and we'd like to be registered for the tournament!"

"Hmm. Very well." The sentinel opened up a leather-bound register and produced a copper pen. "Write down your name, place of birth, and sword style."

"…S-style, too?" Eugeo asked, pausing mid-reach. Kirito snatched the pen away instead. Unlike the high-durability parchment, the register's paper was cheap and made of threadgrass, and it was full of the names of all the participants who had already signed up.

The black-haired youth filled out the name *Kirito* and place of birth *Rulid* in the common language of the Human Empire, then paused before scrawling down *Aincrad style.*

The observer had been curious about a number of things in its five months of surveillance, and this strange name was first and foremost among them. There were around thirty different schools of swordsmanship in the human lands, and the name *Aincrad style* did not appear anywhere else.

At first, the observer wondered if bold, confident Kirito had decided to start this style all on his own, but over time, that turned out not to be the case. The mysterious Aincrad style did not have just one "secret form" like all the others but more than ten...

Kirito and Eugeo finished jotting down their information—Eugeo indicated the same style—and returned the pen to the sentinel. He put it in the holder, turned the register to face him, and raised an eyebrow again.

"Hrmm. I've been swinging a sword for many years, and I've never heard of this style before. Is this from around Rulid?"

His suspicion was warranted. There were over fifty names on the register already, and half of them belonged to the Zakkarite style founded by the original lord of Zakkaria. The other half belonged to the Norkia style spread far and wide within the Norlangarth Empire. No other participants registered under a little-known name like this one.

But Kirito proudly announced, "It's a pretty new school, from what I understand."

Eugeo could only nod, his face growing paler by the moment. The sentinel merely grunted—it certainly wasn't a reason to turn them away—and handed each a thin bronze placard. Kirito's had the number 55 engraved on it, while Eugeo's said 56.

"Be in the waiting room of the grounds by eleven thirty. First thing, you'll be sorted by lots into the East Block and West Block. That's where you'll get your dueling sword. When the bells ring noon, that's when the preliminary round starts. You'll demonstrate your forms until each block is whittled down to eight. The forms from one to ten were announced ahead of time; I trust you know what to do?"

Eugeo nodded lightly; Kirito, a little oddly.

"Very good. The final competition will begin at two o'clock. You will duel such that eight becomes four, then two, then one. That one winner—in other words, the two from West and East—will be given the calling of a Zakkarian sentinel."

This time, both boys nodded with vigor. From within Kirito's bangs, the observer went back to its thoughts of several hours ago.

The boys sought to join the garrison here. That required them to be placed separately, in either block, then pass the prelims and combat rounds to win. But if the luck of the draw had them in the same block to start with, their scheme was ruined right from the start. Had they even considered that? What was their plan if that happened...?

As it happened, that very topic came up after the boys finished the registration process, while they ate their lunch of meat buns and skewers in the square.

"...So here's the question, Eugeo...What will we do...if we're in the same block?" Kirito asked in between bites of the split meat bun.

"...What *will* we do?" asked Eugeo after finishing his first skewer.

Neither of them had given it any thought. The observer had had an inkling of this, but it was still so shocking to hear that it nearly tumbled out of Kirito's hair. It channeled its raging demand to *think!* into gripping the hair even harder—but just then, Kirito raised his right hand, and the observer had to make a quick evacuation of his head. Kirito scratched at his bangs and came to his grand conclusion.

"Well, whatever happens happens. It's fine; I'm sure we'll wind up in separate blocks. Besides, I prayed to Stacia and Solus and Te...Terror..."

"Terraria!"

"Right. I prayed to Terroria for this to happen."

Eugeo sighed loudly at the same moment as a tiny, inaudible sigh in Kirito's hair. It returned to its usual position and told itself, *Well, if you say so. But this really could be it, boys.*

*   *   *

Thirty minutes later, just before the ringing of the half-past-eleven bells, they made their way into the waiting room.

On the western side of the large chamber, twenty mels to a side, there were four long benches, upon which sat the tournament participants, facing east. On the east wall were four rather fine chairs. They were still empty, but a sentinel stood at the registration window.

The instant Kirito and Eugeo stepped into the room, fifty-four pairs of eyeballs turned upon them.

All of them were large, powerful, confident men. About ten wore the tunics of Zakkaria's sentinels-in-training, most of whom were young, but the majority of the guards from neighboring towns and villages were in their prime. Some wore whiskers that covered most of their faces, while others proudly bore ugly scars.

Eugeo flinched under all the attention, but Kirito just stared around at the large chamber and murmured, "Ah, good..."

"Wh-what's good?" Eugeo hissed back at him.

He turned and whispered, "There aren't any female entries."

"...Come on, Kirito..."

"Hey, you don't want to have to fight a girl, either, do you?"

"W-well, no, but...I wasn't even thinking about that."

"Hopefully we won't have to worry about fighting girls until that unified, four-empire whatsitcalled."

"I wouldn't be so sure. I heard a story once about a band of knights that was entirely made up of women."

"...Ooooh."

The fifty-four warriors quickly lost interest in the two boys and their frivolous conversation. They would be gone in the prelims soon enough. The men returned to their inspection and care of the supplied swords and leather gloves.

Kirito gave the room another once-over and left Eugeo's side to walk straight to the long benches where the participants sat. He walked from bench to bench, sniffing the air repeatedly. It was anyone's guess as to what this meant.

For five minutes, he strolled around all the competitors, then returned to Eugeo's side. His partner gave him a suspicious look, so he leaned in and whispered, "Don't turn your head. Can you see the young guy at the very end of the second bench?"

Eugeo swiveled his eyes to the spot. "Yeah. The one wearing the sentinel apprentice uniform?"

"If you face off against him, watch out. He might try something."

Like Eugeo, the observer peered doubtfully out of Kirito's bangs. Seated in the spot in question was a young man with long, sandy hair, wearing a brick-red tunic with the Zakkarian insignia on it. According to his Stacia Window, he was eighteen years old. His life numbers and object control authority were below average, suggesting that he wasn't particularly noteworthy.

"Huh...? Do you know him?" Eugeo asked. Kirito shook his head.

"No. But...maybe this will explain it to you. I'm pretty sure he's got a personality like Zink's."

The observer knew that the unit named Zink was the current chief man-at-arms of Rulid, their home. He had a personality index that these two did not particularly want to associate with.

Human units strictly followed the laws and accords of the world, but that did not mean they all acted with perfect benevolence. Some units were like the Walde family, taking in suspicious wanderers and treating them generously, while others might intercept, manipulate, or insult others with whatever words they could use that did not violate any laws. Zink in Rulid was one of the latter type, so if Kirito's statement was correct, that harmless-looking apprentice was, too.

"...Like Zink's, you say? Then before my match, he'll probably try to smear bittergrass sap on my blade," Eugeo said, scowling.

"Wouldn't that be against the rules?" Kirito wondered.

"It wouldn't affect the life of the sword; if anything, it'd add a shine effect. But when freshly applied, it stinks like crazy. Zink got me with that one many times as a kid, and I could barely focus on the exercise."

"I see...Better make sure not to let go of the swords they give us. Don't lose focus in the match, either. Hopefully he's on my block instead..."

"If that happens and he tries some nonsense, *you'd* better be careful not to get angry and mess everything up, Kirito."

"...I'll try." Kirito grinned weakly. He and Eugeo headed for the registration window, handed over their placards, and received the swords that all participants would use. They were metal blades rather than wooden and had plenty enough power to lower a human's life, despite their low-priority value. Naturally, the rule said that they had to stop at the last second, so there would absolutely, positively be no bloodshed.

With their swords, the boys returned and sat on the very front bench, right around the time that four new units proceeded through the door in the back. They were proper sentinels in their dazzling red uniforms. One of them was the grizzled old sentinel from the desk out front.

A fortysomething man wearing the golden shoulder badge of a captain gave a quick greeting, and then a younger sentinel brought in a large box. The captain patted the box and said, "Inside this, we have red and blue balls, each with a number from 1 to 28, so that there's one for all fifty-six of you. You will reach in through the hole at the top and take out a ball. Red is for the East Block; blue is for the West Block. Your preliminary form demonstrations will happen in the order of your numbers. If there are no questions, then starting from the front bench, you may now draw your—"

Before he could finish his sentence, Kirito shot to his feet and rushed to the box. Eugeo hurriedly followed him, and the rest of the participants clanked to their feet as well.

The observer leaned out to see that there was a little hatch about ten cens across in the lid of the box. The interior was dark enough that even its powerful eyes couldn't identify any individual balls. Kirito clicked his tongue in disappointment; this explained his haste to be first to draw. He was hoping that when full, the box would allow him some measure of identifying the ball color before he drew it.

For being so lackadaisical, the boy certainly had a devious side, just not the knowledge he needed. In this world, lottery boxes built to avoid being seen into were impenetrable to the naked eye. Only with some element that eliminated the box's properties—such as creating a light element inside the box or casting an art of visual strengthening—could the contents be seen.

"Go on, draw your ball, youngster," said the captain. Kirito slowly reached inside. Without being able to see the color, it would be up to luck to ensure that he and Eugeo weren't in the same block. But…

…*I'll help him out this time.*

Just before Kirito reached into the hole, the observer leaped from his bangs to the lid of the box. It raced along the shadow cast by the boy's arm and into the hole.

Kirito's hand rushed into the box after it, grabbed the first ball it touched, and pulled it out. Once inside the box, the colors were easily visible. Kirito had pulled out a blue ball—putting him in the West Block.

The observer shifted the size of its body, going from the minimum of five mels to ten cens, twenty times the size. It was still small in comparison to its original size, but this would do. It used two arms to lift up a five-cen wooden ball—colored red, of course.

Seconds later, a fumbling white hand entered, obviously Eugeo's. Unlike Kirito's direct grab, his fingers wandered around timidly, so the observer pushed the red ball up toward them. The fingers flinched at first, then grasped the ball and yanked it out of the box. The boy even let out a cute little *"Yah!"* as he pulled.

A few seconds later, he finally opened his hand and exclaimed, "Look, Kirito! It's red!" The next sound was of hasty footsteps as the following contestant ushered them out of the way.

What a handful…

The observer was about to shrink down again and leave the box, but it paused to think first.

The young, sandy-haired apprentice. Why had Kirito focused on that particular unit? The observer had a professional interest in this. Perhaps that apprentice ought to face off against Kirito, rather than Eugeo.

It decided to wait in the corner of the box rather than leave. If anyone opened the lid, the sight would shock him. It was only ten cens in size, but there were no living things of this shape in the world of the human units.

It lay in wait for several minutes. After a few dozen other searching hands had taken their turns, a weak, spindly limb entered the box, its window specifying that it belonged to the sentinel trainee in question. As the fingers rubbed nervously over the bunch, the observer slid its prepared blue ball into them. He grabbed the ball without suspicion and pulled it out, much to the observer's relief. This time it shrank down to minimum size and clung to the sleeve of the next arm that entered the box.

It rode on the sleeve back to the waiting benches, then raced across the floor with some amount of risk to the feet of the boys sitting at the end. It climbed up the worn leather boots, the back of the dark-blue tunic, and then into the black hair hanging over the back collar. Once it was back in its usual spot near the front hairline, it sighed.

Manipulating drawing results was completely out of line with its duties. If Master found out, it might even suffer a word of rebuke.

No…Separating Kirito and Eugeo into different blocks would make observation more efficient, and it might learn something by arranging for Kirito to be in the block with that apprentice. These actions were certainly *not* from a line of thought that violated its duty. It most definitely was not considering a possible sacred arts interference if the apprentice tried any funny business in a match against Kirito. Not at all.

4

When the bells of the Zakkaria church chimed the melody of midday, a roar arose from the stands.

Amid the applause and bursting of smokegrass, fifty-six contestants left the waiting room in two lines. Eugeo's line curved to the right toward the eastern stage, while Kirito's line headed left to the western stage. The groups of twenty-eight contestants filed into lines on their respective stages, then turned to the VIP seating on the south side to salute the Zakkarian lord's family.

Kelgam Zakkarite, liege lord of the town, gave a speech that went on just a bit too long, received a brief round of applause from the impatient crowd, and then the event began. First came the preliminary round that would whittle each block from twenty-eight down to eight contestants. The contestants would go in order of their ball numbers, taking turns exhibiting the designated swordfighting forms onstage.

A "form" was a set string of movements, including sword path, arm placement, and footwork. Contestants were judged on precision, boldness, and beauty.

Over five months of observing the boys, it was not worried about Eugeo, but Kirito was a different story. Yes, he had his mysterious, unique "Aincrad style," but all of the designated forms in this event were Zakkarite style. On top of that, the judges were senior members of the garrison and town hall. If anything, they would be *more* inclined to harshly judge the wielder of a strange, unfamiliar style, not less.

The preliminaries proceeded, the observer feeling a bit nervous, until Eugeo's number was called. He looked a bit pale, as was his tendency, but he had the fortitude to get up on the stage, salute, and draw his sword in a smooth, confident motion.

Each form took about ten seconds, making the entire demonstration a hundred seconds long. Eugeo made not a single mistake and executed his routine with grace and skill. The furious morning practices were a part of that success, no doubt, but it was also thanks to his very high object control authority. To him, that sparring sword had to feel as light and airy as a fallen twig.

The roar of applause he received was far greater than any for the men-at-arms or sentinels-in-training. The judges would not be eager to give a suspicious wanderer high marks, but given that they were bound by the tournament rule that all contestants should be judged solely on the merits of their performance, they could not penalize him for their own reasons. An imperial noble unbound by lesser laws would be a different story, but the only noble in town was Kelgam Zakkarite, a fifth-rank peer, who was not one of the judges.

Eugeo stepped down from the stage, wiped the sweat from his brow, and flashed a huge smile to his partner waiting next to the western stage. Kirito shot him a thumbs-up, but if anything, *he* was the one to worry about.

Two minutes later, Kirito's number was called at last. He strode up the steps without a hint of nerves—which was precisely the worrying part. The observer wanted to command, *Just do it normally today; don't get any crazy ideas.*

He stood in the middle of the stage, which was made out of fitted blocks of polished red marble rather than the usual sandstone, bowed to the lord in his special stands, and promptly drew his sword. The judges sitting in the nearby tent scowled at his haste. But he ignored them, lifted his right arm, and proceeded into the first form...

Zmmf! The grounds trembled with his powerful step. *Vwum!* The rush of air from his swing reached the stands twenty mels away. Amid shouts and screams of surprise, the dressed-up VIPs bolted out of their chairs. It was hard to blame them; Kirito had just executed a ten-second form, at full power, in barely two seconds.

The observer nearly pulled out the boy's hair and screamed, *What are you thinking?!* Then it recalled that the instructions regarding the form only designated that it be completed within a certain number of seconds. Therefore, there should be no penalty for early completion. But still…

Kirito spun around from where he had finished his swing and faced the north stands for his second form. The next powerful breeze ruffled the hair of the audience in front. There were more yelps and screams but also an increase in cheers. As he demonstrated the third and fourth forms in quick succession, the cheers turned to roars and applause. It made sense; watching dozens of contestants perform the same movements one after the other was a tepid opening act for an excited audience. Perhaps that was why they had both stages performing at the same time, to lessen the time required.

Kirito finished his ten forms without slowing in the least, sheathed his sword, bowed, and left the central grounds rumbling with applause. There was a portion of the stands screaming in a higher pitch than the rest, owing to the presence of Teline and Telure, the twins from Walde Farm. Their parents had brought them to cheer, just as promised.

He waved to them and confidently descended the steps, only to meet the onrushing Eugeo. The other boy looked fit to grab him by the shirt in anger, but instead he merely hissed, "Wh-what are you thinking?!"

"Oh, I just noticed that there was some variety in the amount of time these demonstrations take, depending on the person…so I figured maybe the quicker, the better."

"W-well, you might not get marked down, but you could have just done it normally!"

"I also figured that if I moved fast enough, the judges might miss some small mistakes in terms of my finger and toe placement..."

"..."

Eugeo looked 70 percent annoyed, 30 percent impressed. His shoulders dropped and he let out a very, very long breath. "Let's just pray that the judges take audience reaction into account..."

Deep in Kirito's hair, the observer had to agree. The preliminary round lasted more than an hour after that and concluded just around the two o'clock bells. The contestants lined up onstage again, and the judges announced the names and numbers of those who qualified for the dueling portion.

The observer was certain that Eugeo would be called. When Kirito's name followed seconds later, it experienced a measure of relief it could not recall feeling in decades and nearly tumbled out of his hair.

How long has it been since I had a mission that affected me so? Perhaps never.

Forty contestants returned to the waiting room in defeat and disappointment, while eight fighters on either stage descended to special waiting areas within the open grounds. They took a light meal and chilled siral water from a well while the audience relaxed. The tournament began thirty minutes later. It consisted of single-elimination blocks of three rounds each, so that there would be an east and west champion.

According to what Vanot Walde had told them while they were workers on his farm, there had been a final match between the east and west winners up until a few decades ago. That custom was removed when one year's final had been so hotly contested that an accident occurred and blood was shed—a forbidden act.

It was the rule of not just Zakkaria but the regional tournaments across Norlangarth—across the entire realm of humanity—that blows should be stopped before they landed.

The Taboo Index ruled that "another's life must not be intentionally shortened for any reason, aside from those listed in a separate verse." Therefore, duels required contradictory strategies, where a duelist had to both subdue the opponent while also protecting their own body.

The reason that sword styles focused on forms so heavily was that they allowed the duelists to time their movements to avoid accidents. Form intercepted form, a kind of strategic, formalized style of fighting, such that the contestant whose stamina and concentration lapsed first would largely disqualify himself. The only places where bloodletting "first-strike" duels were allowed were at the higher tournaments in Centoria or during practices at the high institutions such as the Imperial Knighthood or Swordcraft Academy.

But unlike other types of moving objects, human units had "emotions." Those gave them great strength but could also make them lose focus and produce unpredictable results at times.

When Vanot Walde said there had been an "accident," he likely meant that one of the two finalists had been so taken by his desire to win that his sword did not stop short; it had hit and drawn blood. Surely it would not have been fatally deep—such an incident would prompt the Axiom Church to intervene, and it would remain in the Cathedral's records—but even a single drop of blood was enough to terrify the townsfolk. It made perfect sense that they would scrap the idea of a singular winner and have two champions instead.

Naturally, the two youngsters were not aware of this. All they cared about was winning this tournament, standing out in the garrison, and earning the right to take the test for the Swordcraft Academy in Centoria. If they squeezed through these gates, one by one, they would eventually be reunited with Alice at Central Cathedral.

Surprisingly, they were going about it the right way. It was incredibly narrow and unfathomably long, but the path they were on now indeed led to the cathedral. But even if they succeeded at stepping into that chalk-white tower, by that time, they would already…

The two-thirty bells interrupted the observer's train of thought. The musicians in a corner of the grounds began to play a thrilling march, signaling the start of the competition.

The boys bolted upright from their folding chairs. Black and green eyes met. They bumped fists, turned their separate directions, and climbed the east and west stages; there was no need for words at this point. The stands hadn't been at full capacity during the preliminary round, but they were packed now, and the roaring of the crowd was like a storm overhead.

A sentinel set up a large board with parchment pulled across it, right next to the judges' tent. On it, in the black letters of the common script, were the tournament bracket and matchups. Eugeo's first-round match was the third in the East Block. Likewise, Kirito's was the third match on the West Block, but more noteworthy was the name Egome opposite his—the apprentice sentinel he had singled out earlier.

The observer's tiny body was filled with an odd sensation that had not arisen when it was actually doing the manipulation of the drawing. It was a baseless anticipation that *something* was going to happen. Such a feature should not have been possible in a nonhuman being.

Meanwhile, Kirito himself gave no reaction of any kind when he saw the name Egome next to his. When the head judge's speech finished, he descended the stage and plopped into a chair in the west-side waiting area. Eugeo had come over during the lunch break, but he had to stay on the east side now, so there was no one to talk with.

The first and second fights finished peacefully and uneventfully. The first attacker tried three or four basic forms, which the defender received easily, blocking the sword with his own. Then they switched; three more clangs. It almost looked like practice, except that they were using real metal swords and both sides would lose a bit of life due to fatigue. After a certain level of fatigue, movements would get sloppy, defense would suffer, one side would falter, and the tip of the sword would stop just short—signaling the end of the duel.

At Centoria tourneys, the feints and timing ploys were much more advanced, but up in the north, this was the best you got. The young man named Egome wasn't particularly noteworthy, so thanks to his exceptional authority level, Kirito should win easily, the observer told itself. When Kirito's name was called, he ascended to the red marble stage.

Seconds later, Eugeo's name was called on the other side, but even at a distance, the sweat running down his opponent's desperate face was clear—Eugeo would have no problem. Meanwhile, Kirito's adversary, Egome, stared at him from behind that sandy hair, never blinking. Once again, the Stacia Window indicated below-average numbers for this tournament. What was it that Kirito was worried about?

They advanced to the starting lines and drew their swords. The adult judge raised his arm, then brought it down and bellowed, "*Start!*"

Egome moved instantaneously. Both duelists were supposed to take a stance, sense who would attack first, then begin, so this move startled the crowd. However, it wasn't against the rules. Catching the opponent off guard was a valid strategy, if an unpopular one.

"*Iyooo!*" Egome howled, slashing from the upper right. Kirito stepped in to intercept it. *Grshing!* The clash of swords sounded unlike any of the others so far, and yellow sparks briefly lit the combatants' faces.

The attacker's sword would normally fly backward, but this one stayed still at the point of impact, trembling. Kirito's ferocious defensive move was late to start, but now he actually applied pressure from above. The sound of the swords grinding rang out across the hushed grounds.

As they pushed, Kirito leaned in closer to Egome's tense face and muttered, "You smell like tanglevine."

"...What if I do?" Egome hissed back, his voice like scraping metal.

"There's only one use for tanglevine. You dry it out, burn it, and use the smoke to paralyze poisonous bugs. Such as...a greater swampfly."

"...!"

Egome's narrowed eyes went wide at the same moment that two tiny ones blinked atop Kirito's head.

That meant Kirito's prowling walk around the waiting room was an attempt to catch the scent of tanglevine. In other words...

"That swampfly that bit the horse outside the west gate this morning...You let it loose, didn't you?" Kirito accused.

Egome only leered back at him. "I don't have to answer to a vagabond like you...but let's say I did do that. All I did was release a harmless bug, rather than kill it. You won't find any rules against that in Basic Imperial Law or the Taboo Index."

The apprentice sentinel's statement was true. If a swampfly was a type of insect that directly afflicted people and lowered their life, it would be forbidden to bring them into areas of human residence. But as the flies attacked only horses, there was no rule against releasing them.

But the situation wasn't that simple. Even the smallest children knew that if they released a living swampfly near one of the horses they fed upon, it would bite the animal and damage its life. Furthermore, that horse could panic and cause major injury to pedestrians nearby.

The majority of human units, understanding this likely consequence, would not be able to release the fly. It would activate the taboo against reducing the life of others. But despite knowing that Kirito or Eugeo could easily be hurt—in fact, *because* he knew that—Egome had done just that. To him, his action was the liberation of a harmless insect, and any further consequences were not his responsibility. That idea outranked the obedience to taboo in his mind.

...Noble blood.

This young man had a strong streak of the negative side of noble genes. He was a unit diametrically opposed to the Waldes; he believed that as long as it wasn't against the law, anything was fair game.

"...Why?" Kirito demanded.

"Because I don't like you. What gives a jobless, homeless wanderer like you the right to compete with the noble Egome Zakkarite? Get into the garrison? They'll never let you. From the moment you applied to the tournament last month, I swore I'd crush you," Egome spat.

"I see...You're in the lord's family. But that noble background isn't going to help you here. Sorry, pal—I'm going to win now."

Kirito was not taken aback in the least by the revelation that his opponent was of noble blood. He pushed back on his sword, hoping to unbalance the other man.

Egome leered again. There was a fine cracking sound, and Kirito tensed. Of the two swords firmly pressed together, Kirito's was faintly, but undoubtedly, cracked and pitted.

They were both dueling swords, so how was only one damaged?! The observer looked closely, pulling up the windows for both swords, and was stunned by the results.

Kirito's sword was a class-10 object. Egome's, however, was class-15. Indeed, upon closer examination, it seemed to have a different shine to it.

"Ugh." Kirito grunted and tried to pull away, but Egome only thrust his weight further. The inferior sword squealed and crackled, its life dwindling rapidly.

"Just so you know, this isn't against the rules, either," Egome gloated. "The rules state that all participants borrow from the swords arranged by the judges. So if a finer blade just so happens to get accidentally included, and I wind up getting to use it, that's not my fault, is it?"

"You got the sentinel in charge of distribution on your side."

"No idea what you're talking about. Anyway, vagabond, aren't you worried about pushing back so hard? Don't you think your cruddy sword will break?" he taunted, pushing with all his might.

But then Kirito did something unexpected.

Rather than push back, he collapsed to the stage and slipped down through Egome's legs. The man's sword slid free and clanged loudly on the marble. As Egome froze from the vibration of the impact, Kirito took the opportunity to leap back and take his distance.

The crowd, which had been holding its breath, now began to stir. This clashing competition of strength and the roll through the legs were new to them. They applauded vigorously, unaware of the argument happening between the combatants.

Egome recovered and faced Kirito, his face twisted with fury.

The observer sensed danger. Of course, even nobles could not break the Taboo Index, so he would not attempt to harm Kirito directly with his sword—but he could certainly be contemplating some *accident* that might coincidentally end up in injury.

Egome's next action solidified that theory.

He had been holding his class-15 sword with both hands before, but now he lifted it with just his right, settling it on his shoulder. He twitched in place for several seconds, as though searching for something. Eventually, the blade began to glow a faint blue color.

That wasn't sacred arts—it was a "secret form" passed down within each style of swordsmanship.

"...Zakkarite-style secret technique—Bluewind Slash."

The stands rumbled again with surprise, including the eastern half this time. The judge onstage looked toward the judging tent for help, but they didn't know what to do, either. As the name *secret form* suggested, these were the deepest secrets of the style and not meant to be thrown about at a moment's notice. But that was entirely up to the user's discretion, not encoded in law, so if Egome decided he wanted to use it, nobody could stop him.

The problem was, these secret techniques were far more powerful than ordinary forms, and once started, they *could not be stopped*. A power apart from the user's will, something similar to yet different from sacred arts, would largely possess the body. In other words, if Kirito failed to block the attack, Egome would not be able to stop himself from cutting flesh and spilling blood—a fact that he knew full well. If he was using the attack at all, he must believe it would be the fault of his target if bloodshed ensued.

In that case, there was a way to halt Egome's form.

Kirito had to lower his sword and leave himself completely defenseless. In that instant, Egome's rationale would collapse, and his use of the secret form would be a clear violation of the Taboo Index. Even the noblest blood could not override the authority of the Axiom Church. It was an absolute boundary etched into the existence of every human unit.

Put down your sword, the observer wanted to command Kirito. Of course, Kirito would realize this himself. *Go on, put it down…*

"…Secret technique, huh?" Kirito whispered, quietly enough that only the being atop his head could hear.

Like Egome, he released his doublehanded grip, but rather than setting it down, he held it at his left side. The moment he paused, his blade flashed a brilliant purple.

Again, the entire crowd and team of judges held their breath. The only exception was Eugeo, who had already won his fight on the other stage and was now shaking his head in disbelief.

Egome's face trembled and warped, and he exposed his teeth.

"*Kyieaaaa!!*"

He screeched like a large avian object, and his form lurched into motion. His left foot stomped forward, and the sword on his right shoulder swung forward on a diagonal path.

For an instant, the observer contemplated interfering. But it was too late for sacred arts now. It would have to leap down from Kirito's head and expose its true form. It would be a complete violation of its orders—but even punishment from Master would be preferable to losing this surveillance target…

But then—

"*Nshh!!*" Kirito hissed, and shot forward.

He plunged straight toward the pale-blue slice. His right hand flashed, tracing a bold purple curve through the air. Left to right. At the same time, right to left.

A tremendous, ringing clash echoed beyond the walls of the central grounds, perhaps even to every corner of the town of Zakkaria.

A silver light shone high in the sky, catching the reflection of Solus at its peak, before falling back to earth. It landed and sank upright into the red-marble stage—a blade snapped at its base.

Kirito's move was so fast, even the observer couldn't catch all the details. But it certainly saw enough.

The sword had swung from left to right, then immediately turned back to go right to left. It was so quick that it was as though two swords were swung at once. But in truth, there was only one metallic reverberation. The doubled swings caught Egome's sword precisely at a point, like the jaws of a wild beast, and crushed it—a dueling sword, half-damaged, destroyed a finer blade five levels its superior in priority.

Egome stared down at the remaining handle of his weapon, his eyes as wide as saucers, trembling slightly. From his own finished position to the left, Kirito murmured into Egome's nearby ear.

"That's the *two-part* Aincrad-style attack…Snakebite."

The instant it heard that, all of the observer's fine hairs stood on end.

This Kirito unit was so far beyond expectations that he was unnerving, alien. In the 378-year history of the Underworld, he was an extremely rare case…Possibly even as noteworthy as Master or the Great One…

It did not know the nature of what was racing through its mind. It did not even register that presence. It just repeated one thought.

I must see Kirito and Eugeo's journey to its end.
Surely, that will lead me to…

*   *   *

The Zakkaria Swordfighting Tournament in the year 378 of the Human Era was won by two youngsters with no calling from a tiny northern village, earning them entrance into the Zakkaria garrison. It was an unprecedented result.

In the end, Kirito only (briefly) struggled in that first fight and did not need to use his two-part attack after that. It should come as no surprise that the following spring, Kirito and Eugeo earned the recommendation needed to test for the Imperial Swordcraft Academy.

CHAPTER FOUR

1

Hopefully we won't have to worry about fighting girls until the Four-Empire Holy Unification Tournament.

I once said something like this to Eugeo, just before the Zakkaria Tournament. That was a year and a half ago.

It was two years ago that we'd felled the Gigas Cedar blocking our way out of Rulid Village. Six months later, we joined the Zakkaria garrison, then ascended to Centoria six months after that, making it one year since we'd knocked on the door of the academy.

They were long, long days that happened in a blink, but thinking back on them made my head spin. Two years was the same amount of time that I had spent in Aincrad, after all.

Fortunately (if you could call it that), this virtual realm called the Underworld, which I was diving into through circumstances unknown, worked on some nearly unimaginable super-tech.

By my estimation, the Fluctlight Acceleration function, which sped up the user's mind and shrank perceived time to a fraction of its regular speed, was working at a factor of around a thousand to one. That meant that for all this time I'd experienced, only eighteen hours had passed for Kazuto Kirigaya in the real world since the start of the dive in the Soul Translator.

The thought that the two years I'd spent—from waking up in the forest near Rulid until reaching Norlangarth's Imperial

Swordcraft Academy in Centoria—had actually happened in less than a day was a mind-bending concept but also a saving grace. It meant that at worst, the amount of time I'd been missing wasn't actually that long.

I didn't want my parents, Suguha, my friends, and certainly not Yui nor Asuna to worry about me. On top of that, I knew that they would never be content with *just* worrying, which was what weighed on my mind.

At any rate, given the possibility that I would cause them distress by doing so, I had vowed to avoid unnecessary feminine contact whenever possible here. I'd sworn it when I left Rulid—thank goodness that Eugeo was male—and it was my intent to honor the pledge that made me say those words in Zakkaria.

How could I have guessed that in the year since coming to Centoria, I would be doing most of my swordfighting against a woman?

"This is a recap of the entire year, so treat it that way."

That cool order came from an older student in a customized uniform, mostly purple, with her dark-brown hair tied into a long ponytail—my upperclassman.

"Understood, Miss Liena," I answered, and drew the wooden practice sword from the leather holder on my left waist. Yes, it was only a wooden sword, but it was made of polished platinum oak, the very finest of materials, shining as though it were metal. It had no edge, meaning that it wouldn't cause any life damage if it brushed clothes, but in terms of item priority, it was far higher than the crude metal swords we had received at the Zakkaria Tournament.

Once I had readied my blade in a normal stance, my opponent smoothly drew hers. Her stance was a bit unorthodox, a sideways lean with her right side forward and the sword held diagonally so that it hid her left arm. While it was strange, this was actually the basic stance for her family's own sword school, the "Serlut Battle Style."

"...Since it's the last time, you can even use your left hand,"

I offered with a cheeky grin. She murmured in the affirmative, totally serious, and reached behind her back and under a large ornamental sash. I had no idea what she would pull out until the duel started.

Despite my aforementioned oath about women, I couldn't deny that the girl standing ten mels ahead was beautiful.

She was even a little bit taller than me, and I was currently five foot six in real life. Her tied-up hair flowed in waves down her back, and the long lilac ribbon that bound it up complemented the dark-brown color well. Her beauty combined the fierceness of a warrior with the pride of nobility. Her dark-blue eyes put me in mind of an evening sky.

She wore a crisp, fitted jacket and a billowing long skirt, both of which were glacial purple. It wasn't a flashy color but, mysteriously enough, on her the uniform looked more dazzling than any dress. Of course, due to my position, I also knew full well how the muscles underneath it were hard as steel.

"...This will be the last one," said Sortiliena Serlut, child of Norlangarth nobility and second-seat elite disciple at the Imperial Swordcraft Academy.

As a primary trainee at the academy and her page, I nodded silently and dropped my center of weight.

My everyday schedule of study and practical exercises lasted from nine in the morning to three in the afternoon, when I began my hour-long duties as her page. I was always mentally and physically exhausted by this point, but when I faced off against Sortiliena, all the fatigue vanished. As it was now after five o'clock, we were the only two people in the training hall of the elite disciples' dorm that stood on high ground within the academy campus.

Right about now, Eugeo would be fretting to himself about the fact that I was breaking the curfew of the common room at the primary trainees' dorm, but he was also serving as a page for another disciple, so he would understand.

I focused on the task at hand and let my sword become an extension of my mind. The color of Liena's eyes darkened, and the air seemed to crackle with tension. The flame in the lamp that lit the wide training hall flickered, unable to stand the pressure.

We moved in unison, our breathing unified, even without a judge there to signal the start.

Liena was called the "Walking Tactics Manual"; tricks and feints would not work on her. I crossed the span between us in a straight line and thrust forward a vertical slash without any warm-up.

If I tried this in the practical exercise portion of the day, the instructor would give me an earful, but in this duel, using a wimpy Norkia-style form was a surefire way to lose. As far as I had experienced, Liena's Serlut style was the most practically suited to battle in all of the Underworld.

She blocked my quick strike with the wooden sword in her right hand. I hardly felt any impact; her wrist, shoulder, and back curved gently to slide the blow along the surface of the blade and disperse the shock. This secret art of the Serlut style was called "Flowing Water," and while I'd been studying it under her tutelage for a year, I still hadn't mastered its use.

As an aside, the written language used in this world was straightforward Japanese (with a few foreign loanwords), but the number of *kanji* they used was rather small—about a third of the JIS first-rank characters, or only about a thousand in total. Given those limitations, the creativity that the Underworldians utilized to name their skills was impressive. For now, they had only fairy tales of the sort told to children, but in another century, they could be writing full-blown novels. If those were pulled out to sell in the real world and became a hit, how crazy would that be…?

I cast aside this mental detour and leaped forward and to the right. I'd learned through hard experience that if I tried to fight the direction of her Flowing Water, I would suffer a painful counter.

I reversed in midair and landed near the wall of the training hall, then launched my right foot off the gleaming black paneling for another charge—when she finally moved her *left* hand.

Her fingers traced an arc of white light from behind her back around to the front. Naturally, it was *not* a light element produced from sacred arts. It belonged to a whip of finely braided white leather: her favorite weapon aside from the sword.

The practice whip made of soft uru goat leather did not cause much life damage on a direct blow, but it was painful enough to bring tears to the eyes. If I tried to parry with my sword, it would wrap around the blade the moment it made contact and render my weapon essentially useless. But if I stepped back, I would have to continue retreating to avoid a second blow, then a third.

I twisted as hard as I could to the left to avoid the whip. It grazed my right cheek and passed, and I hurtled forward. The end of the whip snapped in midair behind me and curled like a snake as it pulled back. I had to close the distance before her next attack. I determined that an ordinary dash wouldn't cut it, so I pulled back instead, holding my sword parallel to my right leg. I leaned low, low, low, and my blade began to glow a sky-blue.

Liena's eyes narrowed. Her left hand snapped open, tossing the whip aside so she could brace the pommel of her sword.

My body shot forward as if struck by a giant invisible hand. It was the Aincrad-style—which was, of course, just a name I had given to the original sword skills of *SAO*—one-handed low-thrust attack Rage Spike. I turned into a gust of wind, closing the twenty feet between us.

For her part, Liena pulled her sword behind her right side and stepped forward with her left foot. The wooden sword glowed a jade-green—the Serlut-style secret technique Ring Vortex.

My sword jumped up from the right, while hers rotated on a level plane, until they connected with a tremendous clash, briefly illuminating the dim training hall with blue and green.

I pushed upward, jamming our swords at the hilt, so that Liena's face was just inches away. Her expression was cool; there wasn't a drop of sweat on her pale forehead. But if I let up on the forward pressure just the tiniest bit, she would easily topple me backward.

Human abilities in this world—our "character stats," if you will—were a bit tricky.

On a Stacia Window, the only numbers listed were the current and maximum life points, an object control (OC) authority level, and a system control (SC) authority level.

My first working theory, which was admittedly simplistic, was that OC level involved manipulating weapons, while SC level involved sacred arts—in other words, physical strength and magic intelligence. But actual physical strength did not correspond directly to OC level. A number of variables affected it, such as age, physique, health status, and long-term experience.

Upon reflection, if OC authority was really all there was to strength, then if a young child's level rose abnormally through some particular event or circumstance, he or she would suddenly be an extremely hardy youth. Based on the reason for this world's existence, such an irregular occurrence would be undesirable.

I hadn't actually checked for myself, but I was pretty certain that my OC level was well above Liena's. The fact that we were at a total standstill spoke to the tremendous amount of training she'd undergone. Eugeo and I hadn't missed our morning practice once in two years, but the word *possessed* didn't even begin to describe her level of self-discipline. That hard work both increased her physical prowess statistic and gave her a different kind of "strength" that could not be expressed with numbers.

But most frightening of all was that out of the twelve elite disciples at the academy, she was still the second seat—meaning there was someone else even *greater*.

Next month, Eugeo and I would take the test to be secondary trainees. The twelve who scored highest would be placed in the ranks of elite disciples—what you might call "scholarship students." We wanted to join their ranks, of course, but ultimately we needed to occupy the first and second seats (essentially the top two ranks of the yearly class). Otherwise, we wouldn't get to participate in the post-graduation tournament in the presence of the emperor—the Norlangarth Imperial Battle Tournament.

In the two-year Swordcraft Academy, there were exactly 120 students in the first year. That meant we had to exceed all 118 other classmates—but the thought that even nearly invincible Liena wasn't the top of her class was honestly making me nervous, if not downright frightened…

"You've grown, Kirito," she said, right next to my ear. It was as though she had read my mind. Pushing back to counter the unrelenting pressure, I managed to shake my head.

"No…I've still got a long way to go."

"Don't be modest. You've at least figured out how to handle my whip."

"And no idea how to use one, myself."

Her shining lips formed a little smile. "You don't need to. And here at the very end, I have a question…There's *more* to your Aincrad style than what you've shown me, isn't there?"

Words caught in my throat. The distraction caused my sword to falter just an inch or two, so that she was looking down at me.

The lady swordsman's dusk-blue eyes stared into me as she said, "The reason I chose you as page a year ago was because I sensed something like a fresh breeze within your sword. Something fundamentally different from the official Norkia style the academy teaches…A type of swordfighting meant to win, not for show. I believe that the Serlut style is also practical, but the last year has taught me that it's still quite stiff compared to yours."

My eyes bulged; I had no response to this confession.

It was only natural that we used our swords differently. I was not from the Underworld. As the name suggested, my Aincrad style of swordsmanship was brought here from that floating castle. From a game of death, where every battle risked the ultimate price.

Here in the Underworld, there was essentially no battle. All fights were competitive "matches"—in the regional tournaments, they ended short of impact, while the higher events in Centoria were finished after the first solid blow. If there was no risk to the combatant's life, it was only natural that their swordplay tended toward the demonstrative.

But that did not mean that the skill of the Underworld's swordsmen was in any way inferior. I had most definitely learned that lesson over the last two years. They practiced their forms infinitely to produce a single perfect technique that could easily overpower a more practically minded fighter who lacked their level of discipline.

It all came down to the power of imagination.

The Underworld was a virtual world, but its fundamental nature was completely different from Aincrad's. Here, the strength of the mental image emitted by the soul, or fluctlight, could sometimes have an influence on events.

The imagination of a swordfighter who had been practicing the same move since childhood, for a decade or two, could be so powerful that it overrode a higher OC authority level—as in this situation, where Liena was overpowering me. The power of the mental image was the true hidden power of this world that couldn't be expressed numerically. And given that I had been in this world for only two years—and Eugeo had started practicing the sword at the same time—we just didn't have that skill yet.

Most of the students at the Swordcraft Academy were born from noble stock, social elites who had received special sword training from the age of three or four. Only a handful of them had gone through truly bloodcurdling training, but we had to surpass them, too, in order to be at the top of the class.

The only weapon I had to my benefit was the Aincrad style. Sword skills.

I still wasn't sure exactly how sword skills had come to be in the Underworld. But for whatever reason, the people here either knew only singular skills or were incapable of doing more than that.

When Egome, the apprentice sentinel, had used the "Bluewind Slash" of the Zakkarite style in the tournament a year and a half ago, it would have been called "Slant" back in *SAO*. Liena's Serlut-style "Ring Vortex" was just the two-handed spinning attack Cyclone. There were others, of course; the Norkia-style "Lightning Slash" was just Vertical, and the High-Norkian "Mountain-Splitting Wave" was the double-handed Avalanche.

These were the secret techniques of the masters of their respective styles, and there were no supersecret or ultrasecret moves beyond that. That meant the two-part and three-part skills I knew were one of the few weapons that could actually counter the tremendous skills of the elites at the school. Yes, it felt a little cheap and sneaky, but we weren't trying to become the most venerable people of this world. All we needed to do was pass through the gate to the Central Cathedral, the Axiom Church's massive tower just a few miles from the academy.

For Eugeo, to reunite with Alice, after she had been taken away as a child.

For me, to find the administrator of this world.

We would do any cheap and cowardly thing we could in every single duel if it meant achieving those goals. I would use the higher sword skills I knew, one match at a time, to continue winning. Whatever it took to win the Unification Tournament and earn the title of Integrity Knight.

That was why I hadn't used any multi-strike skills over the last year. And even if I had, it was always a charge attack like Rage Spike.

But somehow, my sneaky, underhanded secrecy was no match for my beautiful upperclassman. Liena leaned in even closer and whispered into my ear conspiratorially.

"Our distant Serlut ancestors earned the displeasure of the emperor at the time and were banished from the official High-Norkia style. For that reason, we had to compensate with whips, knives, and other irregular tools, crafting a style that relied more on softness than strength. That is the Serlut way...Do not get me wrong. I am not unhappy about this. In fact, I am proud to be the only one to carry on our style. It's what I've spent my life studying..."

Despite her strong words, her hands were trembling, causing our wooden swords to creak with pressure. It could have been my chance to push back, but I didn't. I stood my ground, waiting for her to continue.

"But my father hopes that I will graduate this academy as first seat, win the imperial event, and restore the honor of the Serlut family. But don't you find that a contradiction? Even if I fulfill his desires and earn us the right to practice the High-Norkia style again...would our family then abandon the Serlut style? If so... then what is the meaning of the pride I have felt in our style since childhood...?"

I had no immediate answer to that question.

I hardly even thought about it anymore, but it was an undeniable fact that Liena, Eugeo, the students and teachers at the academy—*all* the people who lived in the Underworld—were not actual human beings. This place was a virtual world, and they were just human units populating it.

And yet, they were not like the NPCs of ordinary VRMMO games. They were artificial fluctlights, copies of human souls saved to a special media format. A totally new form of AI created by someone in the real world, probably the mysterious venture capital project Rath...

Yet somehow, their emotive capability sometimes appeared much *richer* than that of real humans. They sensed, worried over, accepted, and occasionally defied this world and their fates within it. Every time I saw this happen, I couldn't help but be amazed. Their existence, the existence of Sortiliena as she ground her wooden blade against mine, felt like an astonishing miracle.

"...Miss Liena," I mumbled. She was wearing the tiniest bit of a sardonic smile.

"I've been carrying that question around with me since long before I came to this school. Not once in these two years did I ever succeed in beating him. Perhaps it's because of that hesitation..."

She was referring to the first-seat elite disciple, the indisputable top student at the school: Volo Levantein. He was the heir of a second-rank noble family that had served as the sword instructors for the Norlangarth Imperial Knights for generations, and he was an appropriately tremendous swordsman. The power of his overhead smashes was far and away the greatest in the academy, and I had witnessed him split a practice log with a wooden sword before.

The top elite students of the academy were ranked, from first seat to twelfth seat. Those ranks were determined based on the results of test matches held four times a year.

Naturally, I had witnessed the three matches so far from the fancy close-up VIP seats. Like the Zakkaria Tournament, the event was put into a bracket. The twelve disciples played through two rounds to produce three finalists, with the highest-ranked of the three according to pre-tournament rankings getting seeded before the other two. All three times, the final of each ended up being Liena versus first-seat Volo. All three times, she was unable to overcome his ability.

As far as I could see, their skills as swordsmen were equal. Volo was strength, and Liena was softness. He struck with incredibly fierce slashes, which she handled with the grace of flowing water, occasionally striking back with acute skill. The matches would continue without a clean hit until time was nearly up—at which point Volo would attempt the High-Norkian secret overhead slash technique, which Liena always failed to block. Twice her wooden sword had been knocked aside, and once it actually broke.

All three matches had to go to judgment, but given these final moments, it was no wonder that the judgment would go to Volo's corner in each case. Thus, for the entire year, Volo had been first seat and Liena had been second seat.

The third seat was also unchanged; the semifinalist who consistently lost against Liena was a large fellow known as Golgorosso Balto. Incidentally, Golgorosso's page was my very good friend Eugeo.

When Liena said this was the last time, just before our duel, she was referring to the fact that her fourth and final "graduation match" was coming up in two days. That would determine the final ranking, and the day after that, the twelve elite disciples and all the secondary trainees would graduate from the academy.

In other words, the match in two days would be Liena's last

chance to finally overcome Volo. Technically, since the top two ranks could appear in the post-graduation Imperial Battle Tournament, she had the opportunity to face off against Volo again, but she didn't seem to feel that she had a chance against him then if she never beat him once at school.

"I'll be honest," she murmured, our swords still pressed against each other, "when I see his Mountain-Splitting Wave stance...I falter. No matter how hard I train and prepare, I cannot convince my body that it is capable of withstanding that blow. It's been that way ever since I was a primary trainee...since the first time I ever saw him fight, in the entrance test..."

I was surprised at this revelation, but I also completely understood her point. There really wasn't a difference in skill between them. The only gap was in the strength of the mind—the amount of confidence.

If my theory was correct and this virtual world was built on mnemonic visual data, then the strength of the mind would be a huge factor in determining the outcome of events. The things that we saw and touched were not polygonal data and textures but memory images extracted from our fluctlights.

How could this mental data, which must surely have fine differences from individual to individual, be shared like this? There was probably something like a "main memory device" that buffered all the fluctlight output data and averaged it. In that case, if a particular fluctlight had a powerful enough mental image to affect that buffer data overall, that would essentially mean that the willpower of an individual could rewrite events.

That was the secret to the overpowering strength of Volo Levantein and others like him. Their absolute confidence in their skills and sword styles led to an unshakeable mental image that manifested in those unstoppable attacks.

On the other hand, Liena had a tiny sliver of self-doubt about her style. The source of that doubt was in the founding and backdrop of the Serlut style, as she had just mentioned. The understanding that her style came about due to her ancestors being forbidden from using the High-Norkia style created something negative, some little element of shame in her heart. Perhaps it was inevitable that she would fall to Volo's absolute confidence.

But this time, I really wanted her to win. Not because of anything to do with the workings of this world or theories about imagination power, but simply because I wanted her to be able to graduate with pride. She had the qualifications and the right to do that. She'd undertaken more training over the last year than any of the other disciples...

"Well...you've been training longer and harder than anyone, even Volo. Is that fact not enough for you to feel confident...?" I asked. She thought for a few moments, then shook her head.

"No...I suppose it isn't. The further I study the Serlut style, the more I think of it. What if this were a true steel fight, not with wooden swords? What if I were allowed to use my whip or knife? Then I would surely be a match for the High-Norkia style. But that's just an excuse. Within the human realm, there is no combat...no true battle. As long as I use that as an excuse, I will never be able to stop Volo's blade..."

Before I could find some response, she smiled and continued, "But you're different, Kirito. You have your own unique style, too, but you don't feel any sense of inferiority toward those of the orthodox styles. I've been watching you for a year now, and I think I finally understand why. Like I brought up earlier... there's much more to your Aincrad style, isn't there? That's why you have such an unshakeable core. Just like that tree from your home forest...the Gigas Cedar."

"Oh...you mean the one I cut down with my own hands," I noted ironically. That one actually got a little laugh out of her.

At some point, the consistent tension had gone out of our arms, and our wooden swords were simply resting against each other. Still, she placed her weight forward, pushing on me. Her voice was deep and smooth for a girl's.

"Then that tree stands within you now, firm against any storm, looking up only to Solus overhead. Kirito...I want to see your hidden inner strength."

" "
...

"It has nothing to do with the fight with Volo. I just want to see it…to know it. I want to know everything that makes you the swordsman you are before I graduate."

Inside those evening-blue eyes, floating just in front of my face, little stars twinkled.

Without realizing it, my face tilted a fraction of an inch closer to that soul-absorbing beauty. Suddenly, there was a sharp little prick of pain at my hairline, jolting me back to my senses. I blinked and restarted my train of thought.

The fact that I hadn't shown Liena the "next step" of the Aincrad style had nothing to do with any frugal ideas about keeping an ace up my sleeve.

It was as simple as this: The class-15 wooden swords we used in duels and sparring could not execute it. The best I could manage was two-part skills like Snakebite and Vertical Arc; no matter how hard I tried, I couldn't pull off three-parters or better. I'd tried it with steel swords of the same class, to no success.

Only when I had used the holy class-45 Blue Rose Sword that had managed to cut down the Gigas Cedar was I able to pull off four-part sword skills. I had no idea why. At the very least, there were no restrictions like that in *SAO*.

At any rate, she wanted to see "everything" I could do, so I didn't want to throw her a bone with an ordinary two-part attack and pretend that was it. It left only one option: to borrow the Blue Rose Sword from Eugeo and execute a five-part attack, the most powerful I could currently use.

Eugeo would probably happily lend it to me, but I felt a bit hesitant about his doing so. The sword belonged to him, and I believed that a sword was the swordsman's soul. I couldn't shake the feeling that as long as I knew I was using another's sword, I couldn't actually deliver the greatest possible attack. And I couldn't just take the highest-priority sword found in the school armory, either; even that wouldn't be *my* sword.

Realizing that there was no option and that I would have to borrow the Blue Rose Sword, I resigned myself to the inevitable choice and said, "All right. But can you give me a day, please? I promise you, at this time tomorrow…I will show you the greatest move I know."

Liena's mouth briefly curled into a smile, which disappeared in favor of a quizzical look. "But tomorrow is our day of rest. Training is forbidden, and this hall will be off-limits."

"…It's not training," I replied.

This intrigued her for some reason. "Oh? What is it, then?"

"W-well…" I started, trying to come up with the right words. Off the top of my head, I said, "It's a thank-you. You've taught me so much over the last year. I've heard that there's a custom at this school, that the day before a disciple graduates, their trainee page gives them some kind of present. I'll make my present a sword attack. That can be given on a day of rest, can't it?"

She smirked. "You'll never change, will you? I've never heard of a sword technique being given as a graduation present. But I suppose this is a good time to make a confession…"

"Uh…what's that?"

"As a matter of fact, I broke with tradition in a way just by choosing you for my page—although the custom is admittedly stupid to begin with. When a noble girl chooses her trainee page, she should choose one from another noble house, but one lower than her own. When I singled you out, the representatives of the higher nobles came to my dorm room in person to complain."

She chuckled at this memory, but I grimaced in horror.

In the privileged classes of the Norlangarth Empire, there were six ranks of nobility, above which was the imperial family. Volo Levantein's family was a second-rank noble house, while the Serluts were third-rank—both multiple levels above the fifth-rank lord of Zakkaria.

I, meanwhile, was as common as common gets (same as the real world), the lowest of social classes. Even without nobility, if you held a certain amount of power within a community or owned significant land—such as Gasfut Zuberg, the Rulid elder, or the farmer Vanot Walde—you earned a last name. The people lower than that didn't even have that right.

What I didn't realize until I had wormed my way into the Imperial Swordcraft Academy was that nearly all the students here were from noble or merchant families; only one in five was of common stock. For one thing, the requirements were completely different. Eugeo and I had had to work our butts off for six months to earn the Zakkarian garrison commander's recommendation just to take the academy entrance test, while nobles had that right by default. When I found that out, I was so angry I could have written a letter of protest to the Ministry of Education.

Once I got in, I learned that the school treated you no differently, whether you were noble or common…but there was still discrimination in various forms. I had withstood all that nonsense over the course of the year without blinking an eye (and so had Eugeo, I expected), but I had no idea they'd gone after Liena as well, just for choosing me as her page.

"If…if that's the custom, then why pick me…? There were six students who scored higher than me on the entrance test. They were all nobles, so you wouldn't have gotten flack for choosing them…"

"But those six scored their points on presentation. I have no interest in the beauty of the form. From what I saw, you were the one who put up the best fight against the testing instructor. In fact, it was more like…"

She paused but did not finish her sentence. Instead, Liena grinned and started over. "No, it's been a year. Don't force me to say why I picked you *now*. I'm about to graduate. Tomorrow is more important. If you're going to present me with a demonstration of the Aincrad style's secret technique, I would be glad to receive it."

"Ah, uh, g-great."

"But…something bothers me. Based on how you brought it up, I could interpret your gift to be something you forgot about and just improvised on the spot…"

"N-no, not at all! I've always meant to give you this, I swear," I claimed.

Liena smugly decided she would take me at face value, then added, "But that aside, we ought to wrap up this sparring session now."

"Huh...? Ah!"

It was only then that I recalled we were in the middle of a practice fight. Before I could react, a powerful shock ran through the wooden sword that I'd just been holding in place. Still Water, a forceful forward step from a locked position, was not a sword skill, but it was one of the few power moves in the Serlut arsenal.

I leaped back rather than fight the flow of force. Unlike Flowing Water earlier, Still Water placed great strain on the legs, so she would be briefly vulnerable after using it. And the whip was not in her free hand anymore.

I whirled my sword back as I landed, hoping to finish the fight with a direct lunge.

Instantly, I felt a chill run down my backbone.

Liena was still holding her wooden sword in both hands—but I couldn't see the whip behind her, where she should have discarded it. Where had it gone?! But there was no stopping the move now. My body activated the overhead lunge Sonic Leap, lighting my weapon a pale blue...

At that exact same moment, Liena removed her left hand from her sword and stretched upward. She grabbed something and swung it down. White light stretched from her hand like a snake, wrapping itself several times around my body just before I could bolt forward.

I had assumed the whip was lying on the floor, but its end had been wrapped around a ceiling beam so that it had dangled overhead the entire time we were locked together.

But I didn't put that all together until after I had toppled sideways and smacked the back of my head against the floor.

As stars burst in front of my eyes, I almost imagined that somebody was sighing in disappointment and exasperation, right around my forehead.

2

Centoria was the biggest city in the Norlangarth Empire—the biggest in the entire human realm, in fact. It was a perfect circle surrounded by walls, measuring ten "kilors" across, in the measurement of this world.

That was just about the length across the very first floor of Aincrad, meaning this city was as large as that massive wilderness map all on its own. It was almost impossibly huge for a virtual city and boasted a population of over twenty thousand, from what I had heard.

On top of that, the city was constructed in a very special way. The circular expanse was split into four by large walls forming an X shape. In essence, it was separated into four wedge-shaped pieces that narrowed down to a ninety-degree point. Even more surprising was that these were known as North Centoria, East Centoria, South Centoria, and West Centoria, and they acted as separate capital cities to the four empires that divided the human realm into cardinal directions.

In other words, the capital cities of the four empires, which mimicked the shape of those larger territories, were all adjacent and separated from one another by a simple wall, at the very center of humanity.

I couldn't help but be shocked when I learned this. The emperors' residences and the headquarters for the knights' brigades that served as the military force of each empire were all located in the capital. If a war ever broke out, the city would immediately explode into chaos. I started to suggest this possibility to Eugeo but realized my mistake in time: There weren't even robberies in this world, much less murders, so war could never break out among the empires.

Of course, in order to pass the giant marble walls—known as Everlasting Walls—that separated the capitals, one needed a special pass. That made sense, given that you were crossing national borders. So the visiting traders and tourists from afar in North Centoria tended to attract a bit of attention: black-haired Easterners, tanned Southerners, and slender Westerners. They were technically foreigners, but since we all spoke the same language (with different accents), there was no real trouble with the locals.

Not only was there no war, there was essentially no friction among the countries at all, and that surely had to do with what sat in the middle of the city—the giant pure-white tower that occupied the center of the human world as a whole.

The Axiom Church's Central Cathedral.

It was so tall that the tip was always indistinct up in the sky. I couldn't begin to guess how many hundreds, if not thousands of feet tall it was. It must have been a tremendous sight looking up from the base, but high walls surrounded the square grounds of the Church, making it impossible. The four Everlasting Walls that split Centoria each intersected with a corner of the Cathedral's white walls…Or perhaps it would be more accurate to say that they flowed *outward* from this center of the realm.

The Everlasting Walls were quite stunning artifacts in their own right, as they ran not just through the city of Centoria but over fields, forests, and deserts, all the way until they ran into the End Mountains nearly five hundred miles away. There were no power shovels or cranes in this world, so it was terrifying to imagine how much time and manpower it had taken to construct the walls by hand.

There could be no better symbol of the absolute authority of the Axiom Church.

The tower in the center of humanity was so grand and vast, looming high over even the palaces of the four emperors, that it was easy to rationalize the way the people of this world overlooked the differences among the empires. It was probably no different than the way I viewed residents of Tokyo versus nearby Saitama.

That raised another question. In this world of less than one hundred thousand residents, why did they need to split up into four empires at all? I hadn't yet found an answer. The rationale for an ultimate church authority presiding over the empires was also a mystery still.

The Axiom Church had civil posts such as priests and senators, along with the Integrity Knights who served as its military rank, but according to what Liena told me, it was not a large organization, consisting of less than a hundred in total. If you totaled up the knights and garrisons of the four empires, they made over two thousand. So the fact that there were no recorded rebellions of the empires against the Church meant that either the emperors themselves could not defy the Church and its Taboo Index, or that those few dozen Integrity Knights were more powerful than an army of two thousand. Possibly both were true.

The glory of the skyscraping Central Cathedral could be viewed from any spot at the Swordcraft Academy. As I left the elite disciples' dorm following my final practice with Liena, hurrying through the chilly spring evening, I glanced up at the chalk-white tower overhead, bathed in orange and blue.

Was whoever stood at the very top of that tower gazing down upon humanity just an onlooker from the real world like me, or yet another Underworldian fluctlight? Even if I continued to clear every single hurdle, it would take another year and a half to find that answer. Yes, in the real world that amounted to only another ten hours and change, but that meant nothing to how I would perceive it.

In the two years since I had woken up in the forest near Rulid, I had spent many nights trembling with the fear of not knowing my situation and the powerful desire to see Asuna, Suguha, my parents, and my friends again.

But on the other hand, there was a part of me, deep down, that feared finding the exit at the top of the Cathedral. Logging out would also mean a parting from all the people I'd met here in this world. That included Selka and the other children of Rulid I hadn't seen in months and months; the few friends I'd met at the academy; Sortiliena, who had tutored me and cared for me as her page for the past year; and most of all, my partner, Eugeo.

I hadn't thought of them as AIs in quite a while. They were just as human as me, only with their souls stored in a different place. The two years I'd spent in Rulid, Zakkaria, and Centoria had taught me this.

In fact, my love wasn't just for them. I felt it for this mysterious, vast, and beautiful world, too…

I summoned a deep breath to stop these thoughts from going any further.

Up ahead was an aging building, a two-story stone structure with green shingle roofing: the North Centoria Swordcraft Academy dorm building housing 120 primary trainees.

I would have preferred to climb straight into my room through the second-story window, but dorm regulations forbade that. Unlike the level of freedom granted to the elite disciples at their dorm, the primary trainee dorm and the secondary trainee dorm on a nearby hill were regimented by rules so strict, even the old Knights of the Blood headquarters would be stunned.

I summoned my courage and climbed the stone steps to the entrance, then carefully pushed the double doors. One silent step inside, then two—and I heard a quiet cough from my right. I turned fearfully to catch sight of a woman sitting across the entrance counter. Her brown hair was neatly arranged, and her features were nothing if not strict and stern. She was likely in her late twenties.

Promptly, I put my left hand to my waist and pounded my right fist over my chest in what they called the "knight's salute" and announced crisply, "Primary Trainee Kirito, returning to dorm!"

"...You are thirty-eight minutes after curfew."

There were no clocks in this world, only special "Bells of Time-Tolling" in every town and major location (including this academy) that played melodies every half hour. The only way to know the precise time would be some special limited-use higher sacred arts, but Azurica, the dorm manager, had to be using some extra-sensory skill to determine that it was exactly 5:38 in the evening.

I held my knight's salute and, quieter this time, said, "My instructor, Elite Disciple Serlut, issued an extension of my instruction time."

Azurica stared at me with her blue-gray eyes. Between her stern disposition and the sound of her name, I couldn't help but be reminded of another person I knew. Before I left this dorm, I wanted the chance to ask her if she had a relative up north named Sister Azalia, but it didn't look like that opportunity would come. Most of our interactions came in the form of scolding—just like this.

"It is the duty of any trainee page to accept the teaching of a disciple. Very well. But Primary Trainee Kirito, I have suspected that you see this not as a duty but a kind of free pass to escape curfew. And after an entire year, I still cannot dispel this suspicion."

I undid my salute, moved my hand behind my head, and put on an awkward smile. "Wh-why, Miss Azurica, my only desire has ever been to improve my skill with the sword. Breaking curfew is simply an unfortunate byproduct of the process and most definitely not its intended purpose. Honest."

"I see. If you've been late all year long to train your skill, you must have made great leaps and bounds. If you wish to determine your level of success, I would be more than happy to serve as a sparring partner."

I froze in place again.

Miss Azurica's calling was being the primary trainee dorm manager at the North Centoria Imperial Swordcraft Academy and not an actual swordcraft instructor. But as a general rule, all adults working at the academy were former graduates. That meant she had greater skill than the average person. Her expertise in the Norkia style and fearsome "one-on-one lessons" for any student caught bending (but never breaking) the dorm rules were well-known by one and all.

That was bad enough, but then what would happen to a student who actually *broke* the dorm rules? Thankfully, I would never find out—because it was impossible. The artificial fluctlights who lived in this world had a peculiar feature that made them incapable of disobeying higher regulations. All except for me, thanks to my different fluctlight vessel.

In a sense, it was really a minor miracle that I had made it an entire year without ever breaking one of the dorm rules. Impressed despite myself, I shook my head in protest. "N-no, Miss Azurica, that won't be necessary. I've only just finished my first year here."

"I see. Then when you have completed your second year's training, I will be ready to judge it."

"…Yes…I would…love that," I said, backing away and praying with all my might that she would not remember this promise for an entire year.

She finally returned to the document in her hands and said, "Dinner is in seventeen minutes. Please try not to be as late this time."

"Y-yes, ma'am! Pardon me!"

I saluted again, spun around, and headed up the main stairs at the maximum allowed speed. Room 206 was where Eugeo and I stayed. It was actually a ten-person room, but the other eight were good guys. Of course, everyone in 206 (and 106 down on the first floor, which was just for the girls) was of common birth, surrounded by nobles and merchant children—so we couldn't afford to squabble among ourselves.

In the upstairs hallway, I made my way through the groups of students chatting and laughing gently on the way to the cafeteria and finally through the door at the very west end, when—

"You're late, Kirito!"

Naturally, that came from a boy—if you could still call him that—with flaxen blond hair, sitting on the bed second from the end on the right. My partner, Eugeo.

He stood up and put his hands on his hips. He'd grown an inch or two since we'd first met two years ago and was more firmly built now. It only made sense, as he would be nineteen this year. Yet his gentle features and sparkling green eyes hadn't changed a bit. The six months at the Zakkaria garrison and this year at the academy had put us through serious challenges, but his honest, hardy soul had never once wavered through all of it.

For my part, I didn't feel like my personality had changed much, either, but the amount of height and muscle I'd put on was startling. I was seventeen when I fell into this world, which meant I felt a two-year gap between my body in the real world and my body in the Underworld. I had felt plenty weird after escaping the two years in *SAO*, but at this rate it was going to be more like three or four this time...

I approached my partner, holding up the sideways hand of apology and saying, "Sorry about the delay. It was a 'special' sparring session with Miss Liena..."

"Well...I get that. It's the last time," Eugeo said with a mild glare. He smiled and continued, "To be honest, I was late by twenty minutes, too. We got to talking in Golgorosso's room."

"Oh, sheesh. I'm surprised, though...I would have figured that Rosso was the type to let his sword do the talking."

I walked past Eugeo to the desk-bed placed against the wall and tossed my practice gloves, elbow pads, and kneepads into the drawer. In the real world, doing this with used kendo gear would quickly produce a very fragrant bouquet, but that wouldn't happen here due to a lack of simulated microorganisms. My uniform had been soaked with sweat at the end of our duel, but now it was completely dry. Liena, of course, had not sweat a single drop the entire time.

I straightened up, feeling much lighter now, and Eugeo smirked and said, "Rosso's actually pretty analytical, if you'd believe it.

Well, let me rephrase that. He considers the state of the mind to be just as important as one's skills…"

"Yeah, I'd believe that. His Baltio style is more focused on the one-hit victory than the Norkia style, even."

"Yeah. And our Aincrad style is more about adapting to the moment. But there are times when a swordsman must be unshakeable and place all his life into a single blow! …Or so he says all the time. Today was just putting a period at the end of that lesson."

"I see. He's got a point. And I feel like your strikes have had extra weight to them recently…But where does that leave *my* adaptive Aincrad style, now that it's getting mixed in with the Serlut style's constant shifting?"

We left the room as we chatted. Our other eight dorm-mates had gone to the mess hall, and the hallway was empty. Meals at the dorm were on a strict time limit, with dinner starting at six o'clock and ending promptly at seven. Showing up after six wasn't against the rules, but we tried not to miss the pre-meal prayer. Anything to avoid trouble—from the noble students' perspective, Eugeo and I were not only commoners in their midst but also taking up two of the twelve valuable page slots.

We headed for the mess hall at maximum battle speed. It couldn't be a coincidence that the dorm rooms reserved for students of common birth were the farthest away. Apparently, the secondary trainee dorm was arranged the same way—but we wouldn't need to worry about that come April. If all went according to plan, we'd score within the top twelve on the advancement test at the end of the month and earn our places within the elite disciples.

Eugeo, thinking about the same thing, muttered, "No more power walking down the hallway after this."

"Yep. The disciples' dorm is way more relaxed about this stuff. But Eugeo…there's one thing that really bothers me about being a disciple…"

"Say no more. It's about the pages, right?"

"Exactly. It was fun having Miss Liena help and instruct me… but I don't know about being in that position myself…"

"Bingo…I don't know what I'll do if I end up with a noble for a page…"

We sighed in unison.

The long hallway came to an end. We pushed through the door and entered a buzzing, lively atmosphere. The mess hall opened up to both floors, and it was the only coed space in the building. The majority of the 120 students were grouped in all-male or all-female tables, but here and there were individuals with the remarkable skill of chatting with mixed company. Just like school in real life, in fact.

Eugeo and I rushed down the stairs and went to the counter to get meal trays. There was an empty table back in the corner that we slid into. Moments later, the six o'clock bells rang, meaning that we had made it in time.

A male student (noble, of course) who served as dorm leader stood up, offered a prayer to the Axiom Church, then led the group in a chant of "Avi Admina." I had no idea what that holy phrase was supposed to mean. With those formalities out of the way, it was time to eat.

Tonight's dinner menu was fried whitefish doused with a fragrant herb sauce, salad, root vegetable soup, and two bread rolls. It wasn't that much different from the food served at the church in Rulid and the farm near Zakkaria, which surprised me, given how many noble students attended this academy. But they treated it as completely normal, with no complaints.

It took me a while to figure out why this would be—and it wasn't because the nobles lived simple, humble lives, too. It had to do with the Underworld's peculiar concept of spatial resources. There was a limit to the quantity and volume of objects generated within a certain range of space and time, which meant that there were only so many crops, livestock, animals, and fish to harvest or hunt at a time.

If the nobles were to monopolize this limited food source, there wouldn't be enough for everyone, and some disadvantaged residents would go hungry. That would cause their life to drop, which was against the Taboo Index law about causing damage to others' lives without justifiable reason—and even nobles and emperors could not defy the Index. Therefore, given its direct link to maintaining life, food was not the subject of fixation and monopolization that it was in real life...Or at least, that was how I interpreted it.

Of course, just because they weren't snooty about food didn't mean that all the nobles were automatically of exemplary character.

"Why, I'm positively *jealous*, Raios!" someone boomed from right behind us. We both made sour faces.

"We poured our own sweat into cleaning this mess hall, and yet some people just get to waltz in afterward and eat! Truly jealous!" the voice continued accusingly.

Another voice chimed in. "Oh, don't be spoiled, Humbert. No doubt the pages are subject to rigors that the rest of us could never understand!"

"Hah! I bet you're right. From what I hear, a page has no choice but to do as their tutoring disciple commands."

"Boy, what if you wound up stuck with a tutor who was of low birth or banned? You never know what they might put you through."

I just sat there, eating my food, understanding that they were just trying to get a rise out of me and responding would be giving them exactly what they wanted. Still, that didn't stop the anger. Not only were they taking it out on us, they also referred to "low birth" to mean Eugeo's tutor, Golgorosso, while the "ban" was referring to Liena's style having come about due to her family's banishment from its original sword style.

That wasn't the only sarcastic needling contained in their statements. The bit about coming in "afterward" was a reference to the fact that there were twelve pages in total, but Eugeo and I were the only ones who showed up just before the dinner bells, identifying us as their targets.

There were creeps like this in Zakkaria, too. Egome Zakkarite had displayed some truly wicked smarts during our tournament duel. But the twisted way that some people had gone after us once we joined the academy was almost impressive. In fact, their totally natural harassment was one of the factors that caused me to forget that all these people were just artificial fluctlights, AIs.

"...We're almost there, Kirito," Eugeo muttered, tearing off a bite of his bread.

He was referring to the fact that we would be disciples soon and live in a different dorm from them. It was a bold statement from Eugeo, to be sure, but it wasn't just idle boasting.

The twelve pages were chosen out of the 120 primary trainees based on their results in the academy's entrance test, meaning that the twelve elite disciples from the second year of the academy got to pick out one page each.

When you were a page, you didn't have to clean the dorm or take care of the practice tools like the other students. Instead, you would clean up the chambers of your tutor disciple, help them with their tasks, and act as their sparring partner.

The two who kept offering up snarky comments hadn't been selected as pages, meaning that their test results were lower than ours. They'd been hovering around the twenties and thirties in rank through the periodic progress tests, so Eugeo was justified in assuming that they would not reach the elite disciple boundary.

But I wasn't so sure about that...

I held up the knife in my right hand and used the reflective flat of the silver blade to see behind my back.

At a nearby table, two male students were continuing their insulting innuendo, throwing occasional glances our way. The one on the left with the slicked-back gray hair was Humbert Zizek, who came from a fourth-rank noble family. The one on the right with flowing blond hair down to his back was Raios Antinous, the eldest son of a third-rank noble line. There were no first-rank nobles at this school—they were prestigious enough to have their own private instruction—and only a few were second-rank, such as Volo Levantein, so third was quite high.

But of course, not all the noble children were like these two. Volo the first seat was the quiet, stoic warrior type—not that I'd interacted with him much. Liena was a third-rank noble like Raios, and she was the very picture of grace.

In that sense, Humbert and Raios fit the mold of the stereotypical pampered rich boys who talked a bigger game than they were actually worth...but I wasn't sure if that told the entire story. Through either good or bad luck, I'd never faced either in a duel, but I couldn't help but wonder if they were slacking off in the seasonal testing periods—perhaps even the original entrance tests, too.

The reason for this was that the top twelve students were automatically thrust into the page's role for the elite disciples. This was treated as an honor within the academy, but given that Raios and Humbert were easily the proudest nobles in the school, they might have gone out of their way to avoid having to take orders from a fellow student.

I had no proof of this, of course. But when I saw their forms during sword practice, I would feel a kind of pressure, a very foreboding chill. It was that sense of mental power again, the absolute self-confidence they possessed by being noble.

"Hey, Kirito, your dish is empty," Eugeo said, nudging me. I looked down and realized that my fork was simply poking an empty salad bowl. To cover up my embarrassment, I lowered the knife to my fried fish, only to see that *it* was gone, too. I'd been so focused on Raios and Humbert that I had eaten my dinner, the second-best part of the day, without enjoying any of it. So much for not letting them get to me.

Worst of all, the best part of my day—the sparring sessions with Liena—was coming to an end today...

Actually, that wasn't quite right. My official duty as page was over, but I did have a big promise to fulfill tomorrow, on our day of rest. I was going to show her everything my style could do.

That reminded me of a very important fact. I set down my knife and fork and leaned over to Eugeo.

"Hey, I need to ask you something. Will you come out to the courtyard after dinner?"

"Yeah, sure. I was just wondering how your little 'garden' was coming along, Kirito."

"Heh! Believe me, it's doing great. Should be ready just in time for graduation."

"I'm looking forward to it."

We finished whispering and stood up with our empty trays. As we passed Raios and Humbert, still prattling on about us, I caught a pungent whiff of the animal-oil perfume they put on their uniforms and rushed past to get away from it.

Once we had returned our dishes to the counter and left the mess hall, we both exhaled mightily. The bells had rung once, just a few minutes ago, which meant it was past six thirty now. That meant we had free time until lights-out at ten, but it really wasn't that free—we couldn't leave the dorm building, and we had to be back in our rooms by eight. There wasn't much else to do but some self-training or studying. I, however, had just one activity after dinner.

On the west wall of the dorm (opposite the mess hall) there was a small door that led to a little yard. High walls without a roof surrounded it, but it was treated as part of the dormitory building.

The square yard was split up into four beds, each sprouting buds of different plants and flowers. There were designated students to tend to the beds, but they weren't just for show. The four different plant species were all materials used as catalysts in sacred arts classes. The plants flowered three months apart, so materials could be harvested year-round. If you crushed a dried-up fruit in your fingers, it would release sacred power into the air, providing the resources necessary for students to practice the arts.

Of course, the earth and sun provided regular resources on their own, but the earth power was diminished in the city, and the sun's strength was affected by weather. In order for 120 students to practice the sacred arts all at once, they needed a more substantial material than spatial power.

Since it was spring, the northeast bed was full of blue anemones in bloom. In summer it would be marigolds, followed by dahlias in the fall and cattleyas in the winter. These were all high-priority, resource-rich flowers.

The Underworld's plant species had evolved in peculiar ways over 380 years of history, but the fact that these flowers still shared the same name and appearance as their real-world counterparts spoke to their importance. I was not as certain that the rest of their biology was so heavily based on reality.

For one thing, once the petals were gone, all the flowers left behind similar rounded fruit. If you plucked and peeled it, you'd wind up with a glass-like ball about an inch across. Pinch it with your fingers, and it would break and release sparkling green light, indicating sacred power…That part was clearly unique to this virtual world.

From what the teacher in sacred arts class said, outside of these Four Holy Flowers, there was one other miraculous species that could bloom throughout the year and grow a particularly lush fruit called the rose. But commoners, nobles, and even emperors were forbidden to cultivate it. If you wanted to see one, you'd have to seek out the rare, secluded locations where it actually bloomed in the wild. That reminded me that I hadn't seen a rose since coming here. Given this description, it made sense that they were reserved for the crafting of divine objects.

We headed west down the little path that split the garden, gazing at the beautiful anemones along the way. Just before the fence, there was a large metal stand laden with gardening tools like shovels and watering cans.

Eugeo and I crouched down around a small, unassuming planter located at the side of the stand.

"It's really growing now. Look, the buds are actually swelling," he noted.

"Well, we've failed at this three times now. I hope that we actually get somewhere this time..."

Growing in the planter was something known as a "zephilia," which had sharply angled leaves that were nearly blue in color. It was probably unique to the Underworld. It apparently did not generate much magical resource...but it *was* very beautiful. The reason it "apparently" didn't have much magic was that neither I, nor Eugeo, nor just about anyone else in Norlangarth had ever seen one before.

The zephilia plants were exclusive to the empire of Wesdarath, beyond the Everlasting Wall. They did not grow in the northern empire; they were not even cultivated.

There was a small but brisk trade among the empires, so you'd think they would sell the flowers or put them in pots, but that was not the case—because there was no calling for "flower traders." They considered it a waste of sacred power to grow inedible flowers for the purpose of commerce. There *were* herb traders who grew their products in their own fields, but they were limited to the Four Holy Flowers. Everything in this world came down to effective use of resources.

So where had the seeds for this zephilia plant come from?

"Did you use up all the seeds you got to produce this seedling, Kirito?" Eugeo asked. I nodded.

"Yeah...this is our last chance. The spice trader said that the next shipment of them wouldn't come until this fall."

They didn't sell the flowers, but they did sell the seeds. Zephilia seeds would produce a vanilla-like scent when crushed into a powder. Therefore, a small amount was imported from Wesdarath as a spice for sweets—a fact I had learned last fall.

I had taken all the *shia* I had—basically, all the salary from the Zakkaria garrison—and bought as much as I could get from a spice trader. All they had in stock was a small bag of seeds, but it was enough for me to try growing them on my own.

There were two reasons that I had suddenly gotten into gardening.

For one, I wanted to do a little experiment about a core nature of this world: what I called the "Imaging System."

The spice trader had told me that zephilias wouldn't grow in Norlangarth soil. I had dug up dirt as close to the western empire's wall as possible to use in the planter, but the first batch of seeds ran out of life without even budding. They simply vanished from the planter.

But that couldn't be a conscious design decision on the part of whichever real-world people (probably Rath's staff) built and managed the Underworld. Unlike anemones and cattleyas, zephilias weren't a real flower.

So why would zephilias grow in the west empire but not the north?

My suspicion was that *the people of this world believed that to be so.* The mental image of their beliefs fixed the properties of the zephilia flower within the buffer data of their main memory device.

If that was the case, could I laser-focus a mental image that was stronger than the people's common knowledge into just a few dozen seeds, causing a temporary overwrite of the buffer data...?

The idea of one person overturning the common sense of thousands and thousands sounded ridiculously arrogant, but it was worth trying out, in my opinion.

I was challenging a piece of ancient knowledge that had been passed down for over a hundred years. In the present day of the Underworld, there likely wasn't a single person bothering to chant, "Zephilias only bloom in Wesdarath!" every single day. In other words, it wasn't like the zephilia data in the main memory device were completely locked from change.

So what if I used my imagination, my mental power, to will it into being...to pray, every single day? Could I actually overturn some ancient bit of common-sense knowledge?

With that idea in mind, I spent six months starting in the fall, giving it water and mental images to feed on.

The first attempt was a failure. The second attempt was a failure. The third attempt had produced tiny little buds. They wilted soon after, but I'd managed something they said was impossible. I had used up the rest of my seeds in the fourth attempt, and now I was going twice a day, in the morning before school and in the evening after dinner, to focus on them like never before. *Soil is soil, and water is water. You're going to sprout, and grow, and bloom.*

At this point, when I silently spoke to it, I could even see the sprout take on a faint glow at times. That was probably just a trick of the eye (or the mind), but by now I was sure of it: the twenty-three plants growing in the planter were going to bloom beautiful flowers this time.

"Here, Kirito, I brought some water."

"…Ah, oh, thanks."

Eugeo had carried over a watering can full to the brim while I'd been lost in thought in front of the planter. I took it from him, and he grinned. "We've been together for two years, Kirito, but I'd never have guessed you had an interest in gardening."

"Neither would I," I said idly. I didn't think much of it, but Eugeo's face suddenly went serious.

"What if it's a sign that your memory's about to come back? What if, before you showed up in Rulid, you had grown flowers back home…? Maybe you had a gardener's calling."

I stared back at him in stunned disbelief, then quickly cleared my throat. "Ah, ahem…I don't know about that. Remember, I didn't know anything about plants. I needed all of Muhle's expertise to get this far."

I'd almost forgotten that I was technically a "lost child of Vecta," a term that Underworldians used to describe people who showed up far from their homes without any memory—which they attributed to a prank of the god of darkness, Vecta. Eugeo was the only one who knew this about me, since I was registered with the academy as being from Rulid Village. And he'd stopped bringing it up recently, so I figured he had essentially moved past it. Apparently I was wrong.

Eugeo nodded slowly and refrained from further comment.

Instead he looked at the plants. "Well, let's give them their water. Don't you hear them begging for it?"

"Oh? Have you learned to hear their voices, too, young Eugeo?"

"Well, I've been going along with this idea of yours for half a year now, Kirito," he joked back. I straightened up and prayed quietly before the planter.

I know it's small, but that's your country. There's nothing there to threaten you. Take in the light, suck up the water, and bloom your beautiful flowers.

Once I felt certain that this wish had permeated the water in the can, I tilted my hand. A spray of droplets issued forth, wetting the fragile bluish leaves and stems, trailing downward, seeping into the black dirt...

I thought I sensed a gentle, warm light infusing the twenty-three sprouts. Another illusion? Or...I glanced over at Eugeo, who was praying with his eyes shut and hadn't noticed anything. By the time I looked back to the plants, the light was gone.

As a matter of fact, I hadn't told Eugeo the truth about my little experiment (disguised as a hobby). He didn't know the flowers were zephilias; I'd told him only that I'd picked out the seeds at the market at random.

My expectation was that if I told Eugeo the truth, his common sense might cancel out my efforts. The experiment wasn't to compare our willpower, and that wasn't what I wanted to do. I was already nervous enough about the possibility that in the testing exams for elite disciples, he and I would end up forced to face each other in a duel...

"...Hey, Kirito."

I spun toward him, surprised. Of course he hadn't really heard my inner voice. But I still wasn't ready for what he asked next.

"What would you do if all your memory came back, Kirito...?"

"Uh...what would I do?"

"I mean, you're here trying to be a disciple...and, ultimately, an Integrity Knight...because you're helping me with my goal, remember? We're trying to look for Alice, since the Axiom

Church took her away eight years ago. But…what if you remember everything—remember your true hometown…"

Would you go back? he finished, speaking with his eyes.

There could be no other answer than, *Yes, I want to go back home.* But home wasn't anywhere in the Underworld. My home, and the people waiting for me, was outside in a country called Japan in the real world.

In order to log out voluntarily, I'd need to find either a system manager or a system console. If I was going to find either of those things anywhere, it would be in the Central Cathedral, the very core of power. So both Eugeo and I needed to become Integrity Knights—just for different reasons.

It hurt to keep a secret from my partner, my friend. I switched the empty watering can to my other hand and patted Eugeo on the back, then left my hand there.

"No…even if my memory does come back, I won't leave. I was a swordsman in my old home. That's the one thing I'm sure of… even if I *did* like flowers. And why wouldn't a swordsman want to compete in the Four-Empire Unification Tournament?"

"…"

Eugeo's back trembled a little bit. His flaxen hair hung low from his bowed head as he hunched. I could just barely hear him say, "I'm…a weak person. If I hadn't met you at the Gigas Cedar, I'd still be swinging my ax at it right now. I'd use that as my excuse, never leave the village…and eventually…I'd forget all about Alice…"

He stared down at the bricks at his feet and continued, "The fact that I got into the Zakkaria garrison…that I made it all the way to Centoria and into the Swordcraft Academy…it was all thanks to you pulling me along. So I've been telling myself…I want to at least be as strong as you by the time we graduate from here. And yet…hearing what you just said…made me so relieved…"

Eugeo trembled again under my palm. I willed strength into my hand, wishing it would flow through my fingers like it had just done for the plants. *You are strong. You are. You're the one who made the decision to leave your home, in this world bound by laws and rules.*

"Let me just say that I certainly couldn't have gotten all this way by myself, either," I said, trying to keep my words lighter than they felt. "I didn't know the way, my memory of Basic Imperial Law is rusty…and I didn't have a single *shia* to my name. The only reason I'm here now is because there were two of us. And it's going to stay that way. If we don't work together, we'll never overcome these elite nobles who have been swinging swords since they learned how to walk. We'll never match the best and brightest of the imperial knights. You can save your thoughts about striking out on our own for after we're Integrity Knights."

"…"

Eugeo didn't have any response to this for a while. When he did speak, his voice was frail. "Yeah. Yeah…you're right. We came this far together. And we'll climb that white tower together."

"That's right. And the next step in that process is placing within the top twelve in this month's test. I might have the physical skill down…but I'm not as sure about the sacred arts. When we get back to the room, teach me more about which catalyst is best for which element."

"…Ha-ha, you got it. Calling in that 'working together' favor early, huh?"

"Hey, why not?"

I slapped Eugeo on the back and got to my feet. When he joined me, he wore his usual genial smile. Then his head tilted a bit, as though he was remembering something.

"Hang on, didn't you have something to talk to me about?"

"Uh…oh, r-right. I completely forgot," I said. I turned to Eugeo and asked formally, "Eugeo, can I borrow the Blue Rose Sword for tomorrow?"

"Yeah, sure," he said, so easily it was almost a letdown. Then he cocked his head again. "But why? Weren't you the one who said we should use the practice swords as much as possible, so as not to throw off our instincts on the test?"

"I did...but then I made a promise to Liena earlier. I said I'd show her the best I can do. And I can only manage up to a two-part attack with the wooden sword."

"Oh, I get it. You want to show her the true power of the Aincrad style. You're free to use the Blue Rose Sword as much as you want, but..."

He paused, looking confused. "But Kirito, have you forgotten? Tomorrow's break is the big day!"

"Huh? What big day...?"

"Come on—the seventh day of the third month. The one you were looking forward to!"

"...Oh, r-right, right. The day it's finally ready! Gosh, it's not like I completely forgot...I just didn't think it would take an entire year..."

"Meaning that you *did* forget." Eugeo laughed and asked, "What's the plan? Will you use the Blue Rose Sword, or..."

"No, I'll use *my* sword. It's all according to Stacia's guidance or whatever. Sorry—just after you said I could borrow yours and everything."

"It's fine. More importantly, let's get back to the room so I can tutor you until lights-out time."

"...Just...go easy on me, okay?" I said, putting the can back on the shelf and following Eugeo back.

I turned for one last look at the planter, glancing at the glistening young buds stretching up to the night sky.

As for the second reason for my zephilia-growing experiment... I didn't even like to acknowledge it. It was just slightly—no, considerably—embarrassing to admit.

3

The Underworld boasted an enormous variety of "callings," life-long professions for its citizens, but almost none of them related in any way to being a traveler.

The closest thing, perhaps, was a trader who would cross the walls into other empires, but it was difficult to define this as "traveling" in a true sense. For one thing, in the circular central city, just carrying goods from North Centoria to East Centoria and back was a trip of five kilometers, at best.

The rural villagers were almost entirely self-sufficient, with the few outside valuables like herbs and fine metalwork coming from the nearest large town (in Rulid's case, Zakkaria) via periodic carriages. There were no traveling artists, poets, or troubadours, and travel for pleasure was impossible due to the "one day of rest per week" system.

The only exception to this rule was the Integrity Knight, who rode on a flying dragon from Centoria all the way to the End Mountains 750 kilometers away—but that was too specialized to be considered a "calling."

Therefore, long-distance travel was anathema to the Under-world, but that didn't mean it was actually forbidden in any way, merely impractical. You just needed a calling that allowed for it—say, a furniture maker in Centoria who traveled to sell wares far up to the north in Zakkaria. I myself had managed to cross the entire empire by following its rules.

In other words, traveling simply came down to the disposition of the individual. And in the case of the Underworld, less than 1 percent of the residents had the disposition to attempt it.

That didn't mean that nobody in the world had a heart full of curiosity and adventure. One of those very people was a craftsman in District Seven of North Centoria named Sadore.

"Just lookit this!"

A number of rectangular stone plates clattered before our eyes. The fine black objects were grindstones from the eastern empire, but they'd all been ground down to a thickness of less than two cens, rendering them useless.

"These black-brick grindstones are supposed to last three years each, and I'm out half a dozen in just a single year!"

"Ah...s-sorry about that," I said, feeling truly apologetic to the red-faced store owner.

Sadore's metalworking business was crammed full of stuff, from raw metal materials, to ornaments, to actual weapons and armor. Most striking was the line of swords on the back wall. Why would a craftsman sell actual swords, we wondered, so we had asked the imposing fellow himself. His answer was simple: He had actually wanted to be a blacksmith.

As a matter of fact, the only difference between blacksmiths and craftsmen in the Underworld was the tools they used. Blacksmiths used furnaces, anvils, and hammers to fashion metal materials into goods. Craftsmen used chisels, drills, and files. In other words, one pounded the metal, the other scraped at it.

In the real world, my mountain bike had different options for the same part that were either forged aluminum or cut aluminum. Figuring this was about the same level of difference, I had suggested that a craftsman could still make a sword. Sadore glared at me furiously and groaned that even the same metal parts would end up performing differently.

According to him, the same metal materials, if used to create a sword through whittling or smithing on an anvil, would be of a higher priority (the class-N object number) in the latter case. Therefore, when he had started trying to make swords, a fellow blacksmith in District Seven had called them "shameless knock-offs that are all look, no quality."

Young, adventurous Sadore had gotten fired up over this. He had created and stocked up an entire year's worth of product, left the management of the business to his wife and apprentice, then gone on a long journey—in search of materials that would make a good sword when cut, not forged.

Craftsmen couldn't get permission to cross borders, so his only choice of destination was north, out of Centoria. For months he walked from town to village, finding promising materials here and there, but none of them satisfied his exacting standards. Eventually he wound up in a forest near the very north, where he met an enormous tree that split the heavens.

No fire could even singe its bark, and a single swing from a metal ax would chip the blade. It simply withstood, tall, hard, and black—the Gigas Cedar.

He had met the "carver" at the time, Old Man Garitta (who was more like Young Man Garitta then), and, energized by his discovery, tried to break off a narrow branch of the Gigas Cedar for use in crafting a sword. Through Garitta's help, he had climbed the trunk to a branch of appropriate size, but despite working with his file for three days and nights, he couldn't create even the tiniest groove in the wood.

Sadore had sadly descended the tree and told Garitta that if it should one day be felled, to let him know, and that he would return to the forest to get that branch.

In the end, Garitta *did* fulfill Sadore's request, but not in the way he imagined.

Last March, after a very long journey, Eugeo and I had finally arrived in Centoria, and as Old Man Garitta had asked, we had visited Sadore's shop in District Seven. I had handed over the branch from the very tip of the Gigas Cedar. Sadore couldn't speak for three whole minutes, and it took him another five to fully examine the wood.

Give me a year, he had said. *With a year, I can turn this branch into one hell of a sword. A sword to surpass even an Integrity Knight's Divine Weapon.*

Exactly one year later, on March 7th, 380 HE, Eugeo and I were back at the red-faced craftsman's shop to pick up the promised item.

"S-so...did you finish the sword?" I asked, cutting through Sadore's grumbling so that it didn't continue forever. He clamped his mouth shut and glared at me, tugging on his gray beard, then snorted and crouched down. He reached with both hands under the counter and pulled out a long, narrow cloth. It took all his burly strength to lift it up.

Gwonk! It clattered heavily on the counter, but he did not let go of it. One hand rested atop the cloth wrapper, while the other returned to his beard.

"Young man. We haven't discussed the price yet."

"*Urg.*"

The empire ran the Swordcraft Academy, so it had no tuition cost, but for the last year, I'd spent my days off going into the city to shop. Most of the *shia* I'd earned at the Zakkaria garrison were gone now. I couldn't begin to guess how much it would cost for the craftsman's fee (plus a year's worth of labor and six grindstones).

"It's all right, Kirito. I brought all my money, too," Eugeo muttered into my ear. That was both a relief and ominous at the same time. What if our combined assets were still far short? Was that against the Taboo Index? Would the police—er, Integrity Knights—swoop in and imprison us...?

"...But I'm willing to waive the cost," Sadore finally finished after a heart-stoppingly long pause. We were just about to exhale when he dramatically continued, "*However!* I will only do so if you can swing this monster, young man. The base material itself was already tremendously heavy, and you carried it all the way from the north to Centoria, so I have faith in you…but consider this a warning. The moment the sword was completed, it got even heavier. Blacksmiths and metal-crafters are able to carry around their finest swords thanks to Terraria's blessing…but even I can't move this thing farther than a mel."

"…Hence the 'monster,' eh?" I murmured, looking down at the cloth.

Even through the heavy woven fabric, there was a powerful sense of presence that practically warped the space around it. It seemed to be inviting me closer…or drawing on some magnetized part of my body to pull me in.

Eugeo and I had headed south on a stormy spring day two years ago.

At Eugeo's waist was the Blue Rose Sword, now safely stashed in the drawer beneath his bed in the primary trainees' dorm. On my back was the freshly snapped black branch of the Gigas Cedar. Old Man Garitta had told us to ask Sadore the craftsman to fashion it into a sword, but there was a part of me that sensed foreboding and urged me to bury it deep in the woods instead.

I still didn't know what it was that had come over me. Obviously it would be more natural and comfortable for two swordsmen to have two swords. Gaining a new weapon as powerful as the Blue Rose Sword should be welcomed, not feared.

Reason overrode my premonition, and I had ultimately carried the branch all the way to Centoria, where I left it with Sadore.

And here we were, one year later. The branch was now a sword, waiting beneath the cloth layer for our first contact.

I took a deep breath, exhaled, and reached out. First I picked up the whole bundle and stood it on the counter. It was indeed quite dense and heavy, but no more so than the Blue Rose Sword.

The cloth was rolled lightly around the sword, not tied, so it fell loose when I stood it up, exposing the hilt.

The pommel was a simple weighted design, and finely trimmed leather was wrapped around the handle. The knuckle guard was on the small side, apparently because it was carved straight out of the wood, rather than being a separately attached part. The exposed parts of the handle were the same semitranslucent black color that I remembered from the branch. The leather was gleaming black, too.

The sheath that swallowed up the blade was also finished with black leather. I reached out, tightening my fingers on the grip one by one, and tensed.

I'd used plenty of swords before, and they were all VRMMO objects, with the sole exception of the dusty old bamboo *shinai* at home. But in spite of that—or perhaps because of it—I felt something when I squeezed the handle. A sensation that went from my palm through my arm and shoulder, then shivered down my back.

The sensation of holding the Anneal Blade when I got it for my first quest on the first floor of Aincrad.

The sensation of holding the Queen's Nightblade the dark elf queen bequeathed me on the ninth floor.

The sensation of holding the black Elucidator longsword that dropped from the fiftieth-floor boss.

The sensation of holding the pale Dark Repulser longsword that Lisbeth forged for me.

Even the sensation of the legendary Excalibur that I earned at great cost in the fairy realm of Alfheim…

A thrill ran through me equal to—perhaps even greater than—the moments I first encountered my various companions throughout my adventures. I was rooted to the spot. When the trembling left, I tensed and yanked the sword out of the black leather sheath.

Jriiiing! The ringing sound was a bit deeper than the Blue Rose Sword's. It was heavy, but without the stiffness of a metallic blade. Yet it was also completely different from a wooden sword. It sounded unbelievably tough and yet fierce. I flipped my wrist up straight, and the end of the sword hummed.

"Hrmm," Sadore grunted.

"Whoaaa," Eugeo marveled.

I held my breath and gazed at the blade.

It looked to be about exactly as long as my old Elucidator. That only made sense, as I was the one who had snapped off the branch at that length and instructed Sadore how long it should be.

The blade was the same deep black as the handle that it was connected to, a single piece of wood. It still had that slight translucence, taking in the light that shone through the window, and occasionally glowing with hints of gold, depending on the angle. It was shaped like an orthodox one-handed longsword, but the flat was a bit wider than the Blue Rose Sword's.

The edge of the bevel slope along the flat had a sharp angle to it and seemed likely to break the skin if you brushed it. The blade itself did not reflect light from any angle; it was as though it cut the light itself.

"...Can you swing it?" Sadore finally rumbled.

By way of answer, I glanced around the shop, making sure there were no other customers present. The young apprentice was in the back workshop, out of sight.

I turned to face parallel to the long counter. There was an empty space at least five mels long ahead of me, plenty enough for a test swing. With my left hand on the sheath, I spread my legs forward and back and crouched. I didn't need to try a sword skill; just a one-handed vertical slice would do.

There was a buckler carved from a steel sheet hanging on the wall. I slowly raised the sword up high, setting my sights on the shield.

After training with nothing but wooden swords for the past year, the black sword was mercilessly heavy in my hand, but it wasn't altogether unpleasant. It was a comforting weight—a challenge to me, a demand that I wield it with skill.

As the tip reached a vertical tilt, I slid my right leg forward, imagining the vector of my weight shifting and the moment of torsion. All the energy stored in that sword tip descending unleashed with a powerful step forward.

"*Shaaa!*"

Black light ran in a straight line, followed by the sound of air being cloven in two. The tip of the sword stopped just short of the floorboard, but the expanding force of the swing caused the board to creak.

I stood up again. Eugeo beamed and applauded, while Sadore snorted ferociously.

"Hmph! So the skinny little academy trainee can swing that thing, eh?"

"It's a good sword," I said, judging that no more needed to be said. The craftsman finally broke into a snarling grin and tugged his beard again.

"Bet your ass it is. Six black-brick grindstones! But...a promise is a promise. No charge for my services—just tell 'em it was the master craftsman Sadore's work, once you get famous! The sword's yours now."

"...Thank you. Thank you very much," I said, bowing deeply. Eugeo joined in. Then I straightened up and sheathed the sword again.

Sadore gazed at the black blade for two seconds, then grinned again. "You've got to think of a name now. And remember, my place is associated with it, so don't go givin' it some weird title."

"Uhh..."

I had no quick answer. Until this point, all the virtual worlds I'd been through were the kind where objects had preset names when you got them. Coming up with names wasn't my strong suit.

"I...I'll think about it," I suggested. "Anyway, if its life starts to drop, I'll be back to get it sharpened again..."

"Sure thing. And it won't be free, I'll tell you that!"

"I—I wouldn't dream of it."

We gave him one last round of bows and took a few steps toward the door.

Suddenly, a loud clanging erupted behind us, and we jumped. Over my shoulder, Sadore was staring at the west wall in shock.

I followed his line of sight to the buckler on the wall, now split into two, with one half clattering on the floor.

*   *   *

① It would be a violation of the Taboo Index to intentionally destroy shop merchandise.

② It would be a violation of the Taboo Index to accidentally destroy merchandise and fail to pay for it.

③ In the case of ②, one may escape punishment only if the shopkeeper forgives the violator.

I rushed back to the academy, poring over these newly learned bits of information. My teacher of all things taboo-related, Eugeo, muttered and complained into my ear as we rushed along.

"…If you were just going to test it out, you didn't need to use one of your top-secret techniques! You should have realized that it was going to ruin some of the wares in there!"

"Er, well…I didn't think I was using a sword sk—er, a technique…"

"I saw what you did, Kirito. The moment you swung it down, the blade glowed just a bit. I have to assume that it was some supersecret Aincrad technique you haven't taught me yet!"

"Er, well…I'm pretty sure there's no such technique in the Aincrad style…"

As we walked and bickered, a sweet scent hit my nostrils and went straight to my brain.

North Centoria was split into ten districts. The farthest south (and closest to Central Cathedral) was District One, home of the imperial palace; then District Two and the imperial government; while Districts Three and Four contained noble houses. The mansions in District Three would make Asuna jealous, but even more surprising was that the nobles from first- to third-rank also owned large private estates outside the city.

Some estates contained their own little villages, the residents of which were essentially servile to the noble family. It was only inevitable that noble children raised in those circumstances eventually went on to produce a few bad eggs like Raios and Humbert.

District Five was a cluster of imperial facilities and buildings:

the knighthood headquarters, the coliseum, and, of course, the Imperial Swordcraft Academy.

Districts Six and Seven were commercial areas. Districts Eight, Nine, and Ten at the north end of the city were civilian residential areas. From what I had learned in geography lessons, this layout was absolutely identical in the east, west, and south portions of Centoria, too. That couldn't be by coincidence, and I doubted that all four emperors had gotten their heads together to plan it out, either. It had to be a unified design choice by someone powerful within the Axiom Church. Being a student meant I was too busy to think about them much, but it was a reminder of the absolute power of the church.

At any rate—in order to get from Sadore's metalworking shop in District Seven to the academy in District Five, we had to pass through District Six, which was packed with tempting food markets and restaurants. Essentially all the money that had fled my wallet over the past year had gone into District Six.

The most dangerous time was around two o'clock on a day of rest. This was right around the time that the Jumping Deer restaurant on East Third Street baked up its famous honey pies and sent the smell wafting out into the street. Every time I caught that smell, I needed to make a high-difficulty saving throw against temptation—and most times, I lost.

"…Hey, Eugeo. It's a good thing we didn't have to pay for the broken shield or the sword itself, isn't it?" I noted, slowing down.

My partner nodded, but with suspicion. "True…After we joined the academy, I found out that Sadore's got certification as a first-class crafts-master. If he'd forced us to pay, our entire savings wouldn't have covered it."

"Ohh…Hey, maybe this is a pointless question, but what would've happened if we didn't have enough? Would they arrest us on the spot?"

"No, that wouldn't happen. It would get put on a tab that we'd have to pay down in monthly amounts."

"Oh, I see…"

Unlike Aincrad, where the Cardinal control system regimented the in-game economy to fix the value of *col*, the *shia* of the Underworld had a more free-flowing value dictated by the residents' activities. Therefore, it was important for even starving students to do their part and stimulate the economy.

Empowered by this noble motive, I suggested, "Well, since we've saved ourselves some extra cash, why don't we swing by and get three each?"

My partner sighed, having seen all of this coming a mile away, and said, "Make it two."

I grinned and nodded, then shifted directions to lead us over toward the left, where a young lady was setting some fresh-baked honey pies at the sales window of the restaurant.

At some point, the weight of the sword package slung over my back had vanished into familiarity, and I didn't even notice it was there. As if it had been there for years.

4

When I returned to the academy, savoring the harmonious after-taste of melting honey and butter, Eugeo split off to visit Gol-gorosso, while I headed for the primary trainee dorm's office. I needed to apply to Miss Azurica to bring in the sword as a per-sonal item.

Bringing any blade three feet long into a real-world school would get you not only scolded by the teacher but possibly arrested. Still, given that the goal of this virtual academy was swordsmanship, students were allowed to possess their own per-sonal weapon.

The number was limited to one, because each sword would periodically absorb trace amounts of sacred power—of spatial resources. In practice, this meant that a weapon damaged in a duel, once polished and returned to its sheath, would gradually regain life—in other words, suck sacred power out of the air. If a blade went so dull that it couldn't automatically repair itself, it needed the help of a professional sharpener. If the damage was bad enough to break or chip the weapon, only a blacksmith could repair it.

If there were no limits on weapon possession, and a particu-larly obsessed student brought in a hundred, the buildup would cause sacred-power anomalies around the room. So theory said that one was the only safe number.

Azurica wasn't working the counter, due to it being a day of rest, but she had left the office door open while she did paperwork. Her blue-gray eyes looked up in surprise when I rapped on the door.

"What is it, Primary Trainee Kirito?"

"Pardon me, ma'am. I've come to get permission to bring in a personal sword," I said with a little bow, stepping through the doorway. Along the walls were a number of shelves stuffed with leather-bound files, a desk, and a single chair. In other words, this one woman managed the primary trainee dorm and its 120 students entirely.

She was a bit confused by my request but got up and immediately went straight to a specific file in the wall of shelves. She pulled a piece of paper out of it and slid it over to me.

"Please fill out the necessary information."

"Er, of course."

I glanced down in apprehension, but all the form wanted was name, student number, and sword priority. Relieved that it didn't have a field for "parent/guardian" or anything like that, I put down the name *Kirito* and the number 7—then came to a stop. Now that I thought of it, I'd even gone so far as to test out the sword, and yet I had never once opened its window.

Miss Azurica watched as I lowered the cloth bundle from my back onto the table and undid the rope tying it up. I could open the window just with the hilt exposed, so I peeled back a corner of the cloth.

"...!"

There was a sharp intake of breath, and I looked up. The normally calm and frank Miss Azurica was staring, wide-eyed.

"Umm...is something wrong?" I asked. She blinked a few times, then shook her head. She did not elaborate any further, so I returned to the sword, made the two-fingered motion command, and tapped the pommel. The properties window appeared with a little bell chime.

It read: *Class 46.*

That was actually one class higher than the divine Blue Rose Sword. No wonder it was so heavy. I wrote down the number on the third line, returned the cloth, and handed her the completed form.

Azurica's gaze slid from the sword to the paper. She stared at the information; she already knew my name and number, so it had to be that priority number she was looking at.

I began to get nervous, wondering if perhaps there was an upper limit to the object priority of any weapon being brought into the dorm, when...

"Trainee Kirito."

"Y-yes?"

"Do you have...that sword's memory...?"

She stopped there, closed her eyes for a bit, then opened them. She was the normal, stern dorm manager again.

"...Never mind. Your form has been received. As I hardly need mention, use of actual swords is limited to private training. It is *not* to be used in tests or group practice under any circumstances. Is that understood?"

"Yes, ma'am!" I replied. As I put the black sword's package over my back again, I wondered if I should ask about her unfinished comment. Then I considered that she wasn't likely to give me an answer, so I made the knight's salute and left the office.

As I walked back toward the front entrance, my mind pored over those words.

That sword's...memory.

It was a strange phrase. True, the sword and everything else in this world was stored in a format called mnemonic visual data. But that was a technology invented by Rath in the real world, and nobody who lived in the Underworld would be aware of it.

So Miss Azurica's comment was more of a literal one. That this black blade held some kind of memory.

But what did that actually mean? What did she see in this black sword...?

I left the building, thoughts and questions swirling in my head, as the bell tower overhead rang out the three o'clock melody. The bells here were far deeper and louder than those in Rulid, but the tune itself was exactly the same.

My meeting with Liena was at five.

Based on my test swing at Sadore's shop, the new sword felt perfectly natural to me—so familiar that it might as well have been my sword from the old *SAO* coming back. But I still needed to confirm that I could actually pull off the high-level sword skills of the Aincrad style first.

On the day of rest, which was the only day of the week we were allowed to leave the academy, most of the Centoria-based students went back home, while the few from farther north went around to visit various spots in the city, leaving the campus rather barren. There was even a small woods and a brook running through the school, creating plenty of places to practice techniques—but I wanted to be absolutely certain that no one would see me. After all, I was about to attempt combination skills, something that no sword school in this entire world possessed.

Why were there sword skills in the Underworld? And why *weren't* there any combination skills?

I'd been here for two years now and was no closer to finding the answer to these questions. The only potential theory I had at the moment was that the Rath engineers had made use of The Seed creation package to construct the Underworld...but even that wasn't a complete explanation.

The freely distributed Seed—a shrunken-down version of the Cardinal system—did not contain sword skills. Out of all the VRMMOs in existence in 2026, the only one with sword skills was *ALfheim Online*, which contained a full copy of the former *SAO* server. But there was no way that *ALO*'s management company, Ymir, was involved with Rath's experiment.

Anything beyond this point was just baseless speculation. If I wanted to know the truth, I had to get to the top of Central Cathedral and make contact with a system manager.

At any rate, the swordsmen of the Underworld could use sword skills as the ultimate techniques of their respective styles, but they were all single-attack skills like Vertical or Avalanche.

I had a guess as to why this was the case: because there was essentially no battle here. The absolute law of the Taboo Index and the invincible Integrity Knights protected the Underworld. Therefore, all "battle" within its borders came in the form of duels. All they sought was clean, beautiful victory. For centuries, the swordsmen of this world had pursued an ideal form—that of the bold pose from a distance, closing the gap, and finishing with one big, decisive blow.

It also served the purpose of defending against the possibility of spontaneous accidents, perhaps. All the regional dueling tournaments used the "stop-short" method, while the higher events in Centoria were ruled over on the first clean hit. That made it somewhat inevitable that they would avoid any combination attacks that were difficult to stop after the first blow.

Under these circumstances, it was no wonder that fighters like Volo Levantein rose to prominence: blessed with size and strength and absolutely confident in the power of their single strike. If I'd been forbidden from using multipart skills in *SAO*, I would never have been able to beat players of the same level who used double-handed weapons.

No doubt that was the reason that Sortiliena had been unable to overcome Volo for the past two years.

She wasn't going to be able to use a multipart attack just because I showed it to her today. Even Eugeo, who hadn't undergone any training in existing styles before he met me, took months to master the two-part Vertical Arc.

But perhaps I could show her that massive overhead swings were not all there was to swordplay. The Serlut style was similar to my Aincrad style, so if I could help erase her preconception of High-Norkia style being more powerful, she might stand a chance in the graduation match.

I headed east through the campus until I was at the edge of the grounds. The walls around the school were fan-shaped and contained a central school building, main practice hall, library, two trainee dorms and instructor housing, and the elite disciple dorm, with plenty of space to spare after that. There were large gates on the north and south walls, a steep little hill to the west, and a spacious forest to the east, neither of which featured any students on a day off.

I chose the forest anyway, thanks to the ample visual cover, and walked until I found a nice little opening. The short, fine grass was as thick as a soccer pitch, the perfect ground to avoid tripping on. I glanced about me again, making sure there was nothing around except for a few floating butterflies, and reached over my back.

I loosened the cloth by feel and grabbed the exposed hilt, savoring the sensation of the wrapped leather sinking into my palm, and yanked.

The pitch-black longsword caught the sun shining through the branches. As it was carved out of the Gigas Cedar branch, I supposed it was technically a wooden sword. But the reflection of the light off the blade was so sharp and tough that it looked like nothing but metal. One glance was all it took to recognize the high priority of the item fashioned over a very long year by Sadore the master craftsman. Yet no matter how I looked at it, I couldn't see how such an object would contain "memories."

I decided to save that question for later and took a normal stance, raising the sword with one hand. Unlike my last practice swing, this time I envisioned a technique—Slant, a diagonal slashing sword skill that I'd used countless times before.

After a brief pause and hold, a vivid light-blue glow rippled across the blade. Pushed and guided by unseen hands, I accelerated the effect with my push-off leg and right arm.

Shwa! The slash rocketed through space. A diagonal line quickly erupted and trickled away into the air like heat haze. The force of the gust flattened all the grass in the clearing to one direction.

I watched the trunk of a tree about fifteen feet ahead from my follow-through pose. But while the skill's effects wore off, no damage appeared on the bark.

That made sense; the range of Slant was maybe eight feet at best. The effect of the move shouldn't last twice that distance.

But if that was the case…why did the buckler in the shop split, if it was the same distance away? Surely it didn't naturally reach the end of its life at that very coincidental second. And I did not use a sword skill then. Eugeo claimed the sword had shone…but I didn't know why.

It just didn't make sense. This world was full of mysteries.

I sighed, straightened up, collected my breathing, and started the motion for my next skill.

A direct overhead slash. Just before the tip touched the ground, it bounced back upward. That was the two-part skill Vertical Arc. A more powerful gust of wind arose this time, rustling the grass violently.

So far, these were moves I could still achieve with a wooden sword. This time, I shifted my legs, held the blade at my waist, and twisted right.

"…!"

With a silent cry, I slashed horizontally left. The blade stopped straight ahead, as though colliding with something invisible, then leaped up and to the right. A step forward, and then a short-range, high-powered slash. The three-part Savage Fulcrum.

The move left a crimson trail like a closed numeral 4 in the air that quickly trailed away. Satisfied, I continued to the next move, holding my sword directly along the median line, then back-swinging up over my head.

High. Low. A connecting forward slash, then a pull all the way over my back for a full-power vertical smash. A blue square floated forward through the air, rotating and spreading apart. That four-part attack had been one of my favorites in *SAO*, due to its wide range and lack of easy exploits—Vertical Square.

All four sword skills went off without a failure or a single hitch.

That was enough to confirm that the sword was at least the same priority level as Eugeo's Blue Rose Sword. Of course, I could have anticipated this back in the dorm office the moment I saw it was a class-46 object.

It looked like I would be able to show Liena a higher sword

skill. I was momentarily relieved, until a different emotion raised its head.

The Blue Rose Sword could achieve four-part skills, but no matter how hard I tried, five-parters would not work. What about this new sword? If I was going to test that out, this private moment was the time to do it.

I squeezed the handle and slid my right foot forward, pulling the sword back to my left shoulder and imagining power building up inside it.

Something at the root of my bangs itched, like a warning sign. I shrugged it off, trying to focus.

Chik. Chik. I caught sight of orange sparks along the blade out of the corner of my eye.

This was a totally new and less impressive style of sword-skill flash, compared to the usual dazzling light effects. I concentrated on the mental image of the technique and held the preliminary motion. The sparks continued to blink uncertainly.

I was running out of stamina to continue the unstable stance, and when my strength finally reached its peak, I unleashed it.

"Whoa!" I mumbled as the ground trembled under my extended right foot. The sword went from upper left to lower right, and the system assistance should have shot it back up just before bottom dead center—except that instead, it drove straight into the ground.

A tremendous impact ran through my right wrist. Instantly, I recognized that I would suffer serious injury if I tried to force the sword. Instead, I gritted my teeth, turned my body, and pulled straight back on the sword, which was sunk about eight inches into the ground.

There was a terrific, heavy boom, and I toppled backward onto the grass as my body turned.

Didn't work. What am I missing? Was it my level? The sword's priority? Perhaps both...?

I lay spread-eagled on the ground, my thoughts racing. Overhead, I saw dirt and grass floating in the air, thrown by the impact of the sword—

And beyond them, a man standing silently at the edge of the clearing.

He was very tall, dressed in a school uniform, though not the academy's normal gray. His was a pearly-white color with brilliant cobalt-blue lines. The right to color-coordinate one's uniform was a privilege allowed only to the school's twelve elite disciples.

Liena's was a dark, grayish purple. Golgorosso's was deep green. And this pearl-white with blue accents belonged to none other than first-seat Volo Levantein.

The dull blond, close-cropped hair and steel-blue eyes stared down impassively, clearly belonging to the unquestioned champion of all students at the academy.

As he watched me lie there, a blob of dirt dislodged by my sword's impact splattered against his pristine white jacket, sending dark flecks out in a circular pattern.

I'd be lying if I said I never considered fleeing the scene.

If this were Aincrad and he was a senior member of the Divine Dragon Alliance guild, I would have scampered off at once. But running after committing an action was the worst possible choice in this world. Crime piled upon crime, certain to eventually grow into a violation of the terrifying Taboo Index.

So a second later, when I recovered, I quickly took a knee and placed my sword on the ground—the sign of absolute deference—and bowed. "Pardon me, Disciple Levantein! Please forgive my rudeness!"

I hadn't made such an impassioned apology since the time Asuna smacked me in her private room on the sixty-first floor of Aincrad. I held my head down, hoping against hope.

"You are Disciple Serlut's page, correct?" he said calmly.

I slowly lifted my head and stared into those blue eyes for an instant, then nodded. "Yes. Primary Trainee Kirito, sir."

"I see," the disciple said, glancing at the black sword laid atop the grass. In his rich tenor, he continued, "According to school rules, throwing mud upon the uniform of a senior student is a grave offense worthy of disciplinary punishment..."

At that point, I groaned on the inside.

Disciplinary punishment was the term for a privilege only the elite disciples had, a stand-in for instructor authority. In other words, when students accidentally committed minor violations of school rules, disciples were allowed to punish them. On a number of occasions, I'd been commanded to do a hundred swings for the crime of showing up late to Liena's room.

As for what happened to students who committed serious offenses—such things did not happen in the Underworld. Major violations did not happen by accident, and artificial fluctlights were incapable of intentionally breaking any law or rule. The only danger of that happening was with me, the natural fluctlight—and I'd made it through a year so far without committing any major faults.

Until now. Splattering mud on the top student's uniform was a critical mistake.

"...However, I am not critical of your dedication to practicing with the sword in secret on our day of rest. Even if such an act is a violation of the academy's rules."

Euuugh. Another silent groan.

In fact, he was right. But if I admitted that, it made disciplinary punishment only more likely. I had to at least try some minimal resistance, whether it worked or not.

"N-no, First Seat. This is not practice. I was, er...trying out my new sword. A weapon I had commissioned in District Seven finally arrived today, and I wasn't able to wait until tomorrow to swing it..."

At that point, I realized something much more important.

How long had the crew-cut blond been watching me? And what was he even doing here in the first place?

I was here in the woods only to practice combination attacks that did not exist in the Underworld's sword teachings, and that was so I could show them off to Liena in an attempt to help her defeat Volo. Now things were completely backward—he was the one witnessing them first.

The strongest student in the academy smirked faintly, as though he had understood my entire thought process.

"I heard some very enthusiastic shouts for a simple test swing. But all that I witnessed was you striking the ground with that sword. Let's say that your feet slipped from using an unfamiliar weapon. I will agree that you were not breaking the rules and practicing on the day of rest, as my reasons for being here are similar."

This both relieved and confused me. "S-similar...you say?"

"I mean that you are not the only one who tries to find a reason to swing his sword on a day of rest," he said, shapely lips curling into an invincible grin. Volo looked around the clearing I'd chosen for a swing test. "But in truth, I found this place first. I promised my page that he would be allowed to use it after my graduation, so you'll need to find a new location."

That explained things for me. He, too, would come up with some non-practice justification to come out here and train on his off days...and I had the sheer bad luck to be using his secret spot right as he was about to show up. No doubt that the pristinely short condition of the grass here was a consequence of him stepping on it every day, resetting its life value.

I made a mental note to find a wilder-looking clearing next time and bowed to him again. "Of course. I will do that, sir. Thank you for your generous understandi—"

"It is too early to be thanking me, Trainee Kirito."

"S-sir?"

"I said I would overlook your use of the sword on a day of rest. I did not say anything about *this*."

My head shot up. He was gesturing with a finger at his uniform breast with a deadly serious expression. At the dark mud stain on the pearl-white fabric.

"B-but, First Seat, you said you weren't critical of my dedication..."

"Indeed, I am not. So I will not discipline you by commanding you to clean the entire disciples' dorm or copy a thousand lines of sacred arts."

Briefly, very briefly, I was relieved.

Then he flicked off some mud and instead commanded, "Primary Trainee Kirito, your discipline shall be a duel with me. Not with wooden swords—you may use that one. I will use this."

That was when I noticed that hanging at his left side was a real sword, seemingly of quite high priority, with a dull-gold pommel and deep-blue sheath.

"...A...a d-duel...sir?"

"I am referring to training in the form of a match, of course. But this is too cramped a location. The main training hall will be empty on a day of rest. We can go there."

And with that said, the first-seat disciple spun around on the spot.

I stood there for two seconds, staring at that white jacket as it slid away from the clearing. When my mind started running properly again, I really did consider just scampering away. But failing to complete a disciplinary punishment turned one's offense from minor into a serious rule-breaking. Given that I wanted to be an elite disciple like Volo after this month's advancement test, I couldn't afford to get expelled now.

I lifted up the sword on the ground, returned it to its sheath, and stood up. After a longing glance at the stone wall of the academy through the trees behind me, I followed after that shaved blond head, resigned.

Volo did not trip on any of the varied weeds and grasses that grew thick and clinging outside the clearing.

Belatedly, very belatedly, I realized, *Gee...it would be the easiest thing in the world for a guy like him to step out of the way of a flying glob of mud.*

5

Right as I left the woods and rejoined the paved footpath, the bells rang four o'clock.

The sky was looking darker now, and some students were around, returning to campus from the city. As they caught sight of the white-and-blue uniform just ahead of me, their eyes bulged.

That was no surprise. Since being named disciple, Volo Levantein had hardly ever left the disciples' dorm. The only times that anyone other than his page saw him were at the four periodic tests throughout the year. Even I had seen him in the hall of the disciples' dorm only a few times, and I went in and out of that building every day to see Liena. This was the first time we had ever spoken.

Now that legendary figure was walking with a common-born primary trainee, apparently heading for the main training hall. No wonder they stared.

More frightening to me was that more than a few of them, upon noticing us walking together, started rushing off to the school building and dorm. Pretty soon people all over the academy would be buzzing about something starting in the training hall.

Curfew on a day of rest was seven o'clock, a bit later than usual, so the majority of students would still be out at this hour. But if I wasn't careful, a whole lot of people might gather to watch us spar. I needed to end things as quickly as possible and escape to Liena's room…

But wait. How was I going to "end things"?

As Volo had explained, in the academy, a duel was something between practice and an official match. The rules stated that a duel was of the "stop-short" variety, but if both parties agreed, they could use the "first-strike" method that I remembered from *SAO*. In other words, it was over after the first solid hit.

In that case, the loser would naturally suffer some damage. It was one of the few exceptions to the Taboo Index's firm law against intentionally damaging the life of another. The first-strike method was forbidden at the Zakkaria garrison, but it was allowed here because they had plenty of expensive healing materials, as well as instructors who could cast powerful sacred arts. In other words, any injury suffered in a duel could be healed.

But Volo had said this should be a duel of real swords, so the stop-short method would have to be in play. That meant that if I wanted to win, I'd have to not only find a way to block or evade that tremendous overhead smash but deliver a counter that stopped just short of landing.

That would be unbelievably tough. And beyond that—should I even *try* to win?

Volo represented the ultimate goal for Liena's hard work of the last two years. Was it right for me, her page and pupil, to beat him? Would she be at all happy knowing that I had won…?

As I trudged along, lost in thought and staring at the ground, two sets of footsteps raced into earshot.

I looked up and to the left. There was Sortiliena Serlut, her skirt billowing as she ran, and behind her, my partner, Eugeo. They crossed a grass hill, not the paved path, on a direct line toward us.

I'd never seen Miss Liena running so hard that she panted like this. I stopped in surprise, and Volo did, too, turning to watch them.

In seconds, Liena had reached the path. She spared me a brief, worried glance, then faced off with Volo. She straightened her purple skirt and her back as she said, "Levantein...what is the meaning of this?"

Liena was the only student in the school who did not use a deferential title toward Volo. The students gathered around the scene began to buzz.

The foremost swordsman in the academy took in the piercing navy gaze of her eyes without flinching. His close-cropped head tilted, and he replied, "As you can see, Serlut, your page caused a bit of offense. I didn't think it was proper to inflict a large disciplinary punishment on a day of rest...so I have challenged him to a single duel."

A larger buzz than before erupted from the crowd.

Liena finally noticed the large, blotchy stain on Volo's uniform jacket and bit her lip, a sign of understanding.

As the first seat and second seat faced off, I scooted sideways over to my partner, who was standing at the lip of the crowd. On his face was a familiar look: a blended expression of "What did you do this time?" and "No...not again..."

"You sure showed up quick," I murmured, and Eugeo nodded.

"I was in the disciples' dorm mess hall when Zoban's page rushed in. They said you were going to fight with the first seat, and while I thought that sounded crazy, I went to tell Miss Serlut...I guess it wasn't crazy after all."

"Er, yeah...Guess not," I said lamely. Eugeo sucked in a deep breath, as though preparing to say something, then held it in for a few seconds and expelled most of it in an exhausted sigh.

"You know...it's a miracle that you didn't cause any trouble here until today. Please tell me you're going to get your year's worth of troublemaking out today."

"Ah, you haven't known me all this time for nothing, partner." I grinned and slapped Eugeo on the back.

Meanwhile, Liena was still staring fiercely at Volo. But even with my poor recollection of all the school rules, I knew there wasn't any evidence that could overturn my fate.

I left Eugeo and headed to my respected tutor's side. "I'm sorry to worry you. I'll be fine, though. If anything...I consider myself lucky to get to face the first seat."

I tried to read her feelings through those dark-blue eyes. What would she think about her trainee page fighting her biggest rival?

A second later, I deeply regretted it. The only thing I saw in those eyes was concern for my well-being.

"Kirito. What are the rules of your duel?" she asked, to my surprise.

"Uh...well, we're using real swords, so I assume it's stop-short—"

"Oh, I forgot to mention," Volo interjected, his face as placid as ever. "I do not engage in stop-short duels. I cannot help that the academy's tests are stop-short as a rule, but in personal matches, I only ever fight first-strike."

"Huh? Th-then..."

At last, the head swordsman at the academy changed expressions. It was a challenge...like a carnivore baring its fangs.

"Of course, a first-strike match requires consent on both sides. So it is written in the Taboo Index and thus takes priority over any disciple's ability to dictate punishment. If you refuse, I will have to settle for a stop-short duel. The choice is yours, Trainee Kirito."

Suddenly, the constant muttering of the crowd around us went silent.

I could practically hear Eugeo behind me, willing, *Go with stop-short!* Naturally, Liena would want the same thing. And even I wasn't reckless enough to accept a first-strike duel against the toughest man in the school using real blades.

Or so I thought.

"...I'll leave the choice up to you, First Seat Levantein. I will accept my punishment," I heard myself say.

Behind me, I sensed Eugeo hanging his head. Liena gasped and held her breath.

And, somewhere atop my head, I got the impression of someone shaking their head in disbelief.

The Main Training Hall of Swordcraft Academy sounded very grand, but behind the name, it was basically just a large gym. The floor was polished white floorboards, with four square match arenas marked out with darker materials. Around them were stands for seating, with enough capacity for all 260 students and faculty during the largest event at the school: the disciple testing tournament.

We stopped near the lines of the southeast arena that Volo had picked out, where at least fifty students had already gathered. Given that it was still before curfew on a day of rest, this probably represented all of the student body currently on campus. There were even three staff members, including—to my surprise—Miss Azurica.

There was another surprise waiting. Among the students were Raios and Humbert, those nasty upper-class nobles. They were probably back early because their mansions were close by. They were seated in the front row, leering with anticipation. The desire to see Volo cut me open was written right on their faces.

I had no regrets about boldly accepting his rules. In that situation, I couldn't possibly have brought myself to any other choice.

Instead, a different kind of indecision now plagued me.

Should I fight Volo or not?

There was definitely a part of me that yearned to challenge the greatest swordsman at the school. In fact, the number-three reason that I'd journeyed from Rulid in the far north down to Centoria was the old-school-gaming desire to fight against mighty opponents.

But at this moment I had a different desire, much stronger than the one to cross swords with Volo.

I wanted Miss Liena to beat him in her final match. I wanted her to win and be free of all the tangles surrounding her family name and style. In the entire year that I'd been serving her, she had never once shown me a true, unburdened smile.

Volo was examining his sword at the other end of the arena while I grappled with my inner dilemma. I heard Liena call my name and snapped around to attention.

Her deep-blue eyes stared right into me. In her normal, firm voice, the second seat said, "Kirito, I believe in your strength. It is with this faith that I warn you: the Levantein family, sword instructors to the imperial knights, have a secret saying. 'Wet your sword with the blood of the mighty, and their strength shall be your own.'"

"B-blood, huh?" I mumbled.

"That is right. Volo has no doubt been through many first-strike duels with naked blades, dating back to before his days here. It is that experience that creates his tremendous power. And he intends to turn your own skill into blood to feed his blade as well."

It was hard to grasp precisely what she meant by that, but I was able to convert her metaphor into terms that were more familiar to me. It all came down to the power of the mental image. Liena's skill was tied down to a mental image that said, "The Serlut style is an offshoot created because we were forbidden from using orthodox styles." While in Volo's case, the Levantein family message was, "The stronger a foe's blood you feed to the sword, the stronger it becomes."

No doubt that when he saw a bit of my combination skill and my high-priority blade in the forest clearing, he figured that he had found a suitable target. If it weren't for the fact that he had picked me out as an easy mark, I might have even been honored by the attention.

In other words, if I took a direct blow from Volo in this duel and shed blood, it would only further strengthen his mental image. And this outcome was highly, highly probable.

I didn't want to give the enemy a morale boost just before Liena's final match. I was just preparing myself to take back my previous statement and beg to use the stop-short rules when her hands patted me on the shoulders.

"I know I said this before, but I believe in you. You're better than letting him demolish you. You...you haven't forgotten yesterday's promise, I trust?"

"Promise..." I mumbled, then nodded. "Right. I promised to show you everything I can do."

"Then fulfill that promise, Kirito. Show it to me here. Unleash all your strength and technique and best Volo Levantein," she said.

Instantly, all the hesitation and fog around my head cleared.

Avoiding a straightforward battle with Volo because it might make him stronger before his fight with her was the worst possible mix of arrogance and pessimistic lack of confidence. And I was nearly about to serve my respected tutor that fatal cocktail. Once the sword was in my grasp, I had no choice but to wield it with all my life and spirit. That was how I had lived in every virtual world to this point.

I gave her a bold, confident look, then turned to my right to glance at Eugeo, who was leaning over the railing of the stands to watch. I shot him a confident grin, and despite his usual worried look, my partner raised a fist in solidarity.

I returned the gesture, then told Liena, "I will fulfill my promise."

She replied with a tip of the head and stepped back. Right on cue, a voice from the other end of the arena asked, "Are you ready now, Trainee Kirito?"

I turned, walked right up to the black floorboard that marked the boundary of the arena, and said, "I'm ready." Volo made a simplified knight's gesture, striking his left breast with his right fist, the back of his hand horizontal. There was no instructor here to serve as judge, but that wouldn't be a problem; whoever bled first, lost.

A step forward into the arena. Two, three, four. I was at the starting line indicated by a white floorboard.

We drew our swords—he from the left waist, I from over my back. Volo's steel-gray sword with its polished golden-brown hilt drew murmurs of appreciation from the crowd. But when they saw mine, that admiration turned to hushed astonishment. None of them had ever seen a sword that was entirely black all over, I was certain.

"Well, well! I wonder if they practice spreading black ink on their blades in the uncivilized regions, Raios!" Humbert said in a stage whisper from the stands.

"Don't be cruel, Humbert. Pages are so busy that they simply don't have time to polish their swords," Raios whispered back, sending up a tizzy of chuckling from the nobles around them.

But as soon as Volo began to move his sword, the crowd went still. It was a sign of respect for the first-seat disciple but also a likely consequence of the vicious presence of his intimidating blade.

To think that wooden and real swords could be so different, I marveled.

I'd seen Volo Levantein's High-Norkian style "Mountain-Splitting Wave" stance three times at close range during the disciple testing matches that had occurred while I served as Liena's page. But seeing Volo with a real sword, rather than a wooden one, and facing off against me personally was a different kind of pressure altogether.

With his shaved blond hair and slender frame, Volo had the appearance of a monk, but I realized in this moment that it was a mistake to judge him based on that. The look in those gray-blue eyes belonged to a demon who sought nothing but to cleave the bodies of his foes with hard steel.

Volo lifted his lengthy sword with both hands; the weapon would be classified as a bastard sword in a video game. The rippling effect around the blade wasn't a hallucination. The sword's high-priority level and the power of its wielder's imagination were vibrating the very air around it.

With a heavy *whoosh*, the first seat lifted the sword high overhead to complete his stance. Just pulling his sword a tiny bit farther back would unleash Mountain-Splitting Wave—the alternate name for the two-handed heavy charging slash attack Avalanche.

In the recent past (which felt like distant times of yore at this point), I had faced off in many one-on-one duels in Aincrad. The most memorable of these fights involving a two-handed-sword wielder was against a man named Kuradeel, who was in charge of Asuna's personal security when she was vice commander of the Knights of the Blood.

When we had faced off, I had correctly predicted that Avalanche would be his first move, and I'd used a different charging skill named Sonic Leap to strike the side of his sword and destroy it.

I briefly considered that stratagem again here but promptly shelved it. I couldn't envision any success in the attempt, only my own sword breaking—or, at the very least, rebounding and leaving my shoulder wide open to his blade's path.

Mountain-Splitting Wave was based on the Avalanche model, but I needed to consider Volo's attack to be a different thing, thanks to its increased weight and speed. His overwhelming confidence gave his skill absolute power. In other words, if I couldn't create a competing mental image that infused my entire body down to the tip of my sword, I had no business standing in the arena with him.

Now was the time to put aside any personal issues and use my combination skills.

So I started the motion for the four-part Vertical Square, the highest attack I could reliably use at the moment. It would require precision control, but if I could strike his Avalanche with the first three hits in order, it should negate his attack. Then the fourth and final swing would finish him.

In contrast to Volo's style, I pulled back my blade in a tight, compact stance. When it came to countering a sword skill with another sword skill, timing was everything. I had to unleash my skill at the exact right moment.

The tip of the black sword slowly passed vertical and began bending backward.

"*Kaaah!!*" Volo screamed, the sound splitting the air.

The bastard sword glowed reddish-gold. With a ferocious rush and the appearance of burning flames, the overhead smash that had thrice beaten Miss Liena's Cyclone barreled toward me.

But I was already moving. I'd begun Vertical Square with the minimum possible pre-movement and pushed into the first slash to provide extra power.

Gyang! A high-pitched clash erupted at the same moment that a tremendous shock ripped into my right hand—my first blow was easily deflected downward. No doubt the students and instructors in the audience assumed that I was using Lightning Slash, the Norkian version of Vertical. If that had been the case, it would be all over already—but I was just getting started.

Even in a clash of skills, the combination would continue as long as the motion itself wasn't completely knocked off alignment. Vertical Square's second attack was an upward slice from down below—exactly where the first hit was deflected. I wasn't done yet.

"*Zeyaa!*"

I spun myself to the left, hurtling the sword upward. Another clash. The blue glow surrounding my sword and the orange around Volo's mingled and flashed white, lighting up the dim training hall.

Again, my sword was knocked backward. But this time, the enemy's Avalanche slowed down. I gritted my teeth, unleashing a vertical slice from top to bottom.

Grinngk! The two swords met with a duller crunch.

As I expected, the third attack didn't deflect his blade, but it did stop the technique. If I pushed back here, it would cancel out the Avalanche and leave me with a fourth and final attack to go.

"*Rrrrah!*"

"*Hrrng!*"

We grunted in unison, trying with all our might to push back the other's attack. At this point, the little details like sword skill attack values and system assistance meant nothing. It was mind against mind, will against will. The connecting point of the swords was white-hot, sizzling and sparking. The thick floorboards of the arena creaked with the incredible force being pushed into them.

I envisioned a person observing the main memory device that contained the entirety of the Underworld and noticing that a certain portion of the light quantum storage was turning a blinding white. The signals being created in our fluctlights were in direct competition, each trying to overwrite the other. There was no more self-assured confidence in Volo's face now, just furrowed brows and gnashing teeth. My face had to look the same to him.

The state of equilibrium lasted for two seconds, three, four...

Then I saw something I never imagined I would see.

Arrayed around the head of Volo Levantein, first-seat elite disciple, were the similar-looking faces of at least five other swordfighters.

Their bodies were vague and transparent, and the only thing I could make out was that they were holding swords in the same pose as Volo, but that was enough to provide instinctual enlightenment. They were the generational heads of the Levantein family, traditional masters of sword teaching for the Imperial Knighthood.

It was the true vision of what Volo the student carried on his back...or was placed on his back for him. The true source of the tremendous power in his swing.

I...cannot afford to lose!! I thought I heard a voice say. The next instant, I felt the weight against my arms grow to many times its previous level.

The bastard sword, now glowing like the fires of hell, gritted and creaked against my black sword. I pushed back as hard as I could to withstand it, but I could feel my feet starting to slide backward.

Another few inches…another inch and my skill would be forced to a close. In that instant, it would throw my weapon aside and leave me vulnerable to a deep, maiming blow.

The words *three hundred and eighty years* echoed in my head.

Nearly four centuries of time had already passed since the creation of the Underworld. Even with the protection of its absolute law system and the absence of any true battle, the swordsmen of this world had created and passed on their swordcraft for all those years. The result far surpassed any kind of mere VRMMO attack skills.

My right foot slid, and the light infusing my black sword began to blink.

But…

I wasn't fighting for the mere sake of experience points, either.

I fought for Eugeo, the friend who had been first to offer a warm hand of help. I fought for Liena, who had spent a year showering me with kindness, discipline, and many lessons. Most of all, I fought for Asuna, Sugu, Klein, Liz, Sinon, Agil, Silica, and all the others who waited for my return to the real world.

"I can't…afford to lose here…either!" I screamed to no one's ears but my own.

In seeming response, the sword in my hand pulsed.

Within the dying blue light enveloping the black blade, a golden point formed. More lights began to appear, until soon the inside of the blade was covered in bright dots. In turn with this phenomenon, the space around me grew darker, but I barely even registered it.

I was more focused on the stunning change in my sword itself.

The blade was growing with little ringing noises. With all the visual effects going on, and the fact that it was just a growth of a few inches, I doubted that anyone noticed except for Volo and me—but it definitely wasn't an illusion.

The hilt grew as well. Automatically, my left hand reached over to squeeze the black leather handle and provide a full two-handed grip.

In the old Aincrad, my sword skill would have automatically ended due to an irregular equipment state. But when I added my left hand, the dying blue Vertical Square glow immediately regained its power, fusing with the golden light within the sword and swirling violently.

Something about the fierce change in the sword put me in mind of the black blade's true form—the Gigas Cedar that loomed over the forest south of Rulid. The obsidian mammoth that had refused to be cut down for over three centuries, sucking up the valuable resources of earth and sun.

…*The sword's…memory.*

The words barely flashed into my mind before my howl overrode them.

"Raaaahhhhh!!"

With all the muscle and willpower I could summon, I stepped—forward.

The moment my foot landed, all the energy packed into that intersection point of the two swords expanded, unable to handle its own density.

Volo and I were both blasted backward, as though by some higher flame-element sacred arts explosion. But we held firm in our forward posture, refusing to fly off our feet. The soles of my hardened boots scraped against the arena floorboards, bringing up smoke. Even with our trails of burned leather, both Volo and I managed to stop just short of the boundary lines.

Our swords were hurled backward with the force of their repulsion. Volo's Avalanche was over, its orange light fading.

But my Vertical Square was still active, even with two hands on it now.

"*Seyaa!!*" I belted, and leaped. The fourth and final attack, a high slice from a pulled-back position, activated. The sword carved a brilliant blue arc through the air as it approached Volo's defenseless chest...

It nicked his jacket and stopped just short of the floor. Vertical Square was not a charging attack. I did all I could to boost the range, but it wasn't enough to reach to the opposite end of the dueling arena.

Volo and I stared into each other's eyes at close range, and after the briefest of intervals, a voice called out, "That's enough!!"

Immediately, I leaped backward to a safe distance and lowered my sword. Up ahead, Volo had similarly disengaged his battle footing.

Once I was sure that it was over, I turned toward the voice, wondering who would step in to play referee in a duel that needed none. The fact that it turned out to be none other than Miss Azurica, the manager of the primary trainee dorm, left me speechless.

Why would a dorm manager—not even an instructor—act like a judge? And why did Volo obey her? These two questions kept me rooted to the spot.

The first seat, meanwhile, walked closer with his sword hanging at his side and murmured, "We cannot disobey *her* judgment."

"Err...why is that...?"

"Because she was the Norlangarth Empire's first sword after the Four-Empire Unification Tournament of seven years ago."

Whaaaaaaat?!

My eyes nearly bulged out of my head. Volo Levantein inclined his monk-like head, displaying none of his earlier ferocity. "Your punishment is hereby concluded. Be more careful not to throw mud onto others from this point onward."

He put his sword back in his sheath and turned around. The white-and-blue uniform crossed the floor and vanished through the door.

Instantly, a roar of shouts and applause erupted, filling the

training hall. To my surprise, there were now nearly a hundred students, and even faculty members, clapping and cheering wildly. In the front row, next to the calmly clapping Azurica, I found my partner, Eugeo, tears streaming from his eyes. I raised my left fist. Next to him was the imposing bulk of his tutor, Golgorosso.

Lastly, I glanced at the sword in my hand to make sure that it was back to its proper size, then slid it into the sheath affixed to my back.

Whap! Someone instantly smacked my shoulders from behind, causing me to jump. Pale hands turned me around, until I was facing Miss Sortiliena, her face even more tear-streaked than Eugeo's.

"...I thought...he'd cut you apart," she whispered, just loud enough for me to hear.

"Yeah...so did I."

"And yet...you didn't surrender...You...you enormous fool."

Her eyes squeezed shut, the long lashes trembling. But she won the saving roll against tears, took a deep breath, and opened them. Those deep-blue eyes were full of a warmth I'd never seen before.

"It was...an incredible battle, Kirito. I want to thank you. I'm sad that it wasn't just for me...but you showed me everything your sword can do, as you promised. Thank you."

"Uh...b-but it was a draw..."

"You're upset about taking Levantein to a draw?"

"I—I didn't mean it that way," I complained, shaking my head.

She favored me with a rare chuckle and leaned close to my ear to whisper, "The outcome of the bout does not matter. I've learned something...something very valuable from your fight. I am now filled with pride at being the heir to the Serlut style...and joy. At being your tutor, as well."

She patted my shoulders again and pulled away, the corners of her mouth still very slightly upturned. "There is still some time until curfew. Come to my room so we can celebrate. Call Eugeo, too...Just this once, I'll allow his tutor to come as well."

I broke into a smile, nodded, and gestured to Eugeo in the stands, pointing to the exit. Once he and Golgorosso got up to leave, I began to walk with Liena across the floor of the still-buzzing training hall.

All the while, the majority of my brain was preoccupied not with visions of Liena's special wine collection, or Golgorosso's endless lectures on the history of sword strategy, but...

You have the option of surrendering in a punishment duel?!

So it was that I barely even noticed Humbert and Raios, sitting in a corner of the stands and shooting me looks of very explicit intent.

6

In the late Aincrad, there had been an abundant variety of wines and ales.

But even an entire barrel of the hardiest, harshest fire whiskey was fundamentally unable to get the drinker inebriated. The user's physical body, resting on its gel bed in the real world, wasn't taking a drop of alcohol, after all.

But to my surprise, alcohol in *this* world did function as intended, to a degree. I suspected that it worked by sending the fluctlights signals intended to simulate a state of inebriation, but in a sign of good conscience uncharacteristic for such a merciless experiment, the effects of being drunk were limited to a level of good cheer, while still retaining rational reason. There were no crying drunks or angry drunks, and no one broke the law on account of the effects of alcohol.

And yet, there was no guarantee those conditions would hold true for me, so when Liena threw her "Draw Celebration Party," I held myself to just two glasses of wine. This was a considerable act of self-control, as Liena had opened up a priceless hundred-year vintage that was so tasty, even a complete newbie like me had to admit that it was fantastic.

Eugeo and Golgorosso joined in the fun, so we reveled in the year's events, made predictions for the year-advancement tests, and even got into the nitty-gritty of different skills and styles. Before I knew it, we had just fifteen minutes until the primary trainee curfew.

We left the disciples' dorm with great regret. Eugeo hadn't yet recovered from his "drunk" status effect, so I dropped him off at the dorm room and headed for the flower beds to the west. Just because it was a day of rest didn't mean the zephilias could go without water. I marched down the staircase and opened the door to the outside.

In the time that I had laid Eugeo into his bed and stashed my sword in the drawer, the last bit of sunlight had vanished, leaving only the shroud of night.

I closed my eyes and drew in a deep breath to savor the chill of the night and the pleasant smell of the anemones in full bloom—but grimaced instead. There was another smell in the air, a clinging odor of some animal-oil perfume. I recognized that smell. I'd experienced it just last night at dinner...but it shouldn't have showed up here.

My eyes snapped open and squinted down the path that split the flowers into four beds, right at the same time that two figures appeared from the darkness. They were wearing the same gray trainee uniforms that we all did, but they both had three buttons of the jackets undone, exposing boldly colored undershirts. The one with the gleaming red shirt was Raios Antinous. The one in fluorescent yellow was Humbert Zizek.

No sooner did I wonder why these two would be out in the garden, given their total lack of interest in plant cultivation, than a nasty foreboding entered my mind. I stood in place, one step in front of the garden door on the west wall of the dorm, as Raios and Humbert walked directly up to face me from a few feet away.

"Well, well, what a pleasant coincidence, Trainee Kirito," Raios drawled, his voice smooth and yet ugly with malice. "We were just thinking of going to find you. Thanks for saving us the trouble."

Humbert giggled gleefully. I looked back at Raios and muttered, "What do you want?"

His friend scowled in fury, but Raios held up a hand to stifle him and answered, "To offer my praise for your splendid battle, naturally. I never would have expected the page to a banned disciple to fight the great Levantein to a draw."

"Absolutely, absolutely. I daresay that the first seat was stunned by the acrobatics of your swordplay," Humbert joined in, cackling.

I kept my tone of voice low. "Are you offering me compliments or insults?"

"Ha-ha-ha, wouldn't dream of it! Higher nobles would never bother to offer commoners anything. We may *provide* some things, however. Ha-ha!" Raios laughed, very pleased with himself, and stuck his hand into his jacket pocket, pulling out something long and narrow. "In honor of your acrobatics—er, your accomplishments—I provide you with this. Please accept it."

He took a step forward, reached out, and placed the object in my front pocket.

"If you'll pardon us, we shall now take our leave. Sweet dreams, Sir Kirito," Raios murmured into my ear, his lips curled into a grin, and passed by me with a wave of golden hair.

Humbert leaned in next and spat, "Don't get full of yourself, you nameless cretin," before following.

They walked into the building and slammed the door behind them, but I was still frozen where I stood.

The object Raios had placed in my pocket was a flower bud with a single bluish leaf. It looked nearly ready to bloom. I plucked it from my pocket with a freezing-cold hand and examined it.

The flower, its stem crudely ripped at the end, belonged to none of the Four Holy Flowers. It was a zephilia, the western flower I'd been trying over and over to grow for the past six months.

With that understanding came a rage so profound, I nearly cracked my molars with the strength of my jaws grinding. If I'd had my sword with me, I'd have rushed into the building and swung it at Raios and Humbert. Instead, I raced for the back of the garden, clutching the pale-blue bud in my trembling fingers. Past the intersecting paths and to the tool shelf on the back wall, where a white planter came into view.

"Ah…aaaah…" I gasped.

The twenty-three zephilia plants that I had bought as spice seeds, raised in unfamiliar soil and very nearly brought to bloom, were all cruelly torn off their stalks.

The round buds were scattered around the planter, their trademark blue color already fading. The stems left in the ground were wilting, clearly losing the last remnants of their life.

Right in the midst of the dying plants stood the tool of their destruction, stuck in the earth like a gravestone: a long metal trowel of the kind used to plant bulbs. Raios and Humbert had used the sharp edges of the tool to sever the fragile plants.

I felt the strength drain out of my legs, and I collapsed to my knees in front of the planter. Through eyes dazed and bleary, staring half-focused at the scattered buds, I tried to think.

Why? The motive and means were obvious, but why did they undertake this course of action? Intentional destruction of another's property was a clear violation of the Taboo Index. It should have been an ironclad rule, even for higher nobles like them.

Object ownership in the Underworld was defined without room for mistake. As I learned when I went out on our journey, the windows for your objects always included a small P field indicating possession. In other words, everything without a P on it was not yours and couldn't be stolen or destroyed.

Yes, there was no possession of plants while they were still rooted to the ground, but that ground itself could be owned. A plant growing in soil owned by someone was that person's property. The flower beds behind me were on Swordcraft Academy land, so the blooming anemones belonged to the school. And I had bought that planter in District Six, so I had always assumed that the zephilia plants growing in it naturally became my property.

Through a mind numbed by rage and despair, I finally hit on the fact of the matter. My eyes bulged.

The dirt. The black soil filling the planter…I hadn't dug that up from the academy ground or bought it at the market. I had brought it back from outside the city, from a patch of land owned by no one. And I had told Muhle about it, as well as several others. Raios and Humbert must have overheard and determined that if they were growing in soil from a distant location without an owner, the plants would belong to no one, too.

If that was true, this was all my fault. I should have thought harder about placing my precious plants in a spot that anyone had the right to access.

Underworldians never broke the law. But that didn't mean they were all fundamentally good people. Some of them followed a personal creed that said anything that wasn't explicitly outlawed was open to interpretation. I was supposed to have learned that in the Zakkaria tournament.

"...I'm sorry..." I grunted.

With one hand, I plucked up the scattered buds around the stand and placed them in my other palm. The brilliant blue of the plants grew grayer as I collected them.

Right after I finished pooling together all twenty-three buds, they died out for good. The little plants crumbled in my palms, spraying a brief, weak blue light, then melted away into the air.

Suddenly, tears flooded my eyes.

I tried to force my mouth into a smile, mocking myself for crying over my precious flowers being ripped up by bullies. But the only thing that happened was a twitching in my cheeks, sending the pooled tears running down them to drip onto the bricks at my feet.

At long last, I realized what meaning I had put into those zephilia sprouts.

The first reason I had tried raising those flowers was to experiment with the power of mental images in the Underworld.

The second reason...was to fulfill Liena's desire to see a real zephilia flower, just once.

But there had been a third reason that I'd never consciously grasped until just now. I saw something of myself in these little flowers, desperately trying to grow in foreign soil. Cut off from the real world, from those I loved and cared about, assailed by the pain and loneliness of not knowing when I might see them again—things I had tried to share with these little flowers...

The tears continued to gush forth, flowing down my cheeks and dripping off.

I huddled into a ball, trying to hold back the sobs, and was about to collapse to the ground when it happened again.

I heard the voice.

Have faith.

Believe in the strength of the flowers you grew so well in this foreign land. Believe in yourself, for getting them to that point.

It was that strange voice I'd heard a number of times on my long journey. It sounded feminine, but it didn't belong to anyone I recognized. It wasn't the voice of the young girl I had heard in the cave through the End Mountains two years ago. It was calm, full of deep knowledge and just the faintest hint of warmth...

"...But...they're all dead," I mumbled.

It's all right, the voice answered quietly. *The roots in the soil are still doing their best to live. Can't you feel it...? All the holy flowers blooming in these flower beds are trying to save their little companions. They want to share their life with them. And you can transfer that wish to the zephilia roots.*

"...I can't. I don't know how to use such high-level sacred arts."

The formal arts are nothing but a tool to harness and refine the "Meaning"—what you call the mental image. At this point, you need neither chants nor catalysts.

Now wipe your tears and get to your feet. Feel the prayer of the flowers.

Feel the ways of the world...

And with that, the voice vanished into the distant night sky.

I took a deep, quavering breath, exhaled, then rubbed at my eyes with the ends of my sleeves. With great force of will, I pulled myself up into a standing position.

Behind me, there was an incredible sight. The holy flowers planted in the four flower beds of the garden—not just the blue anemones in full bloom but the bud-less marigolds, the short stalks growing from the dahlia bulbs, and the cattleyas with their crawling roots—were glowing faintly green in the darkness.

Sacred power. Spatial resources. These words were crass and pointless in the presence of that gentle, warm, powerful glow.

Guided by the light, I spread my hands to the four species of flowers and whispered, "Please…give them your strength…just a bit of your life."

I focused on an image—the life force coming from the flowers running through me like a conduit and into the zephilia roots left in the planter.

Narrow, glowing green lines rose in countless numbers from the flower beds. They gathered and wove together, forming a number of thick ribbons. I waved my fingers, and they danced silently through the air, flowing toward a single point.

All that was left was to close the final distance. The ribbon of light infused the planter of broken stalks, wrapping around it multiple times to look like one enormous flower, then melting into the ground and vanishing.

Slowly but surely, the twenty-three stalks began to rebuild and regrow. Leaves like sharp little swords split off from them, spreading to protect round, bulging buds.

Once again, my eyes filled with tears.

What a mysterious, wondrous world. It was all, all of it, a collection of virtual objects, and yet it was equipped with beauty… with life…with will that far surpassed the real world's.

"…Thank you," I whispered to the Four Holy Flowers and to the owner of the mysterious voice. After some brief consideration, I took the sigil pin off my uniform collar and placed it at the edge of the planter. It was a sign that this land belonged to *me*.

When I got back to the room, I would apologize to the branch of the Gigas Cedar I'd turned into a sword, for cutting it down. And I would thank it, for helping me in the match against Volo.

For a long while, I gazed at the zephilia buds, now fully regrown. When the bells rang seven thirty, I got up and started walking back to the dorm.

Just before I reached the door, I glanced to the south, over the stone wall surrounding the garden, over the roof of the training hall, at the massive Central Cathedral that split the starry sky in half. The way the countless windows shone orange was just like a skyscraper in the real world, only this one was far taller and more beautiful.

Just at that moment, one light separated itself from the tower, very high up.

I squinted, unable to believe it. But it wasn't an illusion or a hallucination. The light was growing, bit by bit, approaching North Centoria. It glided through the night sky, maintaining altitude…

"…A dragon!" I gasped.

No doubt about it. The light was from one of the enormous lanterns that hung from the flying dragon's armor. It wasn't a headlight or a warning signal, merely a light meant to inspire the proper fear and respect in the people on the ground by night, as they did during the day. Riding on the back of that dragon was an Integrity Knight, highest agent of control and order in the world.

The gigantic beast crossed the sky, its wings held outstretched, moving in the northeast direction. It was likely heading for the End Mountains to undertake its duties of protecting the human realm. The dragon would cross that 750-kilometer expanse in a single day—a trip that had taken Eugeo and me an entire year.

Once the light of the lantern had vanished into the night, I craned my neck to gaze upon the cathedral tower again. The knight had taken off from about three-quarters of the way up. Perhaps there was something like a flight pad up there. I tried looking higher than that, but the top of the tower was lost in the darkness.

What I sought had to be up there: the door to the real world.

But was it my imagination, or did the thirst to return grow weaker and weaker by the day? And was it a trick of the mind that it seemed to be replaced by a growing desire to see more of this mysterious and beautiful world, to know it more intimately…?

I breathed in a lungful of the flowers' sweet scent, exhaled slowly, and tore my gaze from the cathedral tower to open the old door and return to the dorm.

At the end of March…

Second-seat disciple Sortiliena Serlut participated in the graduation tournament and, in her final opportunity, bested first-seat disciple Volo Levantein, thus graduating from the North Centoria Imperial Swordcraft Academy as its top student.

When we parted ways, I presented her with the planter full of blooming zephilias, and she presented me with the first dazzling smile and tears that I had ever seen from her.

Two weeks after her graduation, she appeared in the Imperial Battle Tournament, but in the first round, she ran into the representative of the Norlangarth Knighthood and lost by a slim margin after a fierce battle.

INTERLUDE II

The bootheels clicked, and a crisp, loud voice filled the large chamber.

"Elite Disciple Eugeo, I have a report to make! Today's cleaning has been completed to satisfaction!"

The voice belonged to a red-haired girl dressed in the gray uniform of a primary trainee, her facial features still containing traces of childhood.

Less than a month had passed since she had traveled through the academy's gate and achieved the honor of being an elite disciple's page, and there was a painful, awkward stiffness to her actions and posture.

Eugeo tried to treat her as warmly and kindly as he could, but he knew from his own experiences that it wasn't that easy to just relax in her situation. To the new students, the twelve elite disciples were a more forbidding, frightening presence than even the strictest teacher.

It took two months at a bare minimum for pages to be able to interact comfortably, and Eugeo hadn't been an exception to the rule. *That* honor went to his partner, who had never met a bit of common sense he couldn't overturn.

Eugeo closed the textbook of sacred arts, stood up from the high-backed chair, and replied, "Thank you, Tiese. You may now return to the dorm. Oh, and…err…"

His eyes moved left from Tiese's red hair to another girl with dark-brown hair, similarly stiff-backed.

"…I'm sorry about this, Ronie. I've told him over and over to be back by the time the room is cleaned," Eugeo apologized, speaking for the partner who had disappeared the moment his drills were finished.

The trainee named Ronie shook her head, eyes wide. "N-not at all! It is my duty to complete my report!"

"Well, I'm afraid you'll be waiting here a bit longer. I don't know what to say…I'm so sorry that I share a room with *him*…"

The North Centoria Imperial Swordcraft Academy may have been the most prestigious swordsmanship school in the empire, attracting the children of noble families and wealthy merchants from all over Norlangarth, but once on the school's soil, even an imperial child started at the same entry level of a primary trainee.

The first year afforded nary a chance to touch a real sword. Instead, students practiced their forms with wooden swords and spent all day learning battle theory and sacred arts. On top of that, primary trainees had to undertake a number of school chores as part of their education.

The type of job depended on the score the student earned in the swordsmanship test just after school started. Ninety percent of them were assigned to cleaning duties, maintaining school supplies, tending to the holy flowers, and so on, but the top twelve scorers were assigned as pages to the twelve disciples, earning them the envy of their peers and two months of very awkward adjustment.

In fact, page duties weren't really that different from the other students', except that instead of cleaning the classrooms or training hall, they cleaned the disciples' rooms. But if that disciple was mean-spirited, or a total slob, or liked to vanish into thin air and not return in a timely fashion, kids like Ronie wound up with a major headache.

"Umm, if you want, Ronie, I can tell the teacher and have you switched to shadow someone else instead...I think you're going to have a very rough year working for him. In fact, I guarantee it."

"N-not at all, sir!" Ronie insisted with another vigorous shake of the head. Just then, a familiar voice spoke up—not through the door but from the open window.

"What are you telling her about me while I'm gone?"

Climbing through the third-story window was his second-year partner, Kirito, dressed in the disciple's uniform. Their styles were exactly the same, except that Eugeo's was a deep blue with a touch of gray, while Kirito's fabric was straight black. One of the many privileges of being an elite disciple was the right to choose one's uniform color.

Ronie's face briefly softened into a relieved grin at the sight of Kirito's return, complete with a delicious-smelling paper bag, then tightened up again as she slammed her bootheel into the floor.

"Elite Disciple Kirito, I have a report to make! Today's cleaning has been completed without incident!"

"Cool, thanks," he replied as he scratched his black hair, still not comfortable with the presence of the trainee pages.

Eugeo snorted and pointed out, "Listen, Kirito, I'm not saying you can't go outside, but they've got tons more work to do than you do, so at least get back before they're done cleaning. And why do you need to use the window in the first place?"

"Because this is the quickest route when coming back from East Third Street. You should tuck that fact away, Ronie and Tiese; it'll come in handy someday."

"Don't fill their heads with nonsense! Oh...if you went to East Third Street, does that mean those are honey pies from the Jumping Deer?"

The sweet smell wafting from Kirito's arms exerted almost violent force on Eugeo's pre-dinner stomach. "Listen, I know they're great, but...you don't have to buy an entire pile of them."

"Hah! If you want some, just be honest and say so, Eugeo." Kirito smirked. He pulled two of the golden, circular pies from the bulging sack, tossing one to his partner and popping the other in his mouth. He dropped the remainder of the sack into Ronie's arms. "Share it with your entire room when you get back to the dorm."

Tiese and Ronie exclaimed like the fifteen- and sixteen-year-old girls they were, then regained their proper posture.

"Th-thank you, Elite Disciple, sir!" Ronie said.

"We shall return to the dorm posthaste so as not to allow our precious cargo's life to drop! Until tomorrow!" Tiese shouted.

With a very quick and abbreviated salute, the two girls marched across the room, boots clicking, and exited into the hall. They bowed again through the doorway, shut the door, and then rushed away, their shrieks of excitement clearly audible.

"..."

Eugeo took a large bite of the fresh-baked pie and threw a sidelong look at Kirito.

"...What?"

"I didn't say anything. I was only wondering to myself if the great Elite Disciple Kirito has forgotten the exact reason we're actually here."

"Hmph! As if I'd forget," Kirito protested. He licked his thumb, already finished with the pie, and turned his black eyes to look out the window at a sight not visible from the primary trainee dorm—the looming tower of the Axiom Church in the very heart of Centoria.

"Three more to go…We've come this far already. First, we beat the other ten disciples at the graduation test match and earn the title of academy representatives. Next, we enter the Imperial Battle Tournament and defeat the old fogeys in the knighthood and imperial guards. Lastly, we both win out at the Four-Empire Unification Tournament. Then you can be an Integrity Knight and walk right through the gate of that tower."

"Yeah…one more year…One more year, and I'll finally…"

Be able to see her. The old friend who was taken away by an Integrity Knight eight years ago.

Eugeo looked away from the Central Cathedral, back at the two swords stored on the wall of the room, white and black.

As long as they had the swords of fate that had brought them to this point, they would never falter.

Eugeo believed it without a shred of doubt.

(Alicization Running—The End)

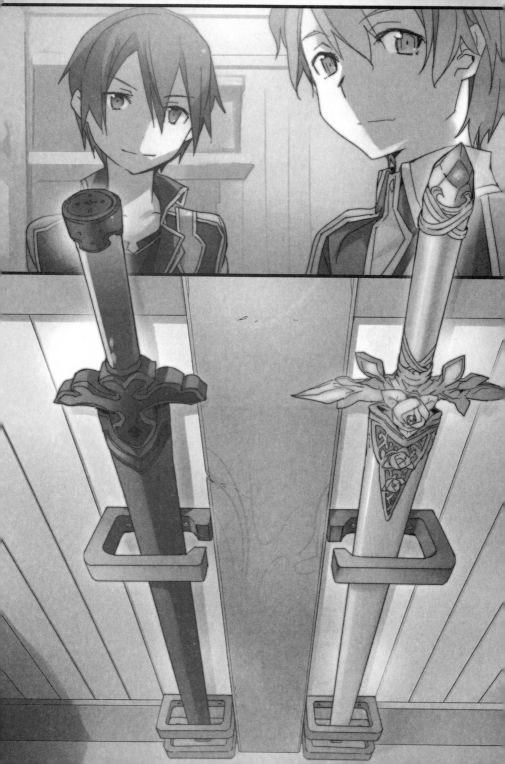

AFTERWORD

Hello, this is Reki Kawahara. Thank you for reading *Sword Art Online 10: Alicization Running*.

The subtitle "Running" is meant to be a reference to something in action or proceeding. A computer program "runs," as you know. On the other hand, this book didn't seem like it was really speeding along to me...In fact, pretty much the entire first half was dedicated to setup and explanation (which often happens with me), so I don't blame any readers for wondering, "When are the swords gonna do their art?!" Allow me to take this opportunity to say something I repeat out of sheer custom: I'm sorry about all the exposition!

On that topic, please allow me to make another apology. In this story arc, the mysterious Mr. Kikuoka's true position is finally revealed, but allow me to be clear that he is not a mouthpiece for the author's worldview. His actions arose as a necessity from his position, and there are many characters in the story who oppose his views—we saw Asuna do this herself. The distance between the character and the author is normally made very clear through the text itself, so that the reader doesn't require a disclaimer like this one, but it seems I have a problem with reaching that level of clarity...I'll try to be better about this sort of thing in the future, but I felt strongly enough about it to bring it up here. Please keep that in mind!

*   *   *

One more apology. The original publication of this book in Japan is on July 10th, 2012, meaning that I've finally broken the streak of every even-numbered month that had lasted since my debut. Part of this was intentional, so we could time it for the premiere of the *SAO* anime series, but it's also true that I wouldn't have finished it in time anyway. So I'm sorry to all of you who expected to see another two-month publication! My idea (my ideal?) is to have *Accel World 12* out in August, where it would have been normally, thus returning me to my every-other-month schedule for the foreseeable future. I'm sure there will come a time where that pace crumbles for good, and I'll be here to apologize for it profusely. In fact...I'm really sorry if that time ends up being before the end of this year...

As I just mentioned, this book should originally be coming out right around the time that the TV anime series begins. The fact that this story I began writing on a website ten years ago is a published series, a manga, a drama CD, and now an anime, is not just a source of joy to me but also a tribute to the mysterious nature of life. It may not be as complex as a video game story, but there have nonetheless been a myriad of different branching options to get to this point. If I didn't have Mr. Miki as my editor, if I didn't have abec as an illustrator, if I hadn't applied for the Fifteenth Dengeki Novel Award, if I hadn't kept writing my web novel, or if I hadn't decided to write a story about a VRMMO game of death ten years ago, I wouldn't be here now. I tend to think that things happen the way they're meant to happen—and don't go the way they're not meant to go. But I can't help but feel as though this *SAO* thing was brought forth to this point by some tremendous power. Naturally, that power includes the strength provided by all your support for my endeavors. The story has a long way to go, so I'd love it if you could follow Kirito's adventures in the years to come.

*   *   *

I'm noticing that this afterword is rapidly expanding in length, so I figured that this would be a good time to provide a personal update, but…there's nothing to write about! Even my one great hobby of biking is still an active one for me, but my riding route is so fixed and predictable that I might as well be riding on bike rollers indoors at this point. When the input drops, naturally the output does as well, so I want to try other stuff all over the place, but I find that my areas of interest are naturally limiting, to say nothing of the lack of time. Honestly, the only thing I want to do with all my heart is write! (*laughs*) If only that made the actual writing speed pick up.

Still, now that it's been over three years since my published debut, I truly think it's a blessing to be able to write the story that I want to write. It sounds like a simple thing, but there are a ton of hurdles to overcome. And there are surprisingly few of those hurdles that you can jump over solely through your own effort… So I want to stay healthy and keep riding my bike. The goal is ninety miles a week!

Well, I've still got a couple of lines of space on this page, but the deadline to submit is in ten minutes, so I should probably wrap it up. Normally, I'd spend about five lines doing my usual thanks and apologies, but I've kind of covered them all, so I'll go over what's next instead…

Volume 11, the third book in the Alicization saga, will feature Kirito and Eugeo's arrival at the center of the Underworld. How the world is shaped and who is controlling it will (probably) be revealed at last…so I hope to see you there.

Please check out the anime adaptation, too, as well as the *SAO* video game currently in development. My guess is that this is one game of death that *won't* be inescapable!

Reki Kawahara—May 2012

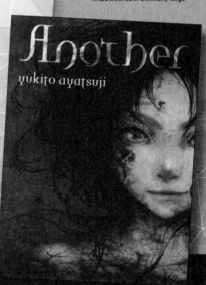

Dive into the latest light novels from
New York Times bestselling author REKI KAWAHARA,
creator of the fan favorite *SWORD ART ONLINE* and
ACCEL WORLD series!

*The Isolator,
Vol.1-2*
©REKI KAWAHARA
ILLUSTRATION:Shimeji

*Sword Art
Online:
Progressive,
Vol.1-3*
©REKI KAWAHARA
ILLUSTRATION:abec

*Sword Art Online,
Vol.1-7*
©REKI KAWAHARA
ILLUSTRATION:abec

*Accel World,
Vol.1-6*
©REKI KAWAHARA
ILLUSTRATION:HIMA

And be sure your shelves are primed with Kawahara's extensive manga selection!

Sword Art Online: Aincrad
©REKI KAWAHARA/ TAMAKO NAKAMURA

*Sword Art Online:
Fairy Dance, Vol. 1-3*
©REKI KAWAHARA/ TSUBASA HADUKI

*Sword Art Online:
Girl Ops, Vol. 1-2*
©REKI KAWAHARA/ NEKO NEKOBYOU

*Sword Art Online:
Progressive, Vol. 1-4*
©REKI KAWAHARA/ KISEKI HIMURA

*Sword Art Online:
Phantom Bullet, Vol. 1-2*
©REKI KAWAHARA/ KOUTAROU YAMADA

*Sword Art Online:
Mother's Rosary, Vol. 1-2*
©REKI KAWAHARA/ TSUBASA HADUKI

Accel World Vol. 1-6
©REKI KAWAHARA/ HIROYUKI AIGAMO

YEN
ON

Yen
Press

www.YenPress.com